I0597159

Eden

The Galatian Exchaange, book 6

Pepper Pace

Contents

A Word From The Author

Hello, and welcome back. I am sure you are familiar with my author notes from the prior five books, so I will change it up a bit and respond to one of the biggest questions I get concerning The Galatian Exchange: Will I continue the story where the Kindle Vella left off.

Yes, I will. I am working hard to publish this series for all to read—especially those who were unable to access Kindle Vella in countries outside of the United States. Also, I have no plans to release this story behind a pay wall such as patreon. In truth, it is nice to take a break from writing twice weekly episodes.

I hope you are enjoying the journey as much as I enjoy writing it. As a reminder, the series should be read in order and is intended for mature readers as it contains adult content such as sex, language, abuse and racism.

-PP

©Pepper Pace Publications

Copyright © 2021, 2022, 2023, 2024, 2025 The Galatian Exchange, book 6 Eden. Pepper Pace.

All rights reserved, including the right to reproduce this book or portions thereof in any form whatsoever, except for short excerpts appearing in book reviews. This novel first appeared on Amazon's Kindle Vella. For reprint or excerpt permission inquiries, please contact the author by e-mail at: pepperpace.author@yahoo.com.

This novel is a work of fiction. Characters – including their names, places, and incidents are products of the author's imagination or are otherwise used fictitiously. Any similarity from this book to events occurring in real life – including locations, or persons living or dead is wholly coincidental. The use of musical titles and the naming of musical artists is not an infringement of copyright per sections 106 and 106A, the fair use of a copyrighted work.

ISBN: 979-8-9909957-3-4

Chaos

Victory demands everything – but can they survive the price?

At long last, Ragna is in the possession of Rafe, Karma, and their team! The odds have never been higher as they face the ruthless forces of the Interplanetary Collection and the Queen's Council. Amid the chaos, Karma's estranged father, James Chambers, resurfaces, bringing his deep-seated hatred for alien life but offering an unexpected advantage in their fight.

As their enemies unravel from within, pushing the boundaries of their depravity, a groundbreaking revelation threatens to reshape everything they know about Galatian history. Do they dare risk life and limb for an opportunity at normalcy?

Part One

Chapter One

"Wait. Lt. Sigur," Garry called after them.

Rafe paused to look at the doctor.

"You can't put her back to sleep so close to the last injection. She's simply too young to take another dose right now." He glanced behind him at the cocoon floating in the swirling Galatian waters.

"I can monitor her vitals here. She can stay in her suit until it's safe to put her back to sleep."

"Are you suggesting that you guard my daughter—here, in the same room with the very same prisoner she's already tried to kill?"

"I'm suggesting that your daughter not be banished to a small chamber for twenty hours while she's wide awake." He gave M an amused look at her shocked expression. Some of the strongest warriors had completely lost it if they awakened while still encased in what would quickly begin to feel like a tomb.

"And, no," Garry continued. "It's not safe for the prisoner to be left unprotected—and by that, I mean the *prisoner* isn't safe. I'm returning her to the transport where the electrical dome in that pool will keep her secured until we arrive in Eden.

"In the meantime, your daughter can remain in her suit and do some chores around here to help work off some of this damage she created."

Rafe considered this non-violent type of punishment. Not that he had ever intended to physically punish her. But since punishing children in any way went against the beliefs of a Galatian, he felt instant relief at this idea.

But then he looked at the doctor dubiously. Perhaps this man underestimates his daughter. It would be unwise to do so. Ragna was a testament to that.

"Or," Garry shrugged. "Just be sure to monitor her vitals—or bring her back here every few hours for me to do it." The doctor turned with a sigh and lifted his wand to continue his work with the prisoner.

Rafe looked at his daughter. "You will stay with Dr. Brookstone. And you will do as he says. For now, he is your Commander, but my eyes will still be on you, Little One. Your monitor is to remain on visual."

Yes, Papa.

He clenched his teeth and then gave her a brief hug before exiting the bay without her. He called out his final instructions over his shoulders, allowing his tail to observe them. "I expect you to be on your best behavior, M. I will send two Galatian Guards to escort Ragna." And then he was gone.

Garry looked at the child. She looked so sweet and innocent, and yet he had seen with his very own eyes what she was capable of. She had whipped the tar out of two full-grown Galatian males!

"Well, you can start by cleaning the specimen containers and pipettes before we recycle them. Everyone tends to complain about the smell of urine and blood in the incinerator."

M's nose went up, but she wasn't complaining. She knew she'd have to face her punishment head-on. The problem is that it would have been worth it to have the bad lady dead. She had hurt her papa, was being punished, and she hadn't even achieved her goal.

They were sitting on rolling stools several hours later, having a meal break. Just as Rafe stated, two Galatian Guards had taken Ragna away, and he was able to confirm through the ship's controls she was secure and her vitals were stable.

There was no eating in the regular way when wearing the full suit. Therefore, they had to take their nourishment through ports in the suit which secreted nutritional enzymes against the flesh. It was only a short-term solution to starvation. But no one had factored in the food cravings while considering the logistics of building the life-sustaining device.

"You're not feeling hungry, are you?"

The little girl shook her head.

"Good, because this suit is equipped to nourish you in every way." He whispered the next. "There's even a flap in the back if you have to use the toilet. But the suit slows all of that down, so you shouldn't need to do any of that."

M tried to look over her shoulder at the back of the suit for this flap. She couldn't see it if it was there. She looked back at the doctor again for her next task.

So far, she had washed like a hundred clear little cups in a solution that was supposed to kill the stink before they were recycled. Her big gloves had made the task hard, but she did it. Afterward, she had to wipe down all the furniture. Dr. Brookside had claimed she had made a mess of things, but it wasn't true. The only thing a mess was the electrical cage that had protected the Black Mask.

At first, she was mad at the doctor. But then he told her that if she had reached the pool and touched the electrical barrier, she would have died instantly. Then he had fussed at her a little.

'I told you about the barrier and that no one could get in or out. Didn't you understand what that meant... ?'

He had been right. Her plan had been to get close enough to throw the electricity into the pool. She would have touched the barrier to do it. She would have died. She had been stupid about her need to get rid of the threat against her family. That is why a true warrior made plans, but was open to change. A warrior didn't just hope for the best!

'Look,' he had said. '*I understand why you did what you did. I even see by that Galatian suit you want to be a warrior.*' Her chest had puffed out. She *was* a warrior. Garry continued as if he understood her expression. '*I have fought for my beliefs—killed for my beliefs. But I make a plan, so I can live to fight another day.*'

Afterwards, M wanted to hear him talk. And talk he did. He talked about his travels, about why he had no pigment, and even about the kids he worked with. What he didn't like talking about was fighting. But she learned that he fought with the Galatians, specifically with Uncle Paris!

But he wouldn't give her details. Still, M decided she liked Dr. Garry.

"You ready for your scan, kiddo?" He asked while standing.

She made a face. She would rather stay awake with the doctor.

Garry sighed when he looked at her monitor. Per her father's requirement, it remained stationary so that he could visually monitor her, but it also meant she had to walk across the room to use the controls to speak to him.

He wished he could take a look at why she was unable to speak. He was sure that Lt. Sigur had gotten the best of the best in physicians, which didn't always mean they were the best in pediatrics. Children's injuries and disabilities often changed with the onset of puberty but definitely as they grew. M's case could use another look.

He felt bad that it wouldn't be him to do it.

Garry scanned her vitals and then nodded in approval. "Yes. You're ready."

She looked distrustfully at one of the chambers.

"Sorry that I can't give you your communicator back, but since you know how to use it as an escape mechanism..."

M shook her head as if to tell him it was okay. She didn't need it.

Garry used her communicator to speak to Rafe. The visual only went one way, but there was no audio unless it was activated. He assumed Rafe was too busy to listen to their idle chatter.

"Lt. Sigur, your daughter is ready to enter the chamber. I will be administering the sedative now."

"M," Rafe's voice came through the communicator. "I am unable to return to the sick bay. Things are very hectic. But I am watching, so I am here with you." M nodded. "You aren't afraid, are you, Little One?" M shook her head adamantly. "Good. We will talk when you wake up." His voice had become a mixture of stern yet filled with love and concern.

M nodded again.

The protocol was to leave her in her suit within the chamber and after making sure she was comfortable; he input a tube into one of the suit's ports and administered the sedative.

She looked a bit lost in the large suit, and Garry's heart went out to her. What life had this little girl led to cause her to do such a thing?

"M. Count backward from ten. You'll be asleep before you reach zero," Garry said.

M gestured for the communicator who was on a rolling cart. She probably wanted to tell her dad bye before she went under. He retrieved it and handed it to her.

But he saw her turn the audio to only be heard in this room. So, it was him she wanted to speak to.

You think I stupid for what I did. I not. Grown-ups think they know best, but they know too much. When you know too much, you have too many choices. And the most important thing is not important anymore.

My daddy say he gonna kill Black Mask. He wants to kill Black Mask. But something will happen that he thinks is more important. And he will say I'll do it later. Then she will heal and get stronger. There is nothing more important than her dying.

Garry thought about her words and then he nodded. "I agree

with you M. I do. I saw what she did and I know terrible people like her; people who kill babies... " He looked away as if he wanted to exorcise distant memories. With a sigh, he looked at her again. "Your father is consumed with hatred and the need for revenge. When the little boy I wanted to adopt was murdered by his father, I annihilated that man. I took his arms, then his legs, and finally his heart—and I kept him alive while I did it.

"I thought it would make me feel better. But it made me into a monster because deep down I knew there was another side to that story. I know he made himself and then Oskar believe that he was evil in order to do what he did. And then he had that child murdered... and he did it because his other children were starving. He didn't take the money and run, he bought food. I saw..."

M watched the doctor, not completely understanding the story, but understanding enough.

Garry let out a soft breath. "That's a road I can't and won't travel down again. I just... want you to know why I'm doing this. You will never have to worry about that lady again. But right is right and wrong is wrong."

M frowned in confusion. But Dr. Garry was already administering the sedative.

Chapter Two

"Rafe Sigur has made a great deal of demands," Amalia stated. "I do not like it."

Commander Einar said nothing. He absolutely did not want to return to Rafe with another request for an interview. Humans had an old saying called 'eating crow'. He didn't understand the origins, but he knew the sentiment. It had taken everything in him not to demand obedience. But Rafe was no longer "his" to command. He didn't want to go back with his tail between his legs begging on behalf of the Queens.

Amalia's brown tint became purple with annoyance. "I suppose there is nothing to be done about it. He knows that in this matter, he has the control."

Einar hid his surprise at that statement. If the Queens thought Rafe had the upper hand, then did that mean he was on the losing team? Einar felt a jolt of regret. It was never a matter of not agreeing with Rafe. But he knew who held all the power because he had done their bidding since joining the military.

But what if he was allowed to think for himself? What if his many decades of service meant he actually knew his job better than Queens, who sat on thrones deciding the fate of others on a whim?

"Einar!" Amalia snarled.

He jerked to attention. "Yes, Most Exalted?"

"Are you listening to me? I said I don't trust Rafe Sigur one bit." She didn't trust Einar, either. He had worked closely with Rafe's team for too long not to think his loyalty might not be in question. "Repeat exactly who he wants present at the parley."

Einar kept his temper even as he replied. "He wants his mate...uh the human mate, his teammates, their Bound Mates and consorts, the entire Queen's Council, The Black Mask war council, the Japoxillian delegates from the Inter-planetary Collective, and finally Mayva Heath to face his mate."

Amalia stared at him for an extended time. "Tell him we accept his terms with one exception: Mayva Heath does not agree to be included. Go." She turned off the communicator and leaned back on her throne.

She didn't think Rafe was behind the disappearance of Mayva Heath. It was obvious the Keengalese had appropriated their human spokesperson. Those types were grateful to be in the good graces of The Collective but also understood their great value. If Pod was ever located, he would be forgiven. His particular abilities were too important.

No, Rafe wasn't behind her disappearance, but Amalia was certain he was behind Ragna's. Why else hadn't he specifically named her to be in attendance at the parley? He was specific about Mayva Heath facing his human. But it was Ragna who had orchestrated the attack, and Rafe knew it was she who had killed his unborn son.

Although the female Galatians did not possess the colorful scales of the males, their emotions did show a bit on their brown scales and hers were tinted pink in good cheer.

Rafe had murdered Ragna—and good riddance. She had never liked that one! But it meant he'd also broken the terms of the amnesty. And that meant he would be put to death—no questions and no trial!

It turned out Ragna was good for something. Her death would end this uprising!

Rafe glanced at the incoming message. It was from Einar. He scowled when he read that Amalia had rejected one of his requirements.

Rafe called Drago. "The Commander has given me Amalia's response. She states that Mayva Heath will not attend the parley."

"She begged for this meeting," Drago replied. "And now she sets conditions. I am sorely tempted to advise you to tell her to kiss your ass."

"But?"

"But...we need to get Haru out of there. How important is it for you to have the ex-consort in attendance?"

Rafe was quiet for a moment. "I wanted her sent to prison for her crimes. It was Einar's decision to give her leniency, which gave her access to our family. Our mates deserve the right to address her...but we must have Haru."

Drago nodded briefly. "Yes. Mayva will meet the same fate as Ragna. Just not as quickly. You should tell Einar you will agree and let us be done with this."

"I agree. I am sorely tempted to change my mind and not even attend once all parties have gathered. But I want to face Amalia and let her know that she no longer rules me—us!"

"Yes, and as I have no reason to be in contact with Isyss, this is where I will sever our bond."

Rafe's eyes widened. "In front of the other Bound-mates? That will not be well received."

"I do not wish her pain," Drago stated. "But she must know this is a decision which has already been made.

"And I am sure Paris will do the same with Thalia."

"Kendrick may be the only one who would return to his Bound-mate," Drago said, only half joking. He worried about his brother. He no longer had a consort, and as things stood, there would not be another Exchange for him to participate in.

He felt as if Kendrick would prefer a human lover. He had always been comfortable around them from the moment he had landed on Earth. And it was apparent his affinity for all things human had not lessened with the death of his consort.

"I will message Einar to set up the meeting once we get to our destination," Rafe stated.

"Rafe. What about Ragna? You said you would end her with no more hesitation."

"Yes," Rafe agreed. "Once the humans awaken. They should be a witness. But we will end Ragna and forever be done with her."

"Yes," Drago said with relief. "Perhaps if we had taken that course earlier, M would not have broken out of her sleep chambers to take matters into her own hands." Drago had an amused tint.

Rafe nodded. "She will be pleased to know we will not keep her." Rafe thought as much as he knew, Ragna's presence caused M fear. In truth, it would be a difficult task to safeguard the prisoner from his daughter.

Rafe made his rounds—first to his quarters where he checked on Karma and his son. They looked at peace, but he wanted to arrive at their destination quickly so he could see them once again lively.

M's empty sleeping chamber caused him to sigh. He would have to institute rules for her. And he would also have to safeguard his weapons. A hunting knife was one thing, but stealing laser guns and electrical batons was quite a different matter. What if she had fired on the Guards? They would have fired back.

He closed his eyes momentarily and then went to the sick bay to speak to the doctor. He'd already interviewed the two guards and was certain things could have ended disastrously had M been anyone other than his daughter.

When he entered the sick bay, he immediately went to M's

sleeping chamber. She looked so small. A wave of love enveloped him. From the moment she had first laid eyes on him, she had wanted to be like him. Rafe smiled a deep pink. And it was probably just as quickly that he had wanted to safeguard her.

He decided her punishment had been served—except for restrictions he would input. It was not only her own safety but also for those around her.

Rafe looked around the quiet room. The doctor was no doubt in the transport monitoring Ragna. He would tell him to stop because there was no need to continue prolonging her life. If she died before they reached their temporary home, then it was the will of the Great Guardian.

Rafe headed for the transport bay to take one last look at the one being he despised more than anyone or anything else in the universe. He would also tell Dr. Brookstone that he was no longer needed and could take his rest in a sleeping chamber.

He received another call from his communicator. There was so much to be done and his communicator was driving him mad!

"Yes, Kendrick?" Rafe almost snapped.

"What is Dr. Brookstone doing?"

"I told you. He's had to place Ragna in the transport's pool to activate the security dome. I am on my way there to tell him our decision not to prolong her death."

"That's not what I mean. Why is he taking the transport out of the bay?"

"What?!"

Kendrick cursed. "The doctor is stealing the transport, and it appears he's stealing our prisoner!"

Chapter Three

Kelsie would have been scared if Mom and Dad weren't sitting beside her bed. Mom stroked her hair, and it was enough to put her to sleep—except they were going to be removing her lungs this morning. Who could sleep when your diseased lungs would be removed forever?

Dr. Maxx said it wouldn't hurt because she would be asleep while they did the transplant. It was scary to think about. People couldn't live without lungs.

But Dad said the surgery happened all the time. He promised after she woke up, she would be able to breathe better than she had in a very long time. There would be a machine that would breathe for her while her lungs continued to mature. She would just wear the little machine in a backpack which she could carry around.

It seemed so crazy there was a technology that could do such a thing. Worse is she would have died while doctors knew all along they could have done something like this for her. There were a lot of people who died from lung disease—but they were poor people and as sad as it was, everybody knew poor people didn't matter as much as everyone else.

The nurse pressed a sticky probe on her neck and then smiled broadly. "Okay, Kelsie. We're ready. You can tell your family goodbye for now."

Mom's smile was broad on her cat-like face. Dad didn't smile but patted her hand. Bain's brow was lifted, as if he was surprised this was happening so fast.

"We'll be here when you wake up," Dorf said.

Kelsie nodded. She needed the oxygen all the time now or else she lost her breath. She opened her hand and Mom slipped her paw into it for a slight squeeze.

"Sleep well, sweet girl," Mom said, and then leaned forward. She thought to kiss her cheek. But instead of a kiss, she felt a soft lick from her warm tongue. It was the first time Mom had ever done that. But she'd seen Mom and Dad do that to each other when they snuggled. It made her feel special. She even wondered if she should lick her mother back, but decided against it. Fur and feathers would get stuck to her tongue!

"Bain," Dad said. "Tell your sister bye."

Bain leaned forward awkwardly. "Bye, Kelsie. See you when you wake up."

She waved at him slightly and then smiled at her family tiredly. The probe... there was something that made her very tired. No pokey needles or nasty-smelling gas.

Another nurse came into the room. This one was Galatian. His face was very severe, but his color was all smiles. Instead of wearing the clothes of the Guards, he wore a long green coat like the other nurses.

"Hi Kelsie, I'm Saskia, and I will be monitoring you during the surgery. I want you to know that everything will be fine. We do this surgery every day." His voice was soft and very pleasant. His presence helped to calm her nerves more than even the presence of her family. When a Galatian told you things would be okay, you believed it.

She nodded.

"Good girl." He patted her shoulder and then quickly studied a scan before carefully placing another patch on the other side of her neck. "Okay. You will be sound asleep shortly." Saskia leaned forward and looked into her eyes. After a moment, he spoke. "Go to sleep, Kelsie."

And with those words, she fell fast asleep.

Bain was looking out the window when his father walked up to him. "Are you tired, son?"

He shook his head. "No."

"Are you wondering what M is doing?"

"I should call her. She'll be worried about Kelsie."

"You won't be able to talk to her until after they arrive on the planet. They have to go into warp speed, so the humans and some others will need to be put into an artificial hibernation."

"How long will it last?"

"About three days."

"She won't like that." Bain frowned.

"Well, it will only feel like falling asleep and waking up the next day. It's not much different from what your sister is going through."

Bain was shaking his head. "No. I mean, she won't want to be asleep while the Black Mask is on the ship."

"Ah. Well. she doesn't have to worry about that one. She arrived at the compound nearly cooked from the inside out. I doubt if she can survive her injuries enough to be a danger to anyone."

Bain sat in a nearby waiting room chair. "M is going to think the Black Mask tricked all the grownups. She thinks bad things are going to happen to her mom and baby brother. Kelsie said at school she sometimes had terrible nightmares. Sometimes she tried to scream but she couldn't."

Dorf closed his eyes and shook his head. He should have paid more attention to her. He cursed himself for being so preoccupied with his own shit. "I'm happy you told me about M. I'll talk to her as soon as I can. I should be able to help her feel safe."

"I hope so. M acts brave, but I think she worries about things too much."

Dorf nodded in agreement and then took the seat next to his son. "She wants to protect everyone. That's why she wants to be a Galatian." He gave Bain a quick look. "That brings me to something I've wanted to speak to you about. Your future."

"My future?" he asked curiously.

"At one point you wanted to be a Guard." Dorf thought about the way he had reacted to the sight of a pistol and he almost wanted to be physically ill. His son may never be comfortable around firearms, all because of one day in his life...

Bain's cheeks had reddened. "I-I don't know what I should do when I grow up."

"What do you want to do?"

"You and mom are protectors..." Bain remembered Dorf proudly stating that he was going into the family business when he announced his intentions to be a Guard like M. But he couldn't be a protector if he didn't want to be around weapons. No matter how much training he received, he could never go up against a laser!

"It doesn't matter what mom and I are. We chose that life when there didn't seem to be anything worth losing."

Bain watched his father, wondering about his sad history. He knew a small amount. Both had each joined the Galatian Guards and were teamed up with a host Guard; Uncle Rafe for his dad and Uncle Drago for his mom after the deaths of their mates.

But he didn't know the real story—not about his father's first wife or about his mother's first love—both killed, which led them each to this eventual destination. But Bain didn't have to have Japoxillian powers to know some things were best left in the past.

"What do you like doing more than anything else?"

"Playing Warlord's Fury. It takes place in the past before...guns. We can fight with swords and knives. Or you can just use hand-to-hand combat. The guy I play, Dirk, never loses a fight—even against the zombies."

"Zombies?"

"Yeah. They are dead people who come back to life."

"Ah," Dorf shook his head in amusement. "I am still rather new to English. I still don't know all the unfamiliar words. But you want to be a weaponless fighter?"

"No. I want to be a computer programmer. Not just so I can make games, but so I can make machines that help people."

Dorf made a pleased sound. "We can begin your training in that field the moment things calm down."

Kemistry came into the waiting room carrying a bag over her shoulders.

"I thought you two might be hungry."

Bain got up and helped her remove the items from the bag. She and Dad were very capable even though they didn't have thumbs, but he could do manual things much quicker and efficiently. Without being asked, he had become his parents' hands.

"There is salmon for us and unless you want a salmon, I got you a burger and fries."

"Burger and fries!" he replied happily. He opened the tops of the beverage containers; flavored water for Mom and Dad and soda for himself. They crowded around the small waiting room table and feasted.

Mayva's stomach growled. She had eaten all the food, even the bruised fruit that should have gone into the trash well before Pod had left.

Pod.

He was no different from any other man. All they ever did was let you down. It had all begun with her father, who wanted her gone so badly he'd convinced himself that turning her into a Galatian's consort was in her best interest. Meanwhile, the males in the family were primed for important government work.

She might not have been happy working every day, but at least she wouldn't be starving in a rundown cabin in the middle of nowhere!

Mayva gathered her items for a nice, hot shower. At least there was plenty of water—He'd done that right. As she rubbed the conditioner into her hair, she was reminded of a tropical fruit basket. She missed the beach and ocean of the little island Heinrich had taken her to. She'd enjoyed her secret lovers, who could stoke her flames when Heinrich invariably missed the boat.

There was plentiful food and drink. Heinrich had gained at least ten pounds during their time in hiding—which certainly hadn't helped his endurance in the bedroom any.

She pushed thoughts of him out of her mind and replaced them with thoughts of the roasted fish the chef prepared several times a week. He made pudding from fruits she'd never before seen. And while she had to be careful about watching her weight, she had enjoyed indulging in a few bites of food at least once a day. If only she were back on that island. She would gorge herself on good food...

When her stomach grumbled again and her mouth began to water, she decided to taste the fruity-smelling hair conditioner. They said it was all naturally made of fruit extract...

Mmm, it was delicious! Instead of using it on her hair, Mayva ate the rest of it. Finally, a bit sated, she dried and then tried to comb her knee-length hair. But it was impossibly gnarled!

She sat at her vanity and tried to work the tangles from the ends, but after about an hour, her stomach began to ache. When she couldn't bear the discomfort a moment longer, she hurried to the bathroom and barely made it to the toilet before her bowels shot from her body like a geyser. Moments later she vomited tropical scented bile.

She dropped to the cool bathroom floor, gripping her knees to her chest. "Why me?" she sobbed as tears spilled from her eyes. "What did I do to deserve this misery?!" She slammed a fist against the tiled floor and broke a fingernail.

"Whaaaaa!" she wailed.

Chapter Four

When M's eyes opened, it was to the sight of her Papa and Mama looking at her. Mama had a concerned expression on her face as she nursed baby Runnar, who lay in the crook of her arm content.

She sat up, her head much clearer than it had been the first time she woke up.

What did Dr. Garry do? But there was no sound. Her communicator! Where was it?

"Ritty," her mama said with a frown. "M doesn't have her communicator."

Papa looked around and saw it sitting on the counter. He quickly grabbed it.

Meanwhile, M had climbed out of the chamber and was shimmying out of the oversized suit. She put on her communicator and spoke quickly.

Did Dr. Garry do something?

Her mother and father exchanged looks, which confirmed the last thoughts she'd had before she'd been put to sleep. Dr. Garry was going to do something he shouldn't.

"That's what we wanted to ask you," Rafe replied. "What did he say to you before he put you to sleep?"

Did he kill her? She asked hopefully, ignoring her father's question.

Her mother was the one who answered. "The doctor transferred that..." she had to pause and inhale before she could continue, "...prisoner to the transport ship. And then he took off with her." M's chest rose and fell rapidly. Karma touched her cheek with the palm of her hand. "Do not worry. Your uncles are searching for them as we speak."

"I need to know what you two talked about," Rafe stated.

M's mouth had gone dry, but she didn't need her mouth to communicate, so she quickly responded.

He talked about a little boy that got killed and that he killed the man that hurt him. I didn't know why he was telling me about the boy. But he said he wanted me to understand why he was doing what he did. He said wrong is wrong and right is right.

Rafe was shaking his head. "What does that mean?"

M frowned. **I don't know, Papa. But he said he understood why I tried to kill the bad lady. Does it mean he's going to kill her so we don't have to wait for her to get better?**

Rafe's jaw clenched. "I don't know. He should have never taken it upon himself to handle this."

He might have taken her someplace where he could kill her, M stated hopefully. **Where you wouldn't punish him. Don't you see? Dr Garry wants her to be dead, too!**

M decided Dr. Garry must have seen how angry Papa was with her for breaking out of the chamber and trying to kill that Black Mask! He was a grownup; he didn't understand! The more time it took to kill her, the more opportunities she had to kill them.

Rafe crouched down in front of her. "Little one, we had already decided that once we arrived on EX-112, we were going to end her. No more waiting for her to wake up to look upon our faces." Her suffering had just extended their own. He should have ended her when she begged for mercy, then they could have all been on the way to putting that part of their lives behind them.

M gave him another hopeful look. **Dr. Garry is not bad. Making people suffer is bad. That's why he took her.**

Karma lightly bit her lip, guilt flaming in her. Their hatred of Ragna had blinded them both. While making her hurt had consumed them, they had lost sight of how every breath she took only built on her daughter's fear.

What kind of mother did it make her that she had been so blinded by revenge she had ignored M's fear? M had formed an attachment to this doctor, which wouldn't bode well for her.

She exchanged looks with Rafe. The doctor's possible good intentions wouldn't save him. When the Galatians caught up with him, they were going to do to him what should have been done to Ragna when they had her in their clutches.

"Maybe you're right," she smiled at M while she lifted Runnar to her shoulder. He had fallen back to sleep after his meal and she patted his back absently. "Your dad will handle that situation. You and I should get ready to join the others. There's a new planet just waiting for us to explore."

M forced a smile onto her face as she took her mother's hand. It was time to pretend again. Grownups needed that.

Ragna was curled up in bed, too tired and hungry to feel motivated to get up. The other day she had gotten dressed in a pair of the ugly camo fatigue slacks that Pod had brought her when they'd first arrived. He'd swiped them from a human soldier. At the time, she'd chastised him for expecting her to wear masculine clothing. She was a consort! Her clothes were made of the finest silks and satins. But he had refused to return to retrieve her real clothing.

She'd punished him...but perhaps she had been too harsh. The pants had come in handy, as well as the boots and jacket. She'd finally gone outside, expecting an animal to jump out at her at every step. Wherever she was in the world, it had gotten cold, so she had snuggled deep into the ugly jacket that, although a bit scratchy, was incredibly warm.

Her hair was now too unruly to comb, so she'd been forced to tie it back just to keep it out of her way. For the first time in her life, Mayva thought about cutting her long locs. She had never had more than a simple trim and, undoubtedly; she had the best hair of anyone in the entire school—maybe even in the history of all the schools. She refused to allow this bump in the road to destroy all the work she had put into being the best of the best.

She'd crept out toward the woods that edged the clearing of the cabin. Every time there was a sound of flapping wings or scurrying critters, it made her wonder if a soldier was coming to return her to Ragna—or worse. Instead of protecting her, Ragna had just allowed them to abuse her! She'd been treated like less than a commoner; she'd been treated like a *minority!*

Despite the fear of the forest, her empty belly had kept her from returning to the house. Obviously, she wasn't equipped to catch a bird or snare a rabbit (and even if she was, there was no one around to clean and cook it!), so she concentrated on finding some fruit or vegetables. What she wouldn't do for an acai bowl! Maybe there was an acai bush somewhere...

But all she found was grass, leaves, and weeds. Any berries had probably died because of the impending winter weather, or they'd already been eaten by the creatures that belonged in a place like this.

She had returned to the cabin empty-handed and feeling even more defeated. After drinking a large glass of water, she realized it had a strange taste. It was cloudy. Damnit, maybe all of her frequent showers had depleted her water supply...

Unable to think about it for the time being, Mayva had climbed into bed, where at least she could sleep and forget her predicament—at least for a while.

But now she was awake, and it was undeniable. She would die if she didn't get out of this place.

She pulled herself out of bed and went to the toilet to pee. Before flushing, she thought about what she'd do if she ran out of water completely. She didn't flush. Somewhere in the back of her mind, she considered that at least the drinking water that had her own pee in it was a better option than being forced to drink the piss and semen-laced water of the soldiers that abused her.

Mayva refused to cry anymore, but she did feel very sorry for herself. She looked in the mirror, horrified at the dark hollows beneath her blue eyes. She was pale (which was fine), but blotchy, and her hair had come undone and was an impossible mess.

She slowly applied makeup, because her movements could be nothing but slow. She was starved. She tied a rag around her head, imagining it looked stylish and trendy. When she was satisfied with her looks, Mayva opened the drawer that contained her communicator.

She sat on the edge of the bed, considering this might be the worst decision of her life. But she had to do something. She made the call. A face immediately appeared on the miniature screen.

"Most Exalted Queen Amalia. I've been kidnapped and tortured. Please help..."

Rafe was just preparing to meet the others to guide them to the planet he hoped they would truly view as Eden when his communicator sounded. His hopes that Drago had gotten a link to the Doctor's location were dashed when he saw the communication was from Einar.

He cursed and looked around. He didn't want Einar to know

anything about his actions, and that included him being on a ship. He moved swiftly into an alcove. Things were quiet as the crew had disembarked or were preparing to.

"Commander." He was preparing to tell the man he had not decided on whether he would accept Amalia's terms for the parley. In fact, he decided that with or without Mayva Heath present, it was more important to secure Haru's safe retreat.

"Lieutenant. I just wanted to inform you there has been a change of mind concerning the parley. Mayva Heath will be present. I am here to secure a time."

Rafe grunted his approval. "One day from now should give us time to gather all parties. You will notify the Japoxillian delegates?"

"They have been notified."

"Then 0100 hours, one day from now."

Einar looked relieved and quickly ended the call.

Rafe opened his scales until they puffed out like porcupine quills. It was something he rarely did around his human family. Not only was it dangerous for them to touch him with his scales 'weaponized', but he looked less humanoid when he did this. But 'ruffling' his scales was like taking a deep sigh.

Things had gone off rails. He would need to call his men back in time to attend the parley because returning Haru to the fold was more important than ending Ragna and the traitor that had taken her.

His scales reddened. He would make sure he achieved each of those goals.

Chapter Five

EX-112 could not be mistaken for Earth. It was too beautiful for anything any of the humans in Rafe's party had ever seen in their world. From the moment they stepped off the ship, M and the former consorts could only think of the planet as Eden.

The moment they stepped onto the loading strip, the group was met with air that was so pleasant it actually seemed to have a flavor. To M, it was like flowers, while others said it tasted the way sunshine felt, and breathing it felt like happiness.

Rafe thought about mentioning the slight difference in the gas vapors that made the air in EX-112. In much higher doses, it could be described as laughing gas. It was completely safe, so in the end, he kept that information in the need-to-know-only file within his head.

M did not think anything could pull her from her concerns for the future until she saw the soft blue sky that seemed so vast because the skyline wasn't cluttered by sprawling skyscrapers and ugly factories. In the distance were tree-covered hills--and did those trees have purple leaves? M was surprised to realize it wasn't just the trees. The grass was purple!

They entered an open-air transport vehicle resembling a trolley, which would take them the short distance to a tall, sprawling building that gleamed like a metallic space station. No one could help but think that it felt out of place in a world that was filled with such color and vibrance.

Around them, other ships were docked, although theirs was the largest. Individuals, mostly aliens, busily loaded or unloaded goods. Even though the workers paid little attention to them, Daya was happy that she had worn long sleeves and a scarf that covered her head and face.

Paris had explained that sunscreen might not be necessary since the atmosphere here was in better condition than Earth's, but she didn't want to take any chances. Now she saw that the temperature was so mild that had she ever traveled outside of the Midwest, she would have known it was tropical. It would be nice to venture around without worrying about damage to her skin, but she would always be conscious of stares.

As they drew closer to the building, tall barriers could be seen separating the loading areas from the view of the building entrances. It was as they rounded the security gates into Eden that they could appreciate the manicured grounds and the humans that moved about. A large stone monument had been erected with a sign that read, "WELCOME TO EDEN".

Karma peered closely at the colorful balls of fluff that pecked at the manicured grass.

"Are those birds?" Several colorful poufs flapped miniature wings and took flight into the lavender sky.

"Yes," Rafe replied. "Although they aren't birds you would be familiar with." He addressed the rest of the small group as they exited the transport.

"While Eden is an amazing planet, there are some things to be aware of."

Maddie clutched Rex closer. But Rex was unconcerned as he quietly strained to look at everything at once.

"Come, and I will explain. I am told there is a room that has been vacated for our use." He gestured for them to follow him through the ornate entrance to the building.

DRIFT SPIRE was intricately carved above the entrance.

A little girl, holding the hand of her mother pointed.

"Mommy, that's a Galatian!"

"Hush," her mother hurried her along.

Karma looked around and realized that Drift Spire was a mall. There were shops of all kinds with signs above their entrances announcing their purpose—although Karma couldn't always decipher what that was. There was a Nexus Hub—perhaps a bar? And the Cosmic Exchange. But the most popular of all was the Starlight Bazaar. Now that was something she understood.

The smell of food and the bustle of shoppers told her that this was the true reason most of the individuals were there.

Karma saw some of their crew, recognizable by their uniforms. Strangely, she saw none of the alien crew—just the humans, and they openly gawked at Rafe.

Earth wasn't allowed to interact with aliens other than the Galatians, but while Eden wasn't technically counted as Earth, these people still seemed to find the different species just as shocking as if they themselves weren't on an alien planet.

Mama? M asked while looking at a group of children who stared at her. **Are these kids Earthlings? Or are they aliens?**

Rafe was now carrying Runnar and Karma gnawed her lip as she considered the question. "I don't know. But I don't think it really matters."

M silently agreed.

Daya unconsciously gathered her scarves to conceal her skin. It was one thing to be confident in the presence of Paris, but quite a different thing when he was not with her.

Justina matched everyone's stare with equal curiosity. Some were men who straightened their posture or jutted out their chests at the sight of her. Some of those men even received an elbow to the ribs from their significant other.

Maddie was not impressed. The entire building was "dramatic", to say the least. One far wall held a mural of outer space, embedded by a large glass-painted planet that resembled Earth. The designers had missed an opportunity to play into the natural beauty of Eden when they created a cold and sterile, space-themed structure.

Maddie thought it was a building that tried too hard to be fine. Of course, a consort would know such things. They had been trained to expect only the best. Once upon a time, she would have been able to list every fashion and decorating *faux pas* that existed. Now, she could only hope that their living arrangements did not mimic this horrible *industrial-space* age design.

Rafe led them through the open area until they reached a security door, which he opened with his communicator. It led them down a long corridor, and at the end was another security door. When he opened this door, they were once again in a bustling area filled with delicious smells, strange music, and a crowd of people. The one stark difference is that this was where the aliens communed.

Aliens of all sizes and shapes moved about. Their shops had signs that she couldn't read although she suspected that if she held up her communicator, it would generate a translation for her.

Finally, Rafe spoke again.

"This is not just a place of trade. It is also a sanctuary for non-humans that are required to do business in Eden. As you have been told, Eden is a closed planet. But unlike Earth, the Edenites are fully aware that extraterrestrials exist."

As the group entered an empty room that looked like it did double duty as a canteen, Daya noted that the aliens did not pay them the least concern. It was the first time that she felt as if she could allow her veils to slip.

They took seats on large stools which could accommodate beings with or without tails.

"This area of Drift Spire is called The Nexus Hub—at least in the human tongue. The intermingling of life forms is strictly prohibited except for Galatians. We are well known here, as we have been assigned to protect this planet and its human inhabitants.

In exchange, we are allowed free movement and are granted something akin to diplomatic treatment."

M had plenty of questions, but it was best to listen first.

"I will provide a quick run-up of what you will need to know to be comfortable here. But you will learn more by living it first-hand." Rafe continued.

"Run down," Karma corrected.

"Ah. Yes." Rafe moved to the front of the room as if he was a professor instructing a class. "EX-112 is now on the second generation of Edenites. As you know, since the Progress Initiative was passed into law, humans are no longer allowed to colonize other planets. Those already here were given the option of staying or returning to Earth. But if they chose to stay, it would be with no expectation of support from planet Earth."

"I remember learning about it in school," Daya said. "Eden was a world intended as an escape for the wealthiest people of Earth." What she didn't add was it turned out to be a fight for supremacy; cultural, political—whatever someone with power thought made them better than another group. And then The Collective shut it down.

Rafe continued. "You'll see that the Edenites are broken into two main factions. The elite and the working class. There is not much interaction between them—and there have been very few outsiders. Many may not have seen new Earthlings in decades and especially not humanoids or aliens.

"So, I will say that while this is not a hostile planet, you should use care when interacting with the natives. They understand that the Galatian Guards enforce law and order throughout this galaxy—and they provide us with certain privileges. But they have their own laws and customs that might seem strange to outsiders."

Justina sighed. "Why can't things just go smoothly for once?"

Maddie's brow went up in agreement. But Karma and Daya were both thinking their own private yet similar thoughts: Compared to the bullshit on Earth, this place sounded like paradise.

Mayva closed her eyes as she luxuriated in the hot bubble bath. An attendant had washed and detangled her hair while another had given her a molecular detox to cleanse her of the impurities after her harrowing ordeal.

Why had she waited so long before contacting Amalia? She'd been afraid initially. Especially when she'd been escorted to a conference room where the entire Queen's Council was present by a holographic feed. They, of course, were in Galatia while she was on Earth, but the room felt like a prison, and for the life of her, she thought it was where she was meant to be kept.

But Amalia had simply questioned her about the whereabouts of Ragna. Mayva was honestly perplexed by the questions until she realized Ragna had run off—probably afraid of the repercussions of losing her!

Even if Amalia and her council weren't present to smell her honesty, the two big Galatian Guards that stayed by her side obviously could. They spoke to the council using strange clicks and throat vibrations, and it was no stretch of the imagination they were confirming her honesty.

Regardless, Amalia had sympathized and ordered her to be given superior accommodations. The first thing she'd done when she'd reached her luxury suite was to eat plates and plates of food. Now she was sated, clean, and ready to climb into the oversized bed beneath a comforter filled with the finest Japoxillian feathers and down. Fleetingly, she wondered if someone had thought to harvest the feathers from the dead Japoxillian that had been caught in the crossfire. It would be such a waste to destroy the valuable feathers when blood could be easily washed off feathers and fur. And even if it did stain, no one would know if they were sewn inside of pillows.

One of the human attendants helped her out of the bath and, after drying her, they slipped a silk robe over her nude body to prepare her for her massage.

She wanted to slip into bed, but who could turn down a full-body massage after all she'd suffered?

Her communicator sounded, indicating an incoming communication. Amalia.

"Most Exalted." Mayva lowered her eyes respectfully.

"Child," Amalia stated while eyeing her critically. "You have grown quite thin—even for a consort. I fear it might be some time before you will be presentable to address our backers."

Mayva looked up quickly. "With a little make-up and the right clothes, I'll be the picture of health. Most Exalted, I am ready and willing to fulfill the duties of my position."

Amalia nodded. "You won't be needed to handle your duties with the Galatian Exchange—the preparations are already well underway."

Mayva blanched, feeling her power slipping. She told herself it didn't matter. She would regain her position within the Exchange. She would show them how invaluable she was.

"I have several speeches prepared-"

"And, of course, you will give them," Amalia said pleasantly. "But I have another duty for you. Tomorrow there is to be an important meeting and I need you to be in attendance—virtually, of course."

"Yes. Of course." Her mind searched for the memories of snippets from previous speeches. Instead of a massage, she would need to think of a winning speech.

"Good," Amalia continued. "You won't have to do anything, child. You just have to be present."

"Okay..." What kind of meeting did she need to attend where she didn't have to speak?

"It's just some ugly business with Rafe Sigur."

"Rafe Sigur..." Mayva looked at the hologram in confusion.

"We're going to have a well-overdue discussion. And the only way he would agree to the parley is if he had certain demands met. One of them was for you to be present."

Mayva's mouth parted. She couldn't find the words to even stutter.

"Do not trouble yourself about it. You will be in one location while he is in another. Of course, he wants the other consorts present. He said he wanted his human to address you directly. But you are under no obligation to speak. In addition, the Japoxillian delegates of The Interplanetary Collective will also be present. But again, you have nothing to worry about from The Collective. You have been placed under our protection and despite their status, you will not be held criminally responsible for the deaths of those Japoxillian. Upholding our laws cannot be a crime in the eyes of the Galatian Court."

Mayva had blanched—What did she mean "criminally" responsible? "But I never killed any of the Japos. That was Ragna! And Auras was the one who shot Titus."

"You are on the side of good, Mayva Heath. And as long as you stay on our side, you will always prevail.

"Now be sure to prepare yourself, for tomorrow you will attend the meeting to face your ex-fellow consorts. Unfortunately, there is no other way." Amalia disconnected and Mayva drew her lip into her mouth and gnawed it until the skin broke and a red tinge of her blood coated her tongue.

Chapter Six

Paris, Drago, and Kendrick arrived at the community center just when the rest of the group was preparing to enter an old-fashioned open-air bus that would take them to their new home.

Paris's eyes scanned the people until they locked onto the image of Daya. Immediately he crossed the room to her, and although he might have preferred a hug and a kiss, he just took her hand in his while smiling with a deep pink tint.

Drago's son saw him from across the room and bounced up and down in his mother's arms.

"Da da da," he exclaimed, reaching out while opening and closing his fat little fists. Drago wasted no time reaching for his woman and son. He took Rex and held him in the crook of one arm as he placed his other around Maddie's shoulders. Instantly, her body relaxed against his. She knew she could handle this alone, but it was so much better having Drago by her side.

Kendrick headed for Justina, who watched him with interest. "How could they get away? Galatians are the best pilots in the entire galaxy."

Rafe had explained he had called the men back to attend an important meeting the following day. He said once they arrived at their new home, he'd explain more.

Kendrick's color was grim. Ending their search for Ragna and Brookstone now would only make more work later. Yet he understood the necessity.

"Yes, but we were at warp speed. It's much harder to track a transport even if we hone in on the exact moment Brookstone made his escape. In time we will find him, but Rafe wanted us to attend tomorrow's meeting."

Justina's expression became even more grim than his. "Yes, that meeting. Do you think we'll have an opportunity to speak to that traitor, Justina?"

"Time permitting. But I believe it was Rafe's purpose for asking her to join the meeting."

Her eyes narrowed. "Good."

They boarded a different transport to take them to their residence. It, too, was an open-air vehicle, but this one was much finer and glided over the ground mysteriously like a child's hoverboard. It also didn't spew exhaust. Back on Earth, only clean fuel was allowed due to the erosion of the ozone layer, but that didn't stop the use of rickety old vehicles in rural and off-grid areas.

A human soldier drove it, while a convoy of military transports flanked them. As Justina gazed out at the beautiful scenery, one truck stayed on pace with them, and one soldier in the truck watched her. She saw that it was Sgt. Kelly—Adrian, they had insisted she call them.

Adrian offered a short nod when they were caught staring. Justina nodded back and smiled. Kendrick observed the interaction using his tail. He remembered once seeing the soldier near Justina and hadn't thought anything of it. But now he could hear the sudden swoosh of blood as it ran through Justina's veins, as well as her rapidly beating heart. She sounded like Daya, Maddie, and Karma when they looked at their mates. Only Justina had not sounded like them when she had looked at him—not now, not ever.

He was quiet as they sat side by side while she pointed out interesting sights. His mind continued to repeat the same thoughts; she didn't want him—not romantically. It was the soldier she wanted…

Garry shut off his thrusters to reserve energy. His vehicle hovered in the deep, dark space. He needed to find a viable place to sit down. Earth was out of the question. There were star charts that specifically listed areas safe for humans and any other alien life form recognized by The Collective. But planets that supported human life were few and far between. The next level of questionable planets had breathable air, but hostile environments: too cold, too hot, predatory, etc.

He'd have to go to a planet like that; where he could hunker down and make his next move. Once he located a comfortable place to land, he could basically stay on the transport and pipe in the air from outdoors.

He closed his eyes and thought about the prisoner. He rubbed his tired eyes and sighed. The easiest and most humane way to kill her was made difficult because she was in that damned chrysalis. Galatians were hard to kill without factoring in the added armor.

He could electrocute her the way the child M had intended. But there would be pain and he knew she was aware enough to feel; emotionally as well as physically. For instance, he knew she was aware they had moved. The monitors showed a spike of adrenalin, which indicated fight, flight, and fear.

It only lasted until she became unconscious, and then the monitors were calm again. But she awakened more and more often. He hadn't exactly lied to the little girl. She might not be a danger to anyone presently, but before long she would be.

Garry intended to keep his promise to the little girl. That child murderer would never hurt her or hers again. But he also had a promise to keep to himself; he would never stand by and wait on formality or expectations because rules invariably benefited the rule maker more than anyone else. If it felt wrong, he didn't care whose rules they were, he would not follow them. Right was right and wrong was wrong. He would not be a party to torturing someone who had begged him for mercy... never again.

Garry opened the maps again and resumed studying them. He was tired and needed a few hours of sleep—but sleeping was a hard thing to do when he knew the most decorated warriors in the galaxy wanted him dead. His hope was once he shipped Ragna's head to them, they would forget about him and move on. Great Guardian knew they had more important things to worry about. A government task force had been formed to investigate Karma Sigur's allegations.

While back on Earth, he had seen that many people were siding with her. And while that was good for Rafe and his separate issues with the Queens, it might not be so good for Karma. She was being summoned to attend a formal hearing to testify against the Black Masks. Influential humans, such as movie stars and singers, were pressuring human lawmakers to do something about the attack and subsequent disappearances. There was a trending hashtag growing in popularity that read #Protectourhumans.

He didn't believe for a minute that human officials cared one bit about Karma. But the officials had never been popular. It was the performers and artists who spoke up against Alien on human violence.

And yet, because Karma hadn't come forward, rumors were now flying. Some thought she was an opportunist and liar, while others feared she'd been captured by the Black Masks in retribution. No, he assumed once Rafe got what they wanted, he and his men would forget about him.

It took a while, but he finally located a planet mined dry by Trinchians who used human slave labor. Acid was a by-product of Trinchian defense, which they spit on their prey or enemies. As a result, the land was riddled with sinkholes, and pools of acid were everywhere. It was no longer viable to support human life when their valuable slaves were rendered lifeless when they lost a foot after stepping into acid.

This minor planet was small and could easily get lost among the thousands of other nearby stars and planets. He started his engine and navigated to it.

As he set his ship to autopilot, Garry napped. He wasn't worried about being tracked. He'd learned a thing or two being a mercenary and one of them was that it was extremely difficult to track someone if hyperspeed was in use... and if the tracking was disabled. Still, it wasn't impossible for them to locate the space trail. All ships left them if you knew how to look for them.

But it would take time, and by then he'd have this business completed.

After what seemed like a long ride compared to the rapidness of space pod travel, Rafe's crew reached their destination. Along the way, they had been awed by fields of flowers that came in every color known to man. There were waterfalls and lakes as red as blood. Strange birds with long legs and necks stood on the shallow bank, plucking up fish and gobbling them down whole.

There were also other critters resembling rabbits or squirrels, and fat grey creatures with long snouts that Maddie thought were called *aard*—something or other. Rex bounced up and down on his father's lap as he looked out the window in wonder. Drago pointed out items naming them to the baby, who tried to mimic him even if it was just a grunt.

Justina watched the black-haired, blue-eyed baby with a strange yearning. She had never wanted to be a mother, but watching Karma and Maddie over the last few weeks had made her long for a new type of love—one that included family.

She thought about Adrian and the way they had promised to be there to watch over her. She realized she was smiling, but if anyone saw, they probably assumed it was because of the cuteness overload of Drago with his son.

M was the first one to climb off the bus because she just leaped over the side even though Karma tried to grab for her. But soldiers were already present, setting up their stations.

M looked up at the mansion. No, mansions were tall, this was just big. One big house for all of them. She liked that.

Paris had escorted Daya down the stairs. "Will we all live here together?" She asked. She couldn't imagine this sprawling property being designated to one family.

"Yes. We will each have a separate wing."

From where she stood, she could see courtyards with open-air rooms. There were lush gardens with stone seating areas. There was even a pool.

Beyond the house was an expanse of water; the ocean? It was pink but inviting.

"Is that okay?" Paris asked. "If not, I can ask Rafe to provide us our own-"

"No! I love this." She'd thought the last compound was nice, albeit rustic. But this was on a completely new level. It reminded her of old Hollywood homes she'd seen in magazines. Having her own home with Paris had been a dream, but his...

"You approve? Paris asked."

Daya just nodded rapidly.

Rafe turned to address the group. He would have looked very authoritative if he hadn't been holding his baby that was trying to grab for his eyes with pudgy little fingers. Rafe would responsively close one or both eyes as he spoke.

"I've sent you each a map of the accommodations. You will find there are more than sufficient quarters for us all. Each has their own kitchen. Unfortunately, there haven't been any modern upgrades, so while there are various appliances, it doesn't include vendor service. This brings up another point; there won't be individual maid services. There is a caretaker who cares for the grounds while his wife maintains the home. She will prepare one dinner meal in the style of her Earth province in Italy. But any other meals will have to be prepared by your own hands. So, in many ways, it is no different from our last accommodations, but I hope you will find them more than adequate."

"It's definitely lusher," Justina said.

"I love it!" Maddie said. "I can't wait to explore. This entire planet is amazing!"

The others quickly agreed.

"Just remember to keep a low profile. No one knows our history on Earth." Rafe said.

But all those people saw us when we came. M stated. **They will know who we are.**

"No," Rafe replied. "This is a closed planet. It is cut off from news from Earth. Also, because of their prohibition of interacting with other life forms, they don't know anything concerning current events."

"When we arrived," he continued, "They saw three women with three children being escorted by one Galatian—your security guard. Our military has been handpicked for this mission. They will not speak our secrets. No one knows who we are unless you tell them." He said the latter, not just to M, but eyed them all. After everyone nodded in agreement, they dispersed to find their suites and to use the toilets.

Chapter Seven

"What are your thoughts about everything?" Rafe asked his family as they entered the home. The others had already disappeared inside, excited to explore their new accommodations. M spun around.

I like it Papa!

"I like it too, but it's so big," Karma said. The room they had just entered had the feel of a lodge with seating for many individuals. Yet it still felt cozy with rustic wooden and stone panels and two over-sized fireplaces. The stone floors were polished and large animal hide rugs adorned it. "Is this another hotel? Are others staying here?"

"Just us. A small military staff will be set up nearby—a larger one will form a compound by week's end."

Karma thought about the many places a Black Mask could hide...

Rafe took her hand as if reading her thoughts.

"It will be fine," he whispered. "We will not allow her to get away."

She offered him a brief smile. "Tamsyn and Haru will arrive soon, won't they?"

"Soon," he replied. "But first we deal with tomorrow's meeting. Have you thought about what you will say?"

"Yes," she said coldly. "I have a few things in mind."

Nurse Guyton rounded the corner. The moment she saw Runnar, a broad smile filled her face, and he bounced in his father's arms. She quickly crossed the room and the baby practically jumped into her arms with a loud squeal. She chuckled.

"I was going to offer to take him off your hands for a while, but it looks like he has the same idea."

Karma reached out and ran her hands through his curls. "Are you sure? You must have a ton of unpacking to do."

The nurse bounced the baby. "Not until after you pick our rooms, so I'll be next to the little one." The nurse gave Rafe an appreciative look. "This is a fine place you selected, Sir."

"Thank you. Humans find this planet most agreeable." He turned to Karma. "I am in dire need of a swim. Do you mind if I leave you for a bit? There are several soldiers already-"

Karma shook her head. "Honey, go. M and I have a lot of exploring to do." She looked around the large room with its fireplaces and overly adorned furnishing. It was certainly rich, but she could clearly see it was also outdated. She had worked in the homes of enough wealthy people to tell. Not that she was complaining. It was still beautiful. But she was curious about where the Galatian pool was located.

"Will there be more than one pool?" She was thinking about the other men.

Rafe had crouched and was removing his boots. "No. These homes were made for humans and didn't include a Galatian den. We have a common area located outdoors."

"Oh. An outhouse."

He came to his feet. "No. It's a cave. It is used by all Galatians in the area. I will call the others to join me."

"Well, how far away is this cave?" she asked in surprise.

"Just a few miles."

"Miles!"

He gave her an amused look. "Which will only take moments to access at a full run." He bent and placed his forehead against hers. "I won't be long. Once you select our quarters, I will bring our belongings. I do not want you attempting to unpack everything yourself. I worry about your legs. They still seem to be in a weakened state."

Mama needs to train with us, M said.

Rafe gave his daughter a stern look. "You and I will have a discussion about your continued training."

M's mouth dropped. Was he going to put a stop to her training as punishment? She thought he had forgotten. Before she could say anything more, he turned and bounded out of the house at a speed no human could have matched.

Karma placed her hand on M's shoulder. "I am so sorry you felt the need to risk your life for us."

Upon hearing Karma's serious tone, the nurse eased out of the area with her charge.

M looked at her mother with a solemn expression.

I'm sorry. I know it was wrong.

"Yes, but you're not the only one who did something wrong. Your dad and I allowed our anger to control us." Her expression darkened. "Now that... that-" she had to purse her lips before she could continue. "That *woman* is gone, and worse, we didn't listen when our family told us how they felt. So, I'm sorry, M. I'm sorry we didn't take care of that problem when we had the opportunity. If our desire for more revenge had resulted in you being injured..." she shook her head and when she continued, her voice was thick with emotion. "I don't know if I could have handled it. I don't want to lose another child."

M saw the strain on her mother's pretty face. She felt ashamed at having done anything to add to her anguish. **I won't do that again, Mama. I promise.**

Karma nodded. "Then I promise to always listen and to hear you. Do we have a deal?"

M nodded and hand in hand, they went deeper into the house.

They found the kitchen and an oversized dining area. They ran into Justina, who had called dibs on a quaint suite of rooms decorated in pastels instead of the rustic wood paneling. And finally, they came upon a set of rooms they would call home for the foreseeable future.

"The mister is going to have a hard time locating us," Nurse said.

M was studying an outdated television screen that hung from the wall. **No. He will smell us,** she replied.

Karma looked around in approval. The master bedroom was spacious and had a balcony overlooking the ocean. French doors were opened to let in the sweet air. M's room had a canopy bed and was decorated in pink and white.

M didn't tell her mother that Kelsie would like it better than her. She liked pretty things.

Runnar's room was across a large corridor and had a smaller adjoining room just large enough for the nanny's bed and dresser. Each room had an adjoining bathroom and, although nice, Karma was simply happy it didn't contain an outdoor toilet.

The bedrooms surrounded a nice-sized living area with about the twentieth fireplace they'd seen since entering the villa. Their quarters opened onto a private lanai. Fruit-bearing trees could be seen with the largest lemons known to man. The families she worked for would vacation in places like this.

Mama, can I call Bain and Kelsie now?

"Kelsie might still be too sick after her surgery to speak much. Remember how you felt when you got your hearing?" M looked crestfallen, but Karma continued. "But I'm sure they'd love to hear from you." M managed a sharp sound of excitement, and then she ran outside to the porch. "Remember the time difference on Earth!" she called, and M waved her hands in acknowledgment.

Karma let out a long breath and turned back to face the empty room.

Her legs did indeed ache. But not too long ago, she had been as close to death as anyone could be and still survive, so she could not complain. She walked tiredly into the master bedroom, past the bed that had been made as if the staff had known this room would be selected by a new family. She walked into the bathroom and closed the door softly. The moment it was closed, Karma slipped to the floor and allowed the tears to finally flow.

She squeezed her eyes closed and made fists and fought against the scream that wanted to burst from her body. Instead, quiet wracking sobs shook her. She put her arms around her belly and cried for her lost child. Runnar was everything; her light, her joy—but one baby did not replace another, and she missed the baby who had grown in her body. She missed him so much.

She drew her knees up and wrapped her arms around them and then rocked with her head placed on them just the way she had done as a child. And she cried for her Daddy and her Mama and the bad things that made his face look the way it did. She also cried because she missed him again as if he had just been taken—because he was. She had lost him again.

Her tears subsided only when she thought about how much she hated Ragna and Mayva. For now, she couldn't do anything about the evil, jealous, so-called woman who had killed her child, but Mayva, who had assisted in the murder of their family and friends, would certainly face her deeds and actions. And although it wouldn't be from behind bars, she was going to know what she'd taken from them.

Hello, Bain?

"M!"

Turn on hologram.

"Okay, let me go outside. Mom and Dad are sleeping," he whispered.

How is Kelsie? Mama said she got her new lungs.

Bain closed the door to a small cottage. It looked like it was made for elves and fairies. Papa would definitely not be able to fit inside.

The hologram showed he was standing in a field of green with the backdrop of a dark sky that sparkled with distant stars.

"She sleeps a lot. But she's not in pain or anything. We come home while she sleeps."

The two friends stood in front of each other, inches apart, while in reality, they were countless light years from the other.

Bain was looking in awe at the landscape that surrounded M. "Wow. Is that a pink ocean?"

Sometimes it's pink, sometimes it's purple. The grass is purple, too! And look at this giant piece of fruit. She plucked one from a low branch. Bain followed her wistfully with his eyes. Even though the monitor was attached to her wrist, once the hologram was initiated, it remained stationary and captured the wearer in a panoramic view. He watched her leap and dart around energetically as she showed him the weird grass and plants.

"Have you seen many aliens?" He asked with interest.

A lot! Not all of them are humanoid, either. I saw a giant wearing a hat and a little fly that could talk. Papa says you have to be very careful not to do harm to innocent beings. He showed us a big chart with all the aliens. I can send it to you.

Bain nodded enthusiastically. "It's so boring here. I can't wait until we can leave."

I know. M sat down on the grass and Bain sat down on the grass opposite her. **How long do you think it will be before you can come?**

"My parents won't say. They just say when Kelsie is better."

Okay.

"M, did you really try to kill that Black Mask?"

I told you I would, didn't I?

Bain's brow rose. M was the only kid he knew that when she said she'd do something, she would make it happen. "I thought you were just talking big."

Well, I didn't do it, and now she's gone.

"Do you think she'll find you?" M thought for a moment before replying.

Not for a while. After she kills poor Dr. Garry, she will steal his transport and find someplace safe to hide while she gets strong.

"Yeah. That's in every alien movie I've ever seen."

Right! M gave him a look of confusion. **Why don't grown-ups know this?**

"Because grown-ups fall in the wrong place. You know, in the movies, but also in real life. Kids don't fall. Kids keep running." Bain held a distant expression.

Maybe Dr. Garry will kill her...but she gave her friend a doubtful look.

Garry settled his transport at one of the high points of a rocky ridge. There were trees that looked like stalagmites. He saw no leaves, in fact, there was no greenery in sight. This was a wasteland. He closed the view from the window, electing to simply use the camera view of the area. There was something very creepy about watching this barren world from the oversized picture window.

He stretched and almost obsessively; he went to check on his patient/prisoner. He did this every few hours, even waking himself when sleeping. The monitors showed she was sleeping and calm. His initial treatment of her had been too good because now it appeared she was in no danger of dying from her wounds. That would have been the optimal outcome—just allowing her body to give up its life forces.

But it was too late for that. With or without him, Ragna would survive her injuries. It is why it was so important to end her life the moment her cocoon allowed him access to her. He'd already prepared the injection. Her heart would stop beating within seconds. It was painless, but more importantly, it was quick.

Standing on the ledge of the pool, he quickly undressed and then dived him. Unlike most humans, he knew of the holistic benefits of the Galatian waters. Some called it the fountain of youth, but the enzymes produced after consuming the waste assisted with any number of ailments. And while he didn't think it would give his skin melanin, he thought it might help with his nystagmus. When he was tired—like now — his vision moved more rapidly back and forth and it **would**, and **did,** make him dizzy.

Garry swam for a while, careful not to disturb the chrysalis. After a few moments of steaming in the sauna area, he floated on his back, lazily kicking his legs and thinking about the good times of his child-hood when he'd swam in a lake doing the same thing. As a child, his world had been set in stone. His friendships had been more meaning-ful. His future was not as questionable.

He dozed, awakening only when he realized the water was moving gently, as if from the ebb and flow of the tide. He looked over at the chrysalis and saw she was awake and rocking her cocoon, causing the gentle, sleepy motion.

Was she looking at him? No...she couldn't see through the thick-ened membrane. But he could tell her head was turned in his direc-tion. He swam to the pool's edge, got out, and quickly dressed.

Chapter Eight

Cheryl glared at the tall woman. "I can't stand that bitch."

Kendra snorted. "That's because she keeps fucking you over in all the challenges."

Cheryl glared at Kendra. "That big fat bitch is a secret man, I bet."

Lottie rolled her eyes. "No one has to be a secret man. This force is good for keeping everybody equal."

Cheryl ignored the woman. If you weren't on her side, then you might as well be her enemy.

Marisol was about to take a seat with her large tray of food when Cheryl called her.

"Yo, Marisol. Over here."

Marisol looked around and quickly recognized the women at one of the distant tables. She headed toward them, and Kendra hissed under her breath.

"What are you doing? You know she ain't right..."

"Neurodivergent doesn't mean she's not right," Lottie snapped. "Many people are on the spectrum, including the Galatians." She was rapidly becoming tired of Cheryl and her group of mean girls.

The only reason she'd sat with them was because her usual team-mates weren't around.

Marisol took an empty seat with the small group of women. "What's up?" she said, paying more attention to her meal than to the people seated at the table. She bit into a fist-sized roll, devouring most of it with one bite.

"Good job in the simulator." Cheryl grinned. Marisol shrugged.

"Thanks." She was a person of few words. But that had been her life, so she didn't realize she came off as abrupt. When there was no one to talk to, listening became her main form of interacting with others.

"You broke the speed record." Cheryl continued as if she couldn't believe the big woman wasn't bragging about it. She would have been.

Marisol shrugged. "Yep." She scooped stew into her mouth.

Tana, another woman, smirked. "She broke plenty of records. Ain't nothing new to her."

"I have, too!" Cheryl snapped.

Marisol finally looked up. "Those challenges don't compare to my daily chores back on the farm." Her country twang had taken the women some time to get used to, as did her odd height and build.

The challenges did not excite Marisol. There wasn't much that tested her abilities. She could do anything the male soldiers did—and more.

Marisol was a big farm girl. Some, such as Cheryl and a few others, called her stupid because of her accent. And while it was true Marisol was on the spectrum, she was far from stupid. She knew Cheryl considered her a competitor. What she didn't understand was the depth of jealousy the woman felt for her.

Marisol didn't see herself as someone to be jealous of—not with her looks. She was built like an ox. And while many Appalachians in her neck of the woods had similar appearances (for various reasons that need not be detailed), Marisol did not. Instead of the thin, waif-like forms of her brothers and sisters, or the silken hair that ran down their backs, she had wiry red hair and freckles with skin as pale as milk. Guardian couldn't even grant her warm brown eyes, but green ones that her father refused to look into. People whispered about the giant, red-haired itinerate worker who had come to the farm the year before she was born. She didn't want to know about him—or if he knew about her. She just wanted to fit in.

Marisol did what she needed to do to become invaluable. But no matter how hard she worked—even when she did the work of three men, her father still made her sleep and eat her meals in the barn with the animals. And Mama only said she should be quiet and keep the peace. But what peace when Daddy still blacked Mama's eye whenever he drank too much. But Marisol had been quiet, and she worked hard and tried to keep the peace—until she couldn't any longer.

When she could take no more of the abuse, she joined the military and was recruited by the Galatians for their special forces. And while she didn't exactly fit in, at least she didn't sleep or eat in a barn.

"How many records have you broken?" Lottie asked with a smirk while glancing at Cheryl, who glared at her.

"Dunno," Marisol said with another shrug. She gave them a dull look before continuing to eat. "Breaking records ain't as hard as breaking steer." She'd brought down steer for sport to back Daddy's bets. And she never lost. Not that Daddy ever gave her praise.

A group of Galatian Guards walked past the open door of the commissary as they headed to the cavern where their den was located.

"You ever seen a Galatian's prick?" Cheryl asked.

"Who hasn't?" Kendra said wistfully. They trained and fought in the nude. They were like sexy animals who didn't really want to wear clothes but had to, otherwise every woman on Earth would be staring at their magnificent pricks.

"Yeah, but have you ever seen it hard?"

"No, and I don't think I want to, not personally," A woman laughed. "It's big enough when it's limp."

"I saw Kendrick with a boner." Cheryl bragged.

"No!" Someone screeched. "How big was it?"

"Well, it was beneath his skirt, but it was huge!" She leaned in to whisper as if she had juicy news. "You know he ain't had a good fuck in months since his consort died."

"He's got a new consort, that chick Paris dumped." Someone whispered while looking around fearfully.

"No," Cheryl said knowingly. "He ain't fucking her. She plays for the other team."

"Shut the fuck up," Kendra replied with wide eyes.

"Of course she is," Lottie replied. "Why else would Kelly be sniffing around her? Kelly's already got themselves assigned to her quadrant."

"Good thing Kelly doesn't need a prick. That consort's probably jacked up down there after fucking Galatian prick. Guys, his boner was poking that skirt out like crazy!"

Marisol just snorted. Cheryl glared at her. "What? Don't tell me you've seen a real Galatian boner?"

"Seen bigger." Marisol used the last of her bread to scrape the sides of her empty stew bowl.

"There ain't nothing bigger than Galatian prick."

"Bull prick is two feet long. There's lots of pricks bigger than Galatians. Ain't nothing special about taking big ones. If them little ladies can do it, then anyone can."

"I dare you, then. Fuck a Galatian-"

"Those women have been altered-" Kendra said.

"Not the Black chick. She snuck her way into the Exchange. You all know she did. She was just a maid—just like any of us." Cheryl's eyes lit up at the forbidden topic, even while the others at the table grew quiet and looked away nervously. This was the kind of talk that got you discharged from the Galatian's handpicked military. They didn't stand for any disloyalty. Her eyes bore into Marisol.

"Let's make a wager. Let's see who can fuck a Galatian first."

Marisol shook her head. "I said I seen big pricks. I ain't say nothing about taking one —"

"You can't even lie and say these big-talking little prick soldiers do it for you. A girl like you probably swallows them whole."

Marisol shrugged. "Not all human males are tiny. I found a few that did pretty well." She didn't know why men liked big women. Sometimes they liked her to boss them around, even pretend to strangle them or other odd abuses. She didn't like that. She liked sex —the intimacy more than the feel. Cheryl was right about one thing— she was big enough that no human had ever truly tested her boundaries.

But while the idea might be intriguing, it was also impossible. Galatians did not interact with humans—well, except for Lt. Kendrick Washington. Since being assigned to the compound back on Earth, Kendrick was quickly recognized as easy to communicate with. He often sought out human interaction such as playing or watching sports—mostly watching as he was too big to compete.

Marisol's frown deepened. "No. Not interested." She stood and took her tray.

"Chicken!" Cheryl called after her. Marisol didn't respond. She was intrigued by Cheryl's wager—but not because she cared about winning a bet, but because she did think it would take a Galatian size prick to test her boundaries.

The boy hid behind a Cherabu tree and watched the brown girl and ghost boy. He wanted to run and tell somebody, but who would he tell? Granny would tan his hide for spying on the elite—well if she could catch him, she would.

For days, everyone had speculated about the transport that was to arrive with human and alien passengers. They were going to be stationed in his town and in the house his family took care of.

They had to be Earthlings. He'd never seen a real Earthling

except in books. There was a movie about Earth they watched at school. It was horrible and only criminals lived there now.

He wondered if the ghost boy actually was a ghost. Because how was he able to see the outline of a house and dark skies around him?

He crept closer, trying to hear what they were talking about.

Maybe your parents will come now that Kelsie has her new lungs, M said.

"I don't know. I think it depends on the situation with the doctors. My dad says that place is behind the times. They live as if they're two hundred years in the past."

Yeah. There's no vendor in the kitchen and all the appliances look like antiques.

"But one thing he said is he wished he had been there when you attacked that Black Mask. He said you wouldn't have done it if he was on the case."

M smiled. She missed Dorf, but she didn't want him to come to Eden to babysit her. She suddenly cocked her head.

"I think my dad underestimates-"

Shh! She snapped.

Bain gave her an inquisitive look, but kept quiet as she scanned the area.

"What is it?" he hissed.

I thought I heard someone.

"Over the sound of those waves?" Bain finally asked. "M, that Black Mask is not lurking around your gardens waiting for an opportunity to grab you."

True, she said while relaxing.

"I better get back to bed. I'll have Kelsie call you when we go to visit. Plus, I'll ask Dad about us moving." Both children rose.

Call me, even if I'm asleep.

"I will." He gave her a quick wave before entering the small cottage and then the feed abruptly ended.

The boy who watched carefully crept away. There was no way he could keep this a secret! He had to tell someone!

Chapter Nine

On the morning of the parley, the family sat quietly at the large dining room table having breakfast. The cook/housekeeper/caretaker cooked an array of local food —just as she had the night before for dinner—which was basically the same dishes.

The Galatians enjoyed the salty stew and savory roasted meats. Maddie and Justina favored the homemade yogurt and fruit, Karma picked at freshly baked bread layered with slices of the roast meat. Daya enjoyed a dish made with tomatoes and eggs—she had two helpings. And M, who didn't recognize any of the food, including the weird-looking fruit, simply had toast with preserves and warm tea flavored with sweet cream. She quickly left to join Nurse, who had promised to take her out exploring.

Nurse had offered to care for Rex and M during the talks, but M would actually be a great help to her in keeping the babies separated. Runnar was too young to control his claws and tail and was just learning he could hurt others. Nurse stoically bore the scratches as proof of this.

"Should we...talk about what we're going to say?" Maddie asked tentatively, as the silence stretched.

"It does not really matter," Kendrick said while gnawing on a rare leg of meat. "It's just a ploy to get Haru out."

"*We* know that," Justina added. "But *they* don't. They will be having a real parley, and I think we should know where we stand."

"They are calling for these talks," Rafe replied. "We can't know exactly what they intend."

"But we can guess," Drago added. "They will want us to stand down."

"They might even offer us a boon," Paris said. "They will probably try to persuade us we cannot win this fight."

"But if they believed that," Daya said, "they wouldn't be so insistent on talking with you."

"I agree with that," Karma said. "They have to tread carefully after that last attack. The Collective is taking their own sweet time to make a ruling on this, but the court of public opinion is siding with us and against them."

"That is thanks to you, my love," Rafe covered her hand with his.

"I only spoke the truth." Karma met his eyes before looking at Maddie. "I think that's all we can do is speak our truth. I don't think we should agree on anything less than what we have already put on the table."

"If we play their game, we can ask for more," Justina said. "Imagine how pissed they'd be if we asked for something like...part of Galatia, or the prosecution of the Black Masks, or equal representation on the Queen's council."

Rafe's eyes lit up. "That gives me thought. I like your ideal Justina."

"You do?" she asked in surprise. "It wasn't really an ideal, but thank you."

"Anyone else looking forward to addressing Mayva?" Maddie asked grimly. She thought about a friendship that had been important to her for most of her life. She thought this was a journey she and Mayva would make together; consorts supporting each other until they were granted their freedom. And from there, they'd live out the rest of their lives as wealthy celebrities—wanting for nothing; best friends to the end.

She would have never dreamed Mayva would risk the lives of her friends, just to be on the side of the Queens.

Justina's eyes narrowed into slits. "That conniving bitch is going to get an earful-"

"She doesn't care what we have to say," Karma said with a quiet intensity. "She made her choice and is receiving her rewards."

"Yeah," Justina grumbled. "Well, that won't stop me from giving her a piece of my mind."

The men were quiet, listening, learning the reactions of their normally mild-mannered counterparts.

Karma stood. "Excuse me. I want to lie down before we head back to the ship."

The women looked on sympathetically, silently acknowledging that no one would be affected harder by this parley than Karma.

Several hours later, when Tamsyn Bano's transport arrived, the entire family was there to meet her at the Drift Spire, although the men stayed out of sight within the transport for the sake of the gossip already spreading.

Tam no longer resembled the slender, meek girl who had dyed her hair blond and wore blue contact lenses just a year before in order to meet the esoteric look of the consorts. She stepped onto the landing wearing black military-style leggings and a t-shirt with the sleeves rolled up to her shoulders that read #Protectourhumans. The shirt revealed that over the last few months; she had bulked up and gotten strong. Her arms were wired with muscles and her short military haircut was pitch black. The biggest transformation was in her skin coloring. Tamsyn was now a beautiful, rich-tanned-skinned woman who was clearly Hispanic.

M broke from the group and was on her first. Tam dropped her bag and caught the little girl in mid-flight. It was as if they were still training together and had spent hours perfecting certain fighting moves.

Surprisingly, she lifted the little girl and swung her around in a bear hug while lathering kisses on her cheeks.

"I missed you, too, *chica*."

Her sisters didn't wait for her to release M before they, too, were hugging her. Daya stood back but wore a happy smile on her face—a face she had decided to shield with a veil. No need to get the locals speculating more than they needed to.

But Tam wasn't having any of that. She reached out for Daya's gloved hand and pulled her into the group hug. She might not know her well, but they had fought for their lives together which made Daya Tam's sister.

Everyone gushed over how good Tam looked. They stroked her hair and squeezed her muscles. Karma pointed at her shirt.

"How did you get that? I hear the term just started trending a few days ago."

Tam grinned broadly at her. "I had to make this in order to have it in time to wear to the parley."

"Oh my Guardian, I love that idea!" Justina exclaimed. "I wish I had one. I'd love to see their stinking faces when we show them the world sees us."

"You don't think it's a bad idea?" Tam asked, but she peeked at Karma. "I don't want to start shit when there is already an overabundance of it."

"I love the idea," Karma replied proudly. "I'm like Justina. I wish we all had one." She, Justina, and Maddie had dressed casually in slacks and blouses far from the revealing silk and satin robes that constituted their consort uniforms. Daya wore a layered dress that swept the tops of her sandal-clad feet—feet that were untouched by the scars covering the rest of her body.

Tam bent to pick up her bag. "I'm happy you said that. Because I made shirts for us all. Even you, M. There's one for Kemistry and Dorf and their kids, too."

The ladies shouted and jumped up and down in excitement while Rafe, Drago, Paris, and Kendrick watched from the vehicle in interest.

"Why are they so excited?" Kendrick asked. "Is it because our movement is now a slogan? Who thought of it? I would have thought of something better."

"I concur," Paris said. "But if they wear that slogan to the parley, just imagine how angry it will make that *sprotken*, Amalia," he spat.

Rafe chuckled. "I do welcome Tamsyn back. My wife was correct. Humans each add a different flavor to the mix."

Drago's expression took on a perplexed expression. Humans had a strange way of making everything a comparison to food.

They boarded the ship as Rafe wanted to hold the meeting in one of the simulators. He wanted to give no one an idea of where they were located and had to set up a backdrop or what the humans called "an environment".

The women had the perfect one in mind.

"It has to be The Conference room," Daya stated.

"Yes, definitely The Conference room," Maddie agreed.

Karma and Justina nodded enthusiastically and with a shrug Rafe loaded 'The Conference room'.

It was a joke, of course—not that the Queens would understand. At one time, humans loved making exotic backdrops, fantasy spaces, or other types of imaginative environments during their virtual conferences. But when a person showed themselves in the old-fashioned conference room—it meant they didn't care enough about the meeting to put forth an effort to even create an inviting environment. Soon the 'conference room' became a passive-aggressive statement: I'm here under duress.

It appeared like any old-fashioned executive conference room that probably appeared in every corporate movie made in circa 1980. There was a huge mahogany table and large office chairs which surrounded it. The walls were paneled wood with a large picture window showing a cityscape with a hodge podge of buildings of different styles so it could have been in Moscow, Japan or Dubai. On the opposite walls were paintings with inspired messages such as: I am freeing myself from all destructive doubt and fear. Or: I am constantly growing and evolving into a better person.

Except in the hands of a passive-aggressive individual, the neutral-sounding affirmations could be changed. And the ladies had a few choice ones: I do not engage with those who try to penetrate my mind with unhelpful thoughts and ideas. And this gem from Justina: I will destroy my enemies—which are thoughts and deeds that do not benefit me.

The ladies had a good laugh, which helped to ease the tension.

They sat in real chairs around a real table, which was created by a special resin that could mimic nearly any inanimate object. After it was no longer needed, it would collapse into something like sand and be absorbed by the simulator until needed for the next simulation.

Rafe sat at one end of the table with Karma on his right. Drago was on his left, and beside him was Maddie. Daya and Paris were next to them, with Justina, Kendrick, and Tam across from them.

There were still a few minutes, but Rafe received an incoming communication. Dorf and Kemistry were ready. He accepted their hologram. The two were sitting on low perches. Their environment was nondescript green, which meant it wouldn't be seen at all once the other members joined the meeting. It would almost appear as if Dorf and Kemistry were in the same room.

Everyone asked about Kelsey's health and, of course, the big question was when he'd be able to join them.

Kelsie needed to be monitored longer, but she was doing well.

"I spoke to the Japoxillian delegates on The Collective," Dorf said. "They are not pleased with the handling of this affair. There has been no justice for our fallen members. As usual, the Japoxillian have been treated as lesser beings!" He looked at Karma. "And I do not mean it to be disrespectful to the humans. I do not see you as lesser. I never have."

She nodded in understanding.

"The Collective claims not to have a hierarchy," Kemistry stated. "But it has always been easy to see which races have been favored. There are whispers that the Japoxillian are planning some very grave changes."

"Do you believe they will be our allies in this fight?"

"Yes," both Dorf and Kemistry nodded.

Rafe hid his pink smile. He checked the monitor. "It is time."

A robotic voice came over the intercom. **The host has accepted the Sigur party. You are now joining the Japoxillian Delegates, and the Queen's War Council.**

The Queen's War Council, i.e.; the Black Masks. An angry chill ran down Karma's body. In that second, she was transformed. It was just like the interview when she had shed the skin of a wife, mother, and friend. In this second, she was a predator looking for an opening to destroy her prey.

Chapter Ten

The parley, initiated by The Most Exalted Queen Amalia, was a strange affair by any outside observer. Rafe's family sat together on one screen with a slightly pixelated Dorf and Kemistry hovering on a large boardroom table.

The Japoxillian delegates from The Interplanetary Collective were on a different screen. They comprised a large cat-bird-like creature with sleek dark feathers as black as a crow's. The plumes sitting atop his head almost seemed to be a decorative headpiece, and yet it was his own shockingly bright red plumage that made him as tall as the average human. Next to him was a bluebird cat, as dainty and small as a wildcat. Despite having wings, the woman differed from any bird because of her yellow eyes—not gold or amber but yellow like rays of the sun. Today, those sunshiny eyes were narrowed in discontent.

On another screen was the Queen's War Council. Most wore black masks, and they were the largest grouping, with over one hundred bodies.

Next were the Bound-Mates of the Galatians who had been

replaced by human consorts. Most could not hide their bitterness as they glared at Rafe Sigur's party.

Finally, there was Amalia and her Queen's Council. A slightly pixelated image of Mayva Heath was seated in a chair nearby, clearly not in the same room (or planet) as the Galatian Queens. As her chair was nowhere near as grandiose as the Queen's thrones.

It suddenly hit Rafe like a mountain of boulders. He'd made a mistake concerning Ragna and shielded his thoughts, relieved he was not in the same room as Amalia or she would have sensed it. As it is, he knew his men had caught his scent of alarm, but had not let on. He wondered if they had caught their mistake as he had.

"Greetings, Rafe Sigur and members," Amalia stated. Her eyes scanned the words written on the shirts of the humans. She felt a warm flush of anger creep over her. She knew the phrase well. The hashtag was growing in popularity and these humans were crass enough to make sure everyone present knew it. "Thank you for agreeing to these talks and to hopefully putting an end to our... mutual discontent."

Rafe nodded slightly. "Greetings," he said, refusing to address her by name. He looked around at the other environments. He was surprised he didn't see Einar, but he quickly recognized many familiar faces.

"Are we still waiting for Ragna?" He asked in feigned curiosity. He could instantly feel a ripple of understanding coming from the other members of his party. They wisely sat unmoving.

But Amalia's expression darkened, and she could not completely hide it, although she eventually suppressed it.

"We can begin with those members present."

Karma heard everything as if it was being recorded in some deep recess of her mind, a place that had crystal clear recollection, a place that replayed the seconds leading up to the murder of her family and her child. Her eyes rested on Mayva without waiver, but the other woman did not meet hers or those of any other member of Karma's family.

"So, you don't intend to say hello, Mayva?" Karma asked. At that moment, there was no fear of the Black Masks or of the Queen who ruled all Galatians. It was as if she and Mayva were alone.

The blond woman finally met her eyes as if drawn to her like a magnet. This was despite her promise to herself that she would pretend none of them existed. They could judge her all they wanted, but she would remain unapologetic about what she needed to do to survive.

Amalia opened her mouth to speak, but Rafe raised his hand to stop her.

"I told you my wife and the others had the right to face this individual. Just as the Japoxillian delegates have the right. And anyone else present that this woman's actions have harmed."

Mayva's eyes widened. For a moment her thoughts flashed to the soldiers who had worked under her, and Heinrich's family who no longer had a husband and father, her parents who had put up the money so she could one day become a woman of means—and even her lover on the island who had been youthful and good in bed. But those thoughts fled when Karma continued.

"You sit there with those Queens thinking you've achieved greatness—and what did it cost you? You have no one!"

"Don't judge me," Mayva snapped. "You're nothing! And all you have comes from your lies!"

"The difference between me and you is that my lies didn't result in the murder of innocents! But you will pay. If it takes the last breath from my body, I swear you will pay."

"I didn't even pull the trigger!" she exclaimed in exasperation. "I didn't kill anybody-"

"You were safe in that bunker!" Karma said, half rising. Rafe watched her tensely. "And you came out—not for your safety, but to side against us!"

"I'm not going to listen to you," Mayva said while shaking her head. "You're nobody. Nothing-"

"No. You can't consider Karma to be nothing," Maddie spoke, her voice tinged with sadness more than anger. "Because everything she is and everything she has is what you've wished for your entire life."

Mayva's eyes darkened in anger. "Shut-up, Maddie! You're just a poor substitute for me! Admit it! You've always wanted to be me; never as pretty, never as rich, never as smart."

Maddie's cheeks reddened at the truth in those words. "Then I grew up and saw you for the pig you really are. From the moment you came back into our lives, I only wished for you to go away."

Mayva's face twisted as she glared at the consort's she'd grown up with—the girls she'd befriended, shared dreams, laughed, and some-times cried with. "All of you were jealous of me. And look at me now! I'm head of the North American Galatian Exchange! I sit with the Queens! Everyone knows my name! I SIT ON TOP OF THE WORLD YOU, PETTY BITCHES!"

"You narcissist, cunt!" Justina snapped. "You're sitting on a pile of shit looking no better than pig turds-"

Mayva just threw her head back and laughed.

But it was the truth, and Maddie was shocked by her ex-friend's appearance. While her make-up was flawless, her hair perfectly coiffed and her clothes the finest that money could buy, she was skin-nier than she had ever been—skinnier than was healthy. Her gaunt face was a huge transformation, with hollowed cheeks and deep-set eyes that twinkled as she cackled. Even her color was no longer porcelain but grey beneath the overly done makeup.

"Who are you trying to impress?!" Justina continued. "The Queens think you're ugly and you are beneath Rafe Sigur."

The laughter died in Mayva's mouth as she glared at the women present.

"I got what I want."

Tam shook her head. "You are sad and pathetic."

"Shut up, Tamsyn! You're a fraud just like her! I knew something was off about you. I should have known you weren't white like us. And you hated it, didn't you? You were jealous because you couldn't be us!"

Tam smirked. "You are dumb if you really believe that. I couldn't wait to shed my fake persona. I never wanted to be you or look like you! I love my heritage and I fucking missed my brown skin!"

Amalia's tail slapped the arm of her throne in exasperation.

"Your women have addressed Mayva Heath as agreed upon. She is guilty of no crime and I will not continue to tolerate this treatment of her!"

Karma's eyes had never moved from Mayva's, but she held out her hands as if to stop her friend's protests.

"She's not worth it. We're done with her...for now."

Mayva was finally able to look at them, and her expression was smug. She'd made the right choice despite a few setbacks.

Rafe's eyes were chilly as he looked at Amalia. "I thought my terms were clear. I asked for the Queen's war council to be present. It is my understanding that Ragna is head of that."

The Queens on Ragna's council became restless, as it was apparent it wouldn't be so easy to capture Rafe in a lie.

"Quite honestly, we assumed you knew the whereabouts of Ragna."

"And how would I know that? Do you not keep tabs on your own?"

Amalia angrily cleared her throat. "I am sure we will address Ragna's 'disappearance' in due time. But first, I want to address the reason for my request to parley." Rafe inclined his head ever-so-slightly. "This business between us can lead to nothing but undo casualties of our already dwindling numbers-"

"And how many Galatian Guards were lost when the Queen's Council tasked us with becoming The Inter-planetary Collective's law enforcers? How many have we lost in pursuit of treacheries that may or may not be endorsed by the same council that was put into place to uphold the law?"

There was a loud outcry from the Queen's council and some members of the War Council. Rafe's impertinence was uncommon. They had never seen a male speak to them in such a manner.

Amalia turned bodily to the Japoxillian delegates that, although were there on behalf of the murdered Japoxillian, also represented the Collective.

But the male who resembled a crow looked non-plussed. "I am Q'uoi, and my companion is Sirii. We acknowledge Lt. Sigur's concerns about the loss of life in pursuit of so-called justice, because we, too, have the same concerns. Although our concerns are a matter of loss of life and the *lack* of justice." Q'uoi was glaring at Mayva, who slowly met his eyes. She quickly looked away.

He wasn't the only one glaring. Daya, who had remained quiet, noticed there was one Queen who stared from her to Paris. She did not have to be in the same room to feel the silent connection, as well as the hatred. This had to be Thalia. Paris had spoken of her; his former Bound-Mate.

Daya was uncomfortable under her scrutiny until Paris took her hand from where it rested beneath the table and squeezed it. Thalia's posture changed as if she could see what he'd done, even though she surely couldn't. Paris didn't give one iota of a care. He was simply happy to be done with that entanglement.

Justina did not notice any of this since Thalia paid her no attention. But Kendrick noticed Evora. He tried to ignore her but found it difficult. He had cared for her. He probably still did in some ways, but she had done nothing to aid him in his fight for freedom. She stood with the Queens and he stood with his brothers. For him, there was no going backward.

Isyss watched Drago with a hurt she could not conceal, although Maddie did not notice this. Maddie was completely sure of her love for Drago and his for her and Rex. Drago stared at his ex with no emotion until finally, Isyss looked away.

The only one present who seemed smug and secure was Caeda because her man was at home ready to pleasure her the way he had done every day since he'd returned to her. Haru had chosen her and their way of life over these sickly humans!

The Bound-Mate not present was Filene, whose mate had been

murdered during the battle to kill Rafe's consort. For various reasons, she had not been invited to attend today's parley. Also not present was Leolo's Bound-mate since he had been returned to her once he rejected his consort, Jayne.

Q'uoi had continued speaking as if his words had not shocked most of the Queens. "Most Exalted Queen, if you are here to speak of justice, then you must acknowledge the fact that several of my members were killed in your attack. And yet the murderers have been allowed to roam freely, with not even a trial by jury."

Murderers? Mayva thought. *I* didn't murder anyone—well...at least not those flying little beasts! Why was she continuously being blamed for that?!

Amalia continued with a defiant lift of her chin. "I acknowledge your people willingly placed themselves in the center of a matter concerning upholding our laws and our way of life. The Interplanetary Collective has had a long-standing rule that they will enforce no laws which interfere with the pursuit of a race's laws and religious beliefs."

"Murdering unborn babies is not upholding a Galatian law," Karma spoke. Amalia turned to her in surprise that she would dare address her directly in a meeting of her superiors. Karma continued. "Your law says there can be no interbreeding between humans and Galatians, which is where your law stops. Your people have taken it upon themselves to enforce their vigilante activities while calling it justice-"

One of the Queen's council members jumped to her feet. "You will tell your human whore to keep her mouth closed-"

Rafe was on his feet in a split second as if he would leap through the monitor and strangle the Queen that had spoken.

Chapter Eleven

"**Y**ou dare to disrespect my wife after you put your war dogs on my family—MINE! Me, who has served you and your fucking Collective for my entire life!"

Amalia turned to her co-council member and hissed something in Galatian which translated to something like, 'sit your ass down!'

Each of Rafe's brothers had leaped to their feet the moment he had. They were standing with him, glaring at the screen, including Dorf, who had his hand on the hilt of a short knife hidden in his weapons belt.

Things had gotten bad quickly and the co-council member quickly took her seat.

"Lt. Sigur," Amalia said while raising her hands contritely. "Please accept my apologies. We did not come here to throw insults." She glared at the Queen, who had spoken intending to have her head on a spike before day's end. If she destroyed this opportunity to bring down Rafe Sigur, she'd wipe out her and her entire creation!

"I want an apology from that one on behalf of my wife!" Rafe demanded, still standing tensely.

Amalia turned to the council member. "Do it!" she hissed.

The Queen gave her a shocked look. Apologize for speaking the truth to a *human?!* But something in Amalia's expression convinced her that although Amalia had no love for humans—had co-signed on the attack to kill the human and the half-breed she carried, she had made a grave error in judgment—perhaps even a deadly one.

The council member came to her feet slowly. "I apologize," she muttered. It sickened her to have to lower herself to a male and his whore.

Rafe continued to glare until Karma placed a hand over his. He turned to meet his wife's eyes and saw by her demeanor that she didn't care one bit what that individual thought of her.

Rafe's shoulders relaxed, and he took his seat. When he did, his brothers did the same. Kemistry ruffled a wing which she placed proudly around her hubby, and his breathing finally evened out.

Amalia took a deep breath. "To address your wife's...accusations, there are no written laws that cover all issues. This is why we have many traditions which we consider to be the law of our land. I am sure your husband advised what the dire results would be should there ever be an offspring resulting from a human and a Galatian's mating."

"And why is that?" Madeline spoke up. It surprised even Drago that she directly addressed this Queen. "Your law is expressly against interbreeding between humans and Galatians. Why not other species? Why only humans?"

Amalia chuckled. "Humans can breed like...well they are very fertile. They could wipe out the existence of Galatians within just a few generations. It is simply a matter of survival."

"Or maybe it could be the answer to your survival," Tam said.

Caeda leaped to her feet. "Coming from a human, your response isn't surprising!" Many Queens voiced their agreement while others wisely remained quiet while silently agreeing.

"QUIET!" Amalia screeched. "No one will speak out of turn unless I give you permission to do so!" She gave Rafe an annoyed look. "It was your decision to bring so many together into these discussions. I suggest we get to the point."

Rafe made a gesture with his hand to continue and it angered Amalia. She despised Rafe Sigur, and she despised his whores and she would do whatever was necessary to bring him down.

"You may not be concerned with the destruction your actions will cause, but many of us are!"

Rafe and Karma exchanged looks, and an unspoken communication was exchanged. Did she seriously think anyone believed she cared about the loss of life when she'd sent hundreds upon hundreds of Black Masks to kill her and whoever got in their way?

Amalia's face was twisted in self-righteous fervor.

"Thousands of years of tradition is suddenly not to your liking, so you will cause a war that not only will finish wiping out an already ravaged Earth but may also end the humans you evidently love so much? End this, Rafe! End this before we destroy not only your little group of dissidents but also the freedom your humans enjoy so much!" Amalia cried passionately.

But instead of upsetting Rafe, she angered someone else. "You have no authority to decree the destruction of a protected world!" Q'uoi shouted in shock.

"I only predict the inevitable!" Amalia said, calming as she remembered the Japoxillian delegates would certainly report back to The Collective.

Karma's icy stare settled on Amalia. "And we predict your warriors will agree that fighting for their freedom will be better than fighting for you *against* it." Karma gestured to the screen. "While I am sure there are more members of your war council than is shown here, I can guarantee the Galatian Guards outnumber you, *and* can outfight you!"

The members of the war council grumbled angrily but were too afraid to speak until Amalia allowed it. However, Amalia remained silent.

Dorf stepped forward. "You cannot tell me you would see your

Queens wiped out simply because you refuse to give your males freedom to act of their own volition." He looked amazed. "As a man who has watched his world destroyed, I guarantee you the loss of everything you love and value is devastating."

"There will be a war if you do not grant our demands," Rafe warned. "But nothing says this war has to take place on Earth. Galatia has an adaptable atmosphere. Our human military can fight with us just as well on Galatia as they can anywhere. And don't delude yourself, Amalia. I *will* bring the destruction of the old ways!"

"The old ways are why we have continued to prosper!" She hissed. For the first time, her face showed her disgust. "Our history had us unprotected while our men went about conquering worlds! You left us behind while you screwed the natives and created bastards at what we were meant to be!"

"Bastards who can procreate without creating clones of ourselves!" Maddie shouted angrily. "You're nothing but the same person over and over due to your interbreeding! Maybe that's why you can't get pregnant! If you weren't so afraid of losing your men to a human mate-"

Isyss leaped to her feet and shouted in Galatian while pointing her clawed fingers at the screen. Her face was red with rage as she spewed Galatian threats against the human. Maddie looked at Drago, fire in her own eyes. But Drago placed a restraining hand over hers, all the while smiling at her with pride.

A council member spoke, momentarily forgetting her fear of Amalia. "And what about what will be left of our kind when weaken our genes with those of human animals?!"

A calm voice interrupted the impending uproar. "I have always found it surprising you believe yourselves to be so much more superior to other species," Sirii stated. "And perhaps you do excel physically. But in other ways, your kind is stunted." Amalia gave her a look of disbelief as she began to sputter. But before she could speak, Sirii continued. "Take, for instance, your inability to compromise. What do you truly lose in denying the males of your species the ability to guide the direction of their own lives, to love who they wish to love? You do not hold power over humans to enforce an edict that they be sterilized in order to be included in the Galatian Exchange."

"As long as our males fall under our jurisdiction, then we can make any rule necessary to protect them and us!"

Amalia knew what others did not—could not, and what was at risk! It wasn't just the fact that humans were resilient. Humans would always survive because they were adaptable. They had adapted to the conditions of Earth and evolved mentally to survive almost any hardship. And it was that ability to adapt that produced their biggest weapon—one so powerful, she dared not think it in mixed company.

It was now the Galatian's purpose to ensure the humans never rose in power over them. Even The Interplanetary Collective understood that man's ability to evolve was dangerous to them all. They were like an invasive vine overtaking everything. Look at how they were already taking their men!

She looked at Rafe, appealing to his sense of self-pride.

"You are Galatian! Are you just going to sit there and let the Japoxillian speak about our race in this way? She is calling you *okpt-numa* and you are showing her that you are!"

Rafe's expression remained calm. He turned to look at Kemistry and Dorf, although he didn't have to. His tail could observe everyone and everything.

"Galatian warriors have worked alongside Japoxillian for decades. I have worked with Sir Dorf since before I ever became a decorated soldier. Without him, I wouldn't be who I am today.

"Unlike you, many of us have allowed other species to influence our thoughts, and it was for the better. And I believe that is why we have evolved while you, who have kept yourselves isolated, have never learned to "play well with others.""

Amalia shook her head while frowning. She hissed in Galatian that he made no sense speaking like a human.

But Sirii continued as if she had never been interrupted.

"Most Exalted One. With all due respect, I am not referring to the male of your species, but specifically to you; the Queens. This is why the Japoxillian across all worlds have agreed that we will aid the Galatian Guards in their fight against the Galatian Queens."

The humans couldn't help themselves. They cheered quietly while Kemistry and Dorf did a quick happy dance.

"Don't be ridiculous!" Amalia sputtered. "Your numbers are small and you are unprotected! It is only The Collective that keeps you untouchable, and it is the Galatian Queens that hold the ear of the Collective!"

Her words affirmed what everyone on Rafe's team had long suspected. But the Japoxillian simply grinned. "Since you have refused to be accountable for the actions that caused the deaths of our fallen comrades until justice is served, we will no longer side on behalf of the Interplanetary Collective. We have placed a moratorium on all translations and readings until our people are vindicated."

Amalia swallowed, seeing the bigger picture. This was no longer just about the Galatians. This now involved the Collective, and they would not be pleased to lose such a great commodity.

"And what about *our* justice?" She asked, pulling out the ace she'd kept in hiding.

"Your justice?" Q'uoi asked. "And what have you lost?"

"It's not what we have lost, but what has been stolen from us! Ragna. It is a known fact that Rafe Sigur and his team kidnapped Ragna and I want him executed for breaking the moratorium between us! You represent The Interplanetary Collective! What are you going to do about *his* misdeeds?!"

Q'uoi and Sirii exchanged looks while Karma gripped Rafe's hand in surprise, but Rafe just snorted.

"You are reaching, Amalia! What evidence do you have that I had anything to do with Ragna's disappearance?"

Amalia stood and pointed to Mayva. "Her! She was there when it happened! She certainly witnessed the entire thing!"

Everyone turned to look at Mayva. "It's true. I saw him kill

Ragna. I saw it with my own eyes." Mayva remained cool on the outside, but on the inside, she was quaking. They hadn't discussed this! What was Amalia doing having her lie before Council delegates —delegates who wanted her dead?!

Karma leaped to her feet. "That's a damn lie. You can smell her lies. Japoxillian can read her lies! All you need to do is to have someone read her!"

Mayva looked expectantly at Amalia, who smiled a soft pink. "We can also read Lt. Sigur. If he says he is innocent, then he should be brought before The Collective, where he can plainly state he had nothing to do with Ragna's disappearance."

Rafe glared at her. "So you can assassinate me in my holding cell? That would be a quick fix for your problems." Just as importantly, they could ask him questions that would incriminate them all...

"You speak as if you don't trust The Collective you've worked most of your life for," she smirked.

"This is ridiculous!" Karma spat. "Rafe is under no obligation to go before The Collective just because you throw out some wild accusations!"

"It isn't a wild accusation," Amalia stated. "He has been heard stating his intent to kill Ragna, which was broadcast nationally. And now Ragna is missing and we have a witness stating she saw her execution at the hands or Rafe Sigur." She turned to give a pleasant smile to the Japoxillian. "Now, of course, we will have you read the human, and if she is found to be lying in this matter... then I suppose she cannot be trusted and must be punished for whatever crimes she may have assisted in. Of course, there would be no need to have your people end their work with The Collective once justice is served."

Wait...*what?!* Mayva's mind went numb at those words. She came weakly to her feet. Her knees felt as if they would buckle.

"Amalia? What are you doing?! Queen! You can't give me to them! They think I'm a killer!"

Amalia glared at her, willing her to sit down and shut up. If she understood the way things worked, then she would see there was no other way. She was to be the sacrificial lamb that would keep the Queens in the goodwill of those damnable Japoxillian! Of course, she would have preferred to keep her as a mouthpiece for their cause. But thankfully, the human had been even more beneficial in other ways.

Amalia turned off the volume to Mayva's feed and now addressed Rafe. "And of course, if the human is found to be a liar, then I will obviously withdraw my accusation against you, Lt. Sigur." She looked from the Japoxillian to Rafe and his party. "So," Amalia continued. "Do we have an agreement?"

Q'uoi inclined his head. "We will accept Mayva Heath for trial on this as well as all other crimes she may have committed. There is the matter of the unexplained death of the former head of the Galatian Exchange." Mayva could hear even if she couldn't be heard, and she screamed no no no no!

"The Japoxillian will continue to form an alliance with the Galatian males, but as justice has been served, we will continue to aid The Collective with readings and translations."

Karma looked at Rafe. Did that mean he didn't have to face The Collective? She didn't trust them and wouldn't want her man anywhere near them. Rafe gave her hand a reassuring squeeze.

"Guards, please escort Mayva Heath to The Collective for a hearing on her truthfulness. And gag her if you must!"

Everyone from Rafe's party watched Mayva's silent screams as two Galatian Guards took her arms and dragged her to the door as she struggled in futile.

Karma relaxed against her seat. She knew they had come very close to losing Rafe to a hearing before The Collective, and she knew if that happened, it would be the end for Rafe. She focused on Mayva, and with a grim shake of her head, she spoke to her.

"Everything you did, and you still ended up being nothing more than a lapdog."

Mayva looked at the consorts in desperation as she screamed either about the injustice, her hatred for them all, or just her regrets.

Chapter Twelve

"Any word from Haru?" Rafe asked as they exited the simulator. Drago checked his communicator.

"No. Nothing." No one said anything, but Maddie took Tam's hand. The slender woman gave her a forced smile. She wanted to say she was sure that everything would be okay, and they'd hear from Haru soon. But the meeting had left her feeling out of sorts; from the way Amalia had lied in front of her council, to the exchange that had taken place with Mayva and how she had been hauled away by the Galatians. None of it felt right, despite the fact she should be happy about the latter. But if she knew anything from what had happened to Ragna, it was that snakes were quick and slippery.

"That head Queen Bitch in charge sure did a number on Mayva." Justina said with a grin.

The severe look on Karma's face disappeared as she smiled. A moment later, she was laughing and so were the other women.

"What do you think the Japoxillian are going to do to her?" Karma asked Rafe.

He placed his arm lightly around her shoulders as they moved to leave the ship.

"The Japoxillian are acting in their own accordance. This is unprecedented, so I do not know the outcome."

"They better not let her off," Justina said.

"She will not be found innocent," Kendrick replied. "She has many secrets we were informed not to probe..."

Karma looked at him grimly. "By Commander Einar?"

"Ai," Kendrick confirmed.

"He should be put on trial, too!" she replied bitterly. "If not for him, then a traitor would not have been in our home!"

"This goes beyond him," Rafe interjected. "He is the mouthpiece of The Collective."

"The Collective needs an overhaul."

Back at the villa, the family gathered in the large living room. Tamsyn filled them in on the happenings of the Rebellion.

"The tide is changing. While the Rebellion didn't take the side of the Queens, they weren't necessarily fans of ours, either. Not all of you know I had infiltrated one of the larger South American cells. I gave Drago the information concerning the weapons and training, but they are very well stocked.

"Do you think they discovered who you were?" Maddie asked.

"No, but they would have figured it out. They could not have imagined a consort would ever know how to fight and have weapons training," she smiled. "They believed I worked within a cartel before joining them." Her smile didn't remain for long. "I can tell you the hatred they harbor for the consorts is unimaginable. To the rebels, we are nothing but..." she glanced at M and then looked away. "Well, anyway, things changed after your interview."

Karma's brow moved upward. "How?"

"They don't like what consorts...do. But they won't abide 'aliens',"
she made air quotes, "hurting human women." Tam's lips moved upward
as if she was smiling, and the other women nodded in understanding.

"So, they'll kill us, but they won't allow anyone else to do it?"
Justina asked.

"Exactly." Tam nodded and then looked at Karma again. "Your
interview showed there is more to consorts than what meets the eye.
"We will fight for what we believe in. We're not weak women who
will just lie down and die. We are warriors."

Even though Tam was speaking mostly to the women, it was the
men who nodded as they quietly listened.

"I know if there is a war, my cell of the Resistance will aid us in
fighting against the Queens. But once the Queens are no longer a
threat, they'll go back to hating us again."

"We need an emissary," Drago said.

"But it can't be you," Rafe said while looking at Tam. Before she
could object, he explained.

"I may not know everything about humans, but I do know about
soldiers. You infiltrated their stronghold and you will only be seen as
a spy. No. We need someone they trust."

"Me." Karma replied. Rafe wanted to say no, but the soldier in
him knew she was the best choice. "I don't want to speak to just
Tam's cell, but to all the rebels—or patriots, as my father called them."

"I want to hear all about that when we get a chance," Tam said
with a frown. "But, sis, you do have the ear of the nation. Movie stars
and music groups are turning you into a celebrity."

"But," Daya added, "You were already on your way to being that
long before the attack. Before I was with Paris," she glanced at him, "I
would hear about your humanitarian efforts and I wanted to know
more. But it wasn't just me. Everyone from the boardinghouse where
I lived talked about you all the time. It was always the same thing;
why do the rich never do anything to help the poor? A lot of street
people look up to you, Karma." Daya's face warmed.

" If you spoke to them directly, I know the street people will listen."

Karma's face held a thoughtful expression. She had always thought it was Rafe who should address the public, but maybe they were right.

"Okay," she nodded. "I think you're right. "And I want the public to know Mayva Heath is being held accountable for her actions."

"But it could backfire on us," Paris said. "If the Collective finds her innocent, then it could taint the public's opinion. And who is to say what The Collective will say and do once they get the Japoxillian delegates alone?"

"I do not think they will bend the will of the Japoxillian," Kendrick stated.

"I agree," Drago added. "They have already involved all of their kind in the decision to side with us. If anything, The Collective will want to mollify them. They will gladly give them a human rather than Ragna."

Karma looked at Drago. Her eyes held a strange light to them, as if a fire burned inside her soul and he could see it through her eyes.

"I want to be a delegate."

"What?" Rafe asked, although he had heard. His heart felt as if it had frozen in his chest. His woman among the treachery and dangers of the aliens who looked at humans as lesser beings? His women facing the Queens who despised her? His woman who...could outthink, outtalk, and outwit any of them!

Karma's smile was radiant as if she was relieved at the conclusion she'd come to. "There should be human delegates, and I want to be one of them. I want to petition for humans to be accepted into the Interplanetary Collective."

Justina jumped to her feet and began pacing as an idea began to bloom in her head. "Rafe, remember when we talked about asking for more so they throw us a bone?"

"I... don't recollect that conversation," Rafe replied with a tilt of his head.

"Remember when I said we should ask for part of Galatia or the prosecution of the Black Masks-"

"Yes!" Rafe exclaimed. "And you are right! We can hit them with demands they do not want to allow in the hopes they will find the Queen's resistance to be more of a hindrance!"

"This bears some consideration," Drago stated. "Let us convene to the pool." The men got up and, with brief touches to their mates, they headed out the door.

Karma shook her head with a soft smile, and Daya grimaced. "I believe your suggestion was meant to be more than a simple ploy," she stated. "I think human delegates are a good idea."

"I do too," Tam concurred.

"We need to be represented so we'll no longer be expendable," Karma said. "The Tybernees kept coming for us long after Earth was deemed off limits, and *they* have delegates who sit on The Collective! If our interests were better represented by more than Queens that hate us, then maybe my father and others like him would not have been stolen and sold into slavery!"

"And maybe Earth wouldn't be run by corrupt officials who don't give a crap about the people, but only about how much they can line their pockets!" Daya said passionately. "We need to do this for the people who don't have a voice."

Karma stood and nodded. "We can't let this time pass without fighting for all our rights!"

M looked at the women in her family with pride. How could she be anything less than kick-ass when all the women she looked up to were warriors?

Rafe and his brothers talked enthusiastically about Karma and Justine's ideas. And then Kendrick saw someone he recognized entering the makeshift canteen; Adrian Kelly.

His scales colored in annoyance. "I will meet you later." Rafe and the others looked after him as he went into the canteen but continued to the pool.

Kendrick wasn't the only Galatian present, but all eyes moved to him the moment he stepped into the area. As one of the commanders, he garnered respect.

"Kelly," he said from behind the soldier. Kelly quickly stepped out of line and saluted their commander.

"Lt. Washington." He was impressed the soldier recognized him. He was relatively new to this team and generally soldiers just referred to him as 'sir' when unable to tell them from another Galatian. Of course, this soldier should know who he was since they'd had the same woman in their sights.

Kendrick looked at the soldier a bit longer before speaking. "At ease." Kelly did as commanded but remained rigid with hands positioned behind their back. They looked at a space behind Lt. Washington but was completely aware of the way the alien eyed every inch of their form.

"Let us speak."

Kendrick led them outside. A few of Adrian's friends shot them a questioning look but Adrian just shrugged, although they had their suspicions about what the Commander wanted to talk about.

Damn. They had liked this gig and would hate to lose it—more, they would hate to never again see the lonely girl who looked so beautiful during the golden hour.

Chapter Thirteen

Kendrick sized up Adrian. "How long have you been in service?"

They looked at the Galatian quickly and then averted their eyes. "Five years, Lieutenant."

"How old are you?"

"Twenty-eight, Lieutenant."

"Why did you join? Do you like Galatians? Or is it the consorts who interest you?"

A shadow crossed Adrian's face, but they fought to maintain a professional demeanor. Adrian answered without hesitation.

"I didn't think about the Galatians or the consorts. I joined the military and was recruited for Special Services...Lieutenant."

"Hmph," Kendrick replied dismissively. "What weapons are you most proficient with?"

"I'm most proficient in hand-to-hand. But fully capable with all firearms, lasers and knives. I have ranked high in the annual archery contest and in the top five of this year's triathlon. Last year I ranked number one...Lieutenant."

"Hmph. And why didn't you rank number one this year?"

Adrian paused, still refusing to look directly at Kendrick. They finally replied. "This year it was deemed inappropriate to separate the trials by gender or species. Galatian Guards won the first four spots. I won the fifth."

Kendrick's head cocked to the side. "And how many Galatians were involved?"

"Seven, Lieutenant."

"Are you saying you out-performed three Galatian Guards?"

"I am saying they ranked after me, Lieutenant."

"Soldier, I want you to report to simulator one." For the first time, Adrian's brow shot up as they looked at the Galatian. "You can explain to your commander that I have placed you on a special project," Kendrick added before turning to head to the ship.

"Uh...sir!" Adrian caught up with the Galatian's long strides. "I don't understand..."

"You will."

Adrian stopped walking and watched the decorated Galatian as they marched toward the ship.

"Shit," Adrian stated while swiping off their hat and running rough hands through their hair. "This is some bullshit," they muttered. Glaring, the human stormed toward the ship to determine how this was supposed to play out.

When Adrian entered the simulator, it was to see Kendrick already there. He had removed his harness and boots, but still wore the long leather skirt that swept the top of his clawed feet.

Adrian gave the commander a questioning look.

"Prepare yourself. Since you are most proficient in hand-to-hand combat, we will fight."

"You want me to *fight* you, sir?"

"Of course. How else am I to size you up?"

Adrian shook their head. "Look, if you plan to cut me from the force just because I requested assignment to Mrs. Frenchman-"

"Oh? Is that what you did?" Kendrick's chest puffed out.

"Yes. I admit to requesting an exchange of duties for the assignment." Adrian's eyes narrowed. "And I now see someone else might feel I *overstepped*. But I assure you regardless of anything else, I am fully capable of protecting Miss Frenchman."

Kendrick didn't respond, just pulled on battle gloves. They shielded his claws during training when the intent wasn't to maim. Adrian felt only somewhat better.

Adrian moved to one side and knelt to remove their boots. The uniform was made of a latex fiber allowing free movement. In addition, it was water and fire-resistant, and nearly impervious to being pierced. Of course, it didn't protect the wearer from a punch to the ribs or a kick to the kidneys. Adrian stretched, cracked their neck, and then faced the jealous Galatian.

Kendrick crouched, and the two opponents circled each other. "Fight me as if I am not your commander."

"I intend to," Adrian muttered. Their attention became a pinpoint focus on nothing but the Galatian. Adrian fully expected to lose this fight, which wasn't the point. The point was to inflict maximum damage before that happened.

Adrian didn't wait or broadcast their intent. With a spin of their hips, the soldier slammed the heel of their feet into the face of the Galatian. Adrian knew from training that spin kicks were one of the most effective ways of knocking a Galatian off balance.

While the kick connected, Kendrick only rocked backward and then used his tail to brace himself and spring forward. He used the heel of his hand to knock the soldier in the chest, sending the smaller human spiraling backward onto their ass. Yet Adrian rolled and regained their footing as if they were doing an acrobatic dance. And without hesitation, dived at the larger man's lower half, gripping his legs and knocking him off balance.

Again, Kendrick's tail prevented him from hitting the floor, despite being knocked off balance. But Adrian did something unexpected. The lithe human kicked upward, hooking their feet onto Kendrick's shoulders, and then used the momentum to spring up until their legs were wrapped around Kendrick's neck!

Surprised, Kendrick gripped the human's legs with his superior strength and tore him from his neck.

"What the...?" he gasped as he flung Adrian to the floor. But Adrian didn't stay down. Again, the human rolled, swung out their legs, and was once more on their feet. And with another rapid attack, Adrian this time went flying at the Galatian with a kick aimed at his chest. Again, the kick landed and again knocked Kendrick off balance. But this time the Galatian did a tight backflip and, in the aftermath of the move, struck out at the human with his tail.

The blow would have shattered bone, could decapitate, had Kendrick willed it so. Which wasn't his purpose. But he was surprised when the soldier spun out of the path of the deadly tail, only to land in a crouch before him.

Adrian was relentless, placing Kendrick on the defense once again as the smaller human went once again for Kendrick's lower half. This little human was fast and limber. Kendrick expected them to go for his legs, but instead, Adrian went between his legs and ended up beneath his skirt.

Kendrick yelped when he felt the sharp yank on his balls. But when he tried to reach down to extricate the little human from his nether region, he was surprised the human had wrapped themself along the underside of his tail and was hanging on for dear life.

"Fuck!" Kendrick yelled. "ARE YOU BITING MY BALLS!"

"I'm about to shove my fist straight up your asshole!"

Kendrick grimaced but stopped, trying to extricate the human from his balls and tail. "Do not do that!"

"Do you give?" Adrian had released the alien's huge ball sack. If they thought too long about having a male's balls in their mouth, they might gag, but later for those thoughts.

"Yes!" Kendrick growled.

Adrian dropped to the floor and scrambled away, just in case the Galatian wasn't as honorable as they proclaimed to be. But Kendrick simply crouched and reached between the pleats of his skirt to cup his balls.

"I didn't break the skin," Adrian said while warily coming to their feet. They spit on the floor and then swiped at their lips distastefully with the back of their hand.

"You fight dirty," Kendrick stated.

"I fight. That's all that matters." And then Adrian saw something amazing. The Galatian was glowing with a bright pink smile—probably the pinkest they'd ever seen.

"Good deal. How do you move so fast?"

Adrian looked away. "Ballet," they said in embarrassment. "Back when my mom thought I was a girl."

Kendrick threw his head back and laughed heartily while Adrian looked on in confusion. When Kendrick noticed Adrian wasn't laughing, the Galatian straightened but remained brightly pink.

"I checked your record. Your father worked for the Kentucky Department of Transportation. You were kicked out of the home after proclaiming your non-binary gender. Never married. No children. And you are mostly a loner."

Adrian crossed their arms and gave Kendrick a hard look. "What is this all about?"

"You are qualified. You may have the position of Justina's personal guard."

Adrian's arms dropped. "Wait..."

Kendrick's smile faded, and his expression grew stern. "I am not saying you have rights to Justina. She chooses the relationships she wants. Becoming her bodyguard doesn't mean you have any rights to her. Do I make myself clear?"

"Uh...yes...Yes, Lieutenant."

"And if you ever hurt her..." Kendrick closed the space between them so rapidly Adrian would have missed it if they had blinked.

Kendrick's face was inches from them. "I will rip your insides to your outsides—and this time I will not hold back."

Adrian looked into the eyes of their Commander. "I understand... sir."

Kendrick stared into the young human's eyes before straightening. "You can begin your new assignment tomorrow. You are dismissed, Sgt. Kelly."

Adrian saluted their commander and then left the simulator. Once the door closed, they walked to the ship's exit, still feeling confused. But after a few moments, a smile crossed their lips. *I'm detailed to be Mrs. Frenchman's protector!*

Adrian hurried to the barracks, too excited to do anything except gather their belongings and prepare for their move to the villa and to Justina.

M and her mother explored the grounds while baby Runnar rode along in his floating carriage. It was the new brand that didn't need a remote control but followed at Karma's side.

Runnar didn't seem nearly as impressed as Karma and M since he kept trying to climb out of the little carriage. He was built like a six-month-old despite being half that, and he was strong enough to wiggle out of the straps so M and Karma sometimes took turns carrying him.

If the villa was large, the grounds were massive. Guards dotted the distant boundaries, letting them know they couldn't cross it without an escort—not that they wanted to. There was enough to see on the grounds.

There was an expansive flower garden with only a few recognizable plants. Most were bigger than what grew on Earth; roses the size of basketballs and daisies, like tiny babies. There was also a vegetable garden, which they avoided because the caretakers looked at them sideways as if they shouldn't be there.

They explored the cliffside overlooking the ocean, marveling at the colorful water. But then Karma became tired and needed to lie down before dinner. As they walked back to the villa, M asked about her uncle Haru.

Aunt Tam is worried about Uncle Haru. Will he be okay, Mama?

Runnar had fallen asleep and although Karma enjoyed feeling his sleeping body resting against her shoulder, he was heavy. She placed him carefully back in his carriage and thought about her daughter's question.

"Your father is still waiting for word from him. It's highly secretive and your uncle has to be discreet. No one can know what he's trying to do."

Can Papa call him just to make sure he's okay?

"No, honey. He might be in hiding or...who knows? It's better if we wait for word from him." She placed an arm around M's shoulder as they walked. "I know you're worried. But your uncle is very capable."

Once at the villa, Karma and Runnar went inside while M remained in the courtyard. She contacted Bain.

"Hey, what's up?" he said as he activated the hologram. Kelsie was beside him in her hospital bed. A big smile crossed her face.

"M! Hi!"

Hi! Are you better? You were sleeping last time I called.

"It feels a little weird. I'm not allowed out of bed yet until I'm sure my lungs are healthy. But my chest feels...empty. It's just weird."

M thought about not having lungs in her chest. **Where are your lungs?**

She pointed to a machine next to her bed. She was connected to it by tubes and wires. "In there. Freaky, huh?"

Yeah. Can you see them?

"No!" Kelsie laughed. "I don't think I want to."

M looked around the hospital room. "Where is uncle Dorf and aunt Kemistry?"

"Dad is talking with your Dad and the others," Bain replied. "Mom is getting dinner."

"Show me around, M," Kelsie asked while straining her head to see the courtyard.

It's really neat. You'll love it. M ran from item to item, pointing out fuzzy trees, huge fruit, purple grass and the cloudless sky.

"Have you met any kids?" Bain asked.

Nope. Just the caretaker and they are old. My Papa says the rich people and the worker people don't mix. I guess we are the rich people even though you couldn't tell from the last place we stayed.

"I liked it," Kelsie proclaimed. I got to help mom do things like cook and take care of the house.

I liked it, too. I liked the trees and grass and being outside. I'm going to be outside all the time! This place is big! When can you come?

"Soon I hope," Kelsie sighed. "I'm tired of being in bed and I can already breathe better than I have in a long time."

The door opened and Kemistry came in carrying two paper sacks. When she saw M, she beamed.

"Hi M. How are you, sweetheart?"

I'm good.

"How are you settling in?"

Fine. I miss Kelsie and Bain.

"I know, honey," she said while setting the sacks on a table. "I promise we will be there before you know it." She opened one of the bags and peered inside. "I'm sorry, kids. I didn't have time to make you anything. Is jerky okay?"

Bain's eyes lit up. Oh, thank the Great Guardian it wasn't salmon! "Yes!" he went over to help her remove the items from the sack, which also included beverages. He passed a bag of jerky to Kelsie, frowning at it. It wasn't brown...

"Mom?" he asked.

Kemistry was already taking a bite of hers. "Salmon jerky. There is a pack of mackerel in there if you want, but I got it for your Dad."

One side of Bain's lip lifted. "No. Salmon is fine." He took a big bite and gave M a wistful look.

I better get cleaned up for dinner, too. Talk to you tomorrow, M said.

"What are you having for dinner?" Bain asked.

M made a face. **Same thing we had for breakfast and yesterday's dinner and lunch; roast beast, yucky weird veggies, pasta and red sauce, eggs, fruit, bread...**

He swallowed. "Oh. See you tomorrow."

As Kendrick left the simulator, he checked to see if any messages had come through concerning Haru. He and Drago were monitoring the ship's communicators and logs but there was no news.

He nearly collided with a woman, but despite his attention being elsewhere, his tale saw the impending collision and he swirled out of her path. He turned to look at her with his eyes when he saw she was bigger than even most human men. But in addition, she had fiery red hair that sprung out in curls around an interesting face, despite the fact it was pulled back into a regulation bun.

What made her face interesting was that her skin wasn't white because it was covered with brown spots, which humans called freckles. There were a lot of freckles. He also saw her eyes were as green as his. He would have kept moving after the brief look, except she had turned to also look at him. Her eyes scanned him slowly, beginning at his bootless feet before settling on his face.

She smiled and then turned and continued to walk away.

Wait...was she checking him out? Kendrick's prick twitched. He resumed his movements heading out of the ship, but before he got too far, he turned and looked back at where the woman had disappeared.

Back in his quarters, he stripped out of his rigging and slipped on a black silk robe. It had probably been made for a Viking-sized human but it fit him nicely. He retrieved one of his cigars and lit it, enjoying a few draws before turning on his entertainment center and selecting some very old music to relax to; they called it heavy metal. He liked that phrase.

He began with Black Sabbath, and sank into a modified easy chair which had been customized to fit his height and to accommodate his tail.

He had selected quarters furthest from anyone else so he could crank his music, which he did. He closed his eyes and bobbed his head to the throbbing beat, singing his favorite lines in his head.

Nobody wants him
He just stares at the world...

Rafe crawled quietly into bed, but Karma turned, coming awake.

He placed a gentle hand on her cheek. "Go back to sleep, honey. It's late."

She snuggled against his chest. "I'm sorry. I meant to stay awake." Any word from Haru?"

He blew out a long breath. "Nothing. Not even our secret distress signal."

"Babe, I have to believe Haru will reach out as soon as he feels it's safe to do so."

"It has only been less than a day." He looked up at the ceiling. "It just seems as if there have been so many setbacks; that bitch Ragna, leaving Earth and separating our families. I miss Dorf and his ability to set my mind right." He quickly drew her closer and placed a kiss on her forehead. "Without you, I would have truly lost my head, and then the Council would have been justified in killing me."

"Don't even think that. You would not have left our kids."

"No," he said resolutely. "In the end, I could not leave them without their mother and their father."

She cupped his cheek and lifted her head to kiss him. "You are a good man, Rafe Sigur."

"My enemies would probably not agree, but coming from my woman, I will happily accept the compliment." They kissed for a few more moments before Rafe gently pulled away. "Let's not make love tonight."

Karma gave him a surprised look. "Why? Are you so tired?"

"It has been a long day," he agreed.

She studied his face for a moment. Except for being in deep sleep aboard the spaceship, they had made love every night since declaring that not a night would pass without sharing pleasure. But it was more than just the declaration. It was also the way she craved him.

Whenever she looked at him, it was as if there was a magnetic draw. No one had ever filled Karma with so much need. She had never known such love as she had since meeting this scary, beautiful being.

So many humans and Galatian alike looked down on such love. It was like in the days when love between different human races could get a person jailed—or worse. There were those who still would rather see them dead than to love freely.

Karma intertwined her fingers with his clawed green ones.

"Okay. A one-night reprieve then."

He smiled a soft pink. What she didn't see was his concern. She wasn't getting better, and while he didn't think daily mating injured her, they also couldn't be easy on her compromised system.

Sanjay said she was in good health, but complete recovery could take as long as a year. But he could see her weakening before his eyes. She was trying to do too much too soon, which was partly his fault.

She was his to care for. It was his vow to the Guardian in

exchange for returning her to him. And this was one vow he refused to ruin the way he had ruined the others.

The next morning, M looked at the array of food on the table. Everyone ate quietly, even her uncles, who usually chatted about things most didn't always understand, like coordinates and challenges.

Mama, do I have to eat these…brain looking things? She looked at the substance on her plate in disgust. **Can I go outside and play before Bain and Kelsie go to bed?**

Karma looked at the bowl of grey… brain-looking things. She had placed some of it on M's plate along with a slice of meat to mask the strangeness. "It's just mashed fruit. You should try it. It's very good. Supposedly, one cup has all the daily nutrients a human needed. Just try a bite."

Rafe broke open a crab and while its legs continued waving, he spoke. "The fruit looks different here, but they are completely edible. Those are supposed to be a hybrid of bananas but sweeter. The people consider it a delicacy."

Are you going to eat some, Papa? M asked hopefully.

He had just slurped up the delicious crab innards before pausing to look at the dish of fruit. He grimaced inwardly, still unsure why humans enjoyed the taste of sweet things. His body and tastebuds much preferred savory and salty items.

He ripped off a raw crab leg and passed it to M. "Just eat this and go out and play."

M accepted it and then hurried out of the large dining room while happily crunching on the crustacean. She'd gladly eat this rather than weird brain-looking food, especially since her Papa didn't trust it, either.

Bain, wanna play Galactic Invader? M asked the moment she was free to turn on her communicator. Of course, she had sent out a communication for Kelsie and Bain, but only Bain was still awake.

"Yeah! Let me connect my VR and laser!"

M ran down the corridor for her gear. **Just wait until you're on the ship! There are simulators where you won't need the VRs. We can fight a hundred space pirates at once!**

A few moments later, the two kids activated their gear, and instead of a sleeping quarters in a military hospital, and a courtyard on an alien planet, M and Bain were defending humankind from space pirates from their post on a moon station. Dressed in their badass black leather and at least ten years older, the children spun, kicked, and cut down their foe as expertly as if they were really a part of an elite fighting force.

Meanwhile, a boy watched from the distance with his spyglass. This time the girl with the robot voice and the ghost boy were fighting invisible people using fancy lasers. They swirled and flipped as if they were performers.

The boy's eyes grew enormous. It was magic! He nearly fell on his butt as he backed away. He turned and ran back to his friends... well they weren't exactly his friends, but after this, they would be. These weren't just Earthlings, they were wizards! Wow!

Tam pushed her breakfast around on her plate before placing her napkin on top of the uneaten food.

Karma gave her a sad look, and Maddy reached out and gently gripped her hand. "It's only been a day. I'm sure we'll hear something before too much longer."

"I'm not sure of anything anymore," Tam said. "I'm sorry. Excuse me, I'm not good company right now."

"To hell with this!" Rafe leaped to his feet, his chair nearly flipping over. He gave Karma an apologetic look, but his expression had grown fierce. "I'm not going to just sit here doing nothing! I'm going to get Haru!"

Tam quickly came to her feet. "Let me get my gear. I'm going with you." Rafe did not object, and they headed out of the dining room. Drago, Paris, and Kendrick were only steps behind them.

The ladies looked at each other, surprised but relieved. "If they hurt Haru...then wouldn't they be guilty of breaking the agreement?" Maddie asked.

"I don't think so," Daya said. "Not if Haru was caught spying..."

Karma dropped her fork and covered her mouth. Rafe had implied he wouldn't risk himself as long as he thought she was dying... but now that she was better, would he put himself at risk?

Once in one of the space pods, Rafe contacted Dorf. The Japoxillian was in his nest, snuggled against Kemistry.

It didn't take long for him to recognize Rafe's crew plus Tamsyn in a pod. He leaped to his feet, making sure his eyepatch was in place.

"Where are we going?" He growled.

"Galatia," Rafe said simply. "Are you coming?"

Dorf's chest puffed out. "I'll meet you halfway!"

Kemistry closed her eyes and smiled, knowing her man was returning to himself.

Chapter Fifteen

Dorf hurried out of the bedroom of the small house that had been assigned to them while Kelsie convalesced. He heard the sounds of fighting coming from his son's bedroom. It was late and he should have been sleeping. But Dorf just sighed, knowing what it was like when you missed your best friend. He missed several of them; some dead, some in far-off lands, and one missing in action.

He grabbed his holster and weapons and then dug through boxes for the symbiot belt, thinking that Rafe on Galatia made for an incredibly dangerous mission—especially with him being the most hated Galatian in the universe. He would need to lock in on him in order to fight for him remotely. His paws came into contact with the belts of his lost friends, and the pain of loss shot through him again. He couldn't dispose of them. He just couldn't do that.

If only Nao was here to hone in on Haru…

He snatched up Nao's belt realizing he was softly humming Nao's song.

"For you, brother!" He belted it over his waist on top of his own symbiot belt. It wouldn't work for anyone but Nao and Haru, but it made him feel closer to the both of them.

So as not to disturb Bain's game—which he had learned a long time ago was tantamount to an actual life-or-death battle, he bypassed the boy's room by slipping out the back door.

Since he was on a military base, Dorf had to head for the underground transport where the vehicles were stowed. Damn, that he only had one wing and couldn't fly! He ran as fast as he could, which was pretty fast when he used all four paws.

The soldiers on duty saw him, but since he was a superior officer, they did not question him, even though he was running at top speed. Only a very few humans understood the Japoxillian race, but all one really needed to understand was this Japoxillian was a decorated officer who had more power than they ever would.

He quickly signed out one of the larger pods since it was fueled and capable of getting to Galatia.

"Command." He communicated to Rafe's team as soon as he had left Earth's atmosphere. Suddenly everyone appeared to each other as holograms.

"Dorf," Rafe replied. "Welcome aboard." They exchanged coordinates. Dorf studied the star map.

"I should arrive 1.3 hours before you," he said.

"We are sure the Queens have changed their security protocol," Drago warned. "You will need to remain far out of range."

"Ai," Dorf acknowledged. "Any word from our Galatian contact?"

"No. Perhaps they are on high alert." Drago continued.

Or perhaps their allies had been discovered... But Dorf refused to speculate on that. The idea of losing another brother was more than he could bear to consider. Humans had a term that was similar to a Japoxillian saying about voicing thoughts and giving them life.

He placed a paw over Nao's and Haru's symbiot belt. "I won't let you down," he vowed.

Ciprio ran until he reached the *burweed* bushes. He then got down on his hands and knees and pushed back some of the more pricklier branches, which he then slipped through unscathed. He kept crawling until he was beneath the security wires. Once he was no longer visible by the security cameras, he could once again begin his fast-paced run. By then, he was on the other side of the villa's property.

If Ciprio had been older than ten, he would have needed to take a breather beneath one of the many trees, but excitement and youth kept him sprinting at top speed toward the swimming hole.

"Guys!" he yelled. There were only four people present; not much of an audience for all he had to tell.

Brooklyn raised her sunglasses and looked toward the screaming boy.

"Damnit, here he comes." She was reclining on one of the chaise lounges which had been situated around a beautiful stone lake. Ages ago, it had been taken over by the teens since the adults found the trek too much when there was a beautiful beach, which was easier to access.

Much too nice for the commoners, the children of the elites soon commandeered the area, setting up loungers and firepits. A waterfall gave a beautiful backdrop to the serene area.

The boys, Germany and Scotland, snickered at the kid's approach. Another girl, London, simply smiled and waved him over.

"Ciprio. Did you bring drinks?" she asked.

Ciprio came to a stumbling halt. "I saw her again! The robot girl!"

"Oh my God. Not with that robot girl nonsense again." Brooklyn said while rolling her blue eyes.

Germany swept back long blond hair and glared at the younger boy. "Didn't we tell you not to come here without refreshments?"

Ciprio straightened and swiped at the sweat rolling down his face. "But listen!" he continued excitedly. "She was fighting invisible monsters with the ghost boy! And they fight like superheroes-"

"Ooh super superheroes!" Scott taunted. "Which ones? Is the girl supposed to be Storm and the boy Spiderman?"

As the only Black person present, London swung around to glare at Scotland. "Why does the girl have to be Storm just because she's Black?" Her braided hair hung down her back, nearly touching her butt. Scott grinned sheepishly and wrapped his arms around her bikini-clad body.

"I didn't mean it in that way," he tried to kiss her, but she pushed him away and then giggled and gave in to a short kiss, but only on her cheek.

"Guys, you have to come see! Now, while she's still there." Ciprio insisted.

"Are you stupid?" Brooklyn glared at him, not shielding her obvious dislike for the commoner. "That place is crawling with military. I'm not getting thrown into the brig just so you can look important."

A shadow fell across Germany's face. "Forget about the brig. It's my dad I'm more concerned with." He absently ran his fingertips over the bruise on his cheek before remembering his friends were watching. His handsome face quickly donned its customary scowl. "But my dad is more elite than any of those women and babies renting out that pseudo-rich beach castle."

"Yeah," Brooklyn agreed. "My mother said only the *nouveau riche* need to flaunt their wealth like that. No one with class would stay at such an over-priced rental."

"But it's not just women and babies!" Ciprio exclaimed. "Galatians live there too!"

The teens looked at the boy before each of them began laughing.

"Everybody knows Galatians don't live in houses," London finally said after her fit of laughter ended. She pitied the little boy. He tried everything to fit in with them, even though he never could as a commoner. She didn't like how the others used him for sport, but he had to learn his place somehow, didn't he? Still, she didn't believe in mistreating the working class the way some others did.

"Besides, how would you know anything about what goes on inside a rich mansion, Cip?" Germany said with a mean scowl. "Your grandparents won't even allow you in the house! Isn't that what you told us? Your grandparents aren't even smart enough to sneak in and live in one of the rooms while the place is vacant. Instead, you all would rather live in that shack behind the barn!"

Ciprio's face burned in embarrassment. It was true his grandparents took their jobs seriously enough that they refused to break the rules by speaking about the residents or even using some of the nicer furniture in their modest little house. It was also true he wasn't allowed inside, since he had once swiped a toy that had been left behind.

It had seemed ridiculous at the time to leave the unwanted item behind when the children who had left it obviously had many more items to play with. But he'd gotten a hiding and then was forbidden to go any further than the kitchen—and only then to help his grandmother with the cooking.

London glared at Germany. "Play nice. I'm stuck here for another month and that kid is the only thing stopping me from having to lug around my own refreshments!"

Brooklyn replaced her sunglasses on her nose and relaxed once more in her chaise. "Ciprio, bring us *bat-nas*. Your grandmother makes them up real good."

"Oh! And some smoothies! It's getting hot!" London added before flopping down into her lounger.

Germany gave him a threatening look. "And this time, you better make sure it's still frosty. I want ice in it!"

"But..." Ciprio wanted to tell them it was hard sneaking food from the house and especially smoothies, which he would have to make on the sly. Besides, he had to make them believe there was something strange going on back at the villa.

Germany's anger flared. How could he manage the family's line of grocery stores if he couldn't even get this little pissant to follow his orders? His father's voice echoed through his mind, *'I'm going to make you into a man, yet!'* SLAP! *'You're weak!'* PUNCH!

Germany placed his hands on the boy's shoulders and squeezed harshly, causing Ciprio to wince. The bigger boy continued applying pressure to the tender flesh between his neck and shoulder until Ciprio cried out and crumpled to his knees.

Germany intended to do more, intended to punch and slap, but someone caught his attention. He frowned at the little Black girl who was approaching from the distance.

"Who's that?" Germany squinted as the girl crossed over the tall grass towards them.

Ciprio's eyes widened. "That's the robot girl!" He tried to come to his feet, but Germany held him in place, kneeling on the ground.

The teens turned to look, and Brooklyn even sat up at the child's approach.

"She doesn't look much like a robot to me," Scott said.

M stopped several feet from Ciprio and Germany.

Let him up. You're hurting him.

"Wait, she does sound like a robot..." London said in awe.

"How is she doing that?" Brooklyn asked.

Germany just sneered and squeezed Ciprio's shoulder again. "Who do you think-?"

The next second he was lying on his back with M crouched over him, ready to punch him in the face after the quick roundhouse kick to his chest. She could have done some damage but had elected not to kick him in the face.

Germany stared at M, stunned, but not so stunned that he dared move. He hadn't even seen the kick coming and could not have prepared for it even if he had seen it. The kid was just that fast.

"What the-?" Scott asked.

Ciprio rubbed his sore shoulder and stared up at M as if she were a goddess.

Drago tried contacting their Galatian agent but there was no response. Rafe rubbed his head and finally addressed his small crew. "If they are holding Haru hostage, then I will make a trade of myself-"

"Do not be so rash!" Kendrick interrupted. "We all want Haru's safe return, but you are too important to this mission-"

"And they won't kill me. They will, however, torture and kill him."

"Rafe," Dorf said. "You have a family. The sacrifices you make affect not only you."

Rafe looked down. "We will not speculate...for now."

It was difficult for the men to hope, but in the end, a swift death might be the best outcome and what any of them could desire.

Dorf pictured Nao, standing so tall with his sleek black feathers. He would often wear a Japanese *hanten* jacket out of respect for Haru's culture. He was always a quiet diplomat but fought better than any of them. There was none more courageous-

Can't...breathe...

Dorf's head cocked to the side. What? He concentrated on the soft whisper of a voice. It wasn't in his pod, nor was it coming from Rafe's pod. The voice was in his head.

No...oxygen...

Dorf's heart sped up. No. It couldn't be.

"Haru?" Dorf looked down at the symbiot belt. Was it possible Nao's belt had picked up on Haru's location?

Chapter Sixteen

"Haru?" Dorf whispered. He waited, but there was no response. He blew out a long breath that caught in his throat a second later.

Dorf? Haru's presence was so faint it was almost like a phantom thought, but there was a thought and he was somehow picking it up!

Dorf exclaimed something that was a curse and a laugh. "Haru! Where are you?! RAFE! HARU IS ALIVE!"

It was Tam who swung around to look at the Japoxillian's hologram. "Dorf? What are you saying?" Everyone on the ship was staring at the small Japoxillian who was staring wide-eyed at nothing.

"Quiet," Dorf said while holding up his paw. "Haru? Can you hear me?" Cocking his head to one side, he waited until there was the faintest sound.

No air...

Dorf's heart was thumping in his chest. "I can hear Haru! He's saying he doesn't have air! HARU WHERE ARE YOU?"

Tam clutched the arms of her seat.

"How do you hear him? Where is he?!" Drago jumped up and moved to the hologram as if Dorf was in the same room with them.

Dorf placed his hand on one of the belts. "I'm wearing his symbiot belt-"

Rafe leaned forward. "Get his coordinates!"

Tell Tam love…

Haru's faint voice ebbed away to nothing in Dorf's head.

Haru! Dorf began speaking internally. **We are speaking in our minds. You do not need to breathe to speak to me, but you need to tell me how to find you. Haru! Do you understand?**

It took a moment, but Haru finally responded. **Yes, I understand Dorf.** His voice was stronger. **I'm in the pool of the transport. There is no more air. I am absorbing what oxygen is left in the waters. I think Mizpaki is dead. He didn't make it to the pool. I have gone into stasis.**

Relief filled Dorf. If his ship was out of air, then going into ecdysis was probably the only thing saving his life. **Give me the coordinates you input and we'll triangulate back to you.**

There was no response. **Haru!**

Dorf…I'm here, but how do I-?

Just picture the controls. I will see what you see.

Dorf had no idea if it would work. Their connection was better, but nearly imperceptible. And without touch, this shouldn't even be possible. And yet he began seeing shadowy images. He concentrated, using one paw to press the belts around his waist and holding up the other to ask the others for quiet.

Rafe's crew seemed to understand, and no one made a sound as they stared at Dorf. Tam didn't realize tears were coursing down her face. *Please, please, please…*

Dorf concentrated. The image of a ship's interface moved in and out of focus. **Just a little more, brother,** he urged. **You have to tell Tamsyn you love her. She's here, you know; right here with us searching for you-**

The images suddenly solidified in Dorf's mind, and he quickly turned and began to rapidly peck into his own control panel.

Kendrick and Paris moved back to their controls. They could mirror Dorf's input. But the images were beginning to fade. Dorf knew Haru had given his last surge of energy, perhaps even his last surge of life, and even though Dorf didn't have all the coordinates, he would get as close as he could.

He moved into hyper-drive without knowing exactly where he was going, just that he was heading in the right direction.

I'm coming Haru. Go back into stasis. I'm coming.

Tam leaped up once Dorf's image disappeared. "What happened to Dorf?!"

Rafe stood and placed a calming hand on her shoulder. "It's okay. The communicator has to be re-initiated if we go into warp or hyper drive." Rafe moved to stand behind Kendrick where he studied his screen. Tam joined him even though she couldn't read the strange figures. "Where is he going?" Rafe asked.

"Look here." Kendrick pointed to a series of coordinates. "This is Galatia, and this is the point where Haru apparently departed. And this series is Earth. Haru was on his way to Earth and Dorf is evidently tracing this path and hoping to intercept his transport."

Paris growled. "But Haru can be anywhere along this path."

"What if he sent out a stress call?" Rafe went back to his own controls to put up a search on their own private networks.

"He might not have trusted doing something the Queens might pick up on," Drago said. He was busily pecking into his own controls but paused and turned to look at Rafe. "If we hit the course Haru's ship was traveling since Dorf is closer to Earth, then it means we must come from the opposite direction."

Rafe met his eyes. "Closer to Galatia..."

"Yes. And maybe ships are searching for him and they might find us instead."

Rafe turned to Tam. "We are going into ultra-warp. You have two minutes to put on a space suit before your eyeballs bleed." Tam was halfway across the ship before Rafe finished speaking. She was dressed within seconds, and Rafe turned to Kendrick. "Initiate warp to Galatia."

Germany rubbed his chest. That kick really hurt! Even though he was sixteen years old and the girl who had attacked him was only about ten years old, he was afraid to get up. At the root of it all, Germany was a coward, and, like most bullies, it was easy for him to pick on younger kids—but only if they were weaker than him.

When M saw the boy wasn't going to get up. She glanced at his friends, who were looking on stunned.

"Who in the hell are you?" Scott asked in awe.

M ignored the question and turned to give Ciprio a severe look. The little boy cringed until M offered her hand. He took it and M helped him to his feet. Just as her attention was turned, Germany frowned and leaped to his feet, and lunged at the little girl. No little girl was going to make him look bad in front of his friends!

M suspected he would do something cowardly like that, but he still managed to push her. She was about to deliver a harsh response but was surprised when one of the teen girls came to her defense.

"Hey!" London yelled. "Stop it Germany!" She hurried to the teen and punched him in the arm, then stood and positioned herself between the two little kids and the older bully.

Germany looked at London in surprise. "But she started it," he whined.

Scott came over to stand next to London. "No, *you* did when you were picking on Ciprio." He probably wouldn't have taken sides if London hadn't but, he wanted to stay in the pretty girl's good graces.

Germany pointed to Ciprio, surprised he was not impressing his friends with his tough attitude. "But he's nobody. He's just a commoner."

"But *she's* not," Brooklyn said from her place on her chaise. "That kid you're about to pick on is an elite whose parents are probably wealthier than all our parents put together."

Everyone looked at M in new appreciation, reminded there was no military assigned to guard *their* vacation homes.

"What's your name, little girl?" London asked.

M didn't answer. They made fun of her voice...

London touched her shoulder, and M refused to flinch. "It's okay? You talk through that thing on your wrist?"

She slowly nodded. **My name is M**.

"Wow!" Scott laughed. "Her mouth is not even moving. How do you do that?"

M was shy about the invisible keyboard that allowed her to type out using words instead of letters. Sometimes it looked like she was just fidgeting as her fingers twitched and moved while at her side. Each finger commanded whole words and if she needed more words then she could switch to letters.

To her, it was now like sign language. If she flexed the fingers on her right hand a certain way, she would say Mama, her left fingers doing the same action as Papa and there were gestures for baby brother and Bain and Kelsie as well as all her uncles and aunts. She'd studied hard to learn to speak smoothly, but not so smoothly that she was the same as other kids.

M held out her hands and moved them in an exaggerated manner. **I talk with my fingers instead of my voice.** She glared at Ciprio. **I'm no robot!**

Ciprio swallowed in embarrassment while the others just exclaimed—all except Germany, who only pouted.

"Let me see that!" Scott reached for the communicator, but M snatched her hand away. It was just like when she'd been at school. London blocked Scott from reaching for the communicator. She might have been an elite, but she wasn't a mean girl.

"Hey," something just dawned on her. "Are you an Earthling?"

M's brow lowered. **Yes. Aren't you?**

Scott laughed. "No. We're Edenites." He stared at her curiously. "I've never seen an Earthling as young as you."

"They're all old," Brooklyn finally came over to join the rest of them, but only because she was staring at M in curiosity.

Crap! M thought. She'd only followed the little boy to see why he was spying, but now it was she who was spilling things no one needed to know.

I have to go home. She turned to leave.

"Wait!" London called. "M! Come back tomorrow. We come here every day!"

M glanced back at them from over her shoulder before going at a full run back to the villa.

Rafe had brought up a 3-D map of the route Dorf had given them. He used his fingers to zoom in until he saw the small bleeping dot indicating Dorf's ship. As he was locked in on the ship, he checked his friend's fuel and air levels. He had enough of both to travel all the way to Galatia but would run out before he could return to Earth. If he traveled too far, he would need to make a stop at a refueling station and the legal ones were under the control of The Interplanetary Collective, while the illegal ones were too dangerous for a lone Japoxillian. Neither option was optimal for outlaws like them.

Tamsyn had come over and was staring at the map intently, willing herself to see any indication of Haru's ship. She looked at Rafe.

"I want to speak to Dorf. I need to know if he's spoken again to Haru."

Rafe nodded and used his communicator to make contact with Dorf. But instead of replying to the call, Dorf spoke to him mentally.

Rafe. I hear you, brother. I am using all my concentration to listen to Haru.

Has he spoken to you again? Rafe asked, using his and Dorf's symbiot belt to speak.

No.

Rafe was quiet, but finally asked the next question. **Do you sense he is no longer–?**

I sense nothing. I need to concentrate!

Dorf retreated, and Rafe sighed.

Tam touched his shoulder, her eyes wide. "What is it, Rafe?"

"I was able to speak to Dorf using this," he touched his belt, "but he needs complete concentration. However, he was able to tell me he has not spoken again to Haru."

She nodded and then returned her attention to the map.

Meanwhile, Dorf was using all of his years of training to connect with Haru. But it wasn't just training but years of experience he needed for what he was trying to do because this went into unprecedented water. No one had ever done what he was doing.

He thought of the way Nao would stare with a stony face intent on guiding Haru through battle. He would sometimes move his own arms and legs as if he was running and fighting because they were so entuned.

A stab of nostalgia struck him so hard he nearly wept, but with it came a stirring in his brain like a feather's tickle. Dorf turned bodily toward the feeling and then moved his ship off course to follow that inkling of life.

Haru! I'm close! I can feel you!

Haru floated and at times he imagined he was in the darkest depths of space, moving aimlessly among the stars. But as he drifted, he would collide with something hard and unyielding—stone and not a star. With a jolt, he would remember he was in the ship, in the pool, and there was no oxygen. He drifted again as awareness ebbed away, but this time when something bumped him, it was different. There was pulling and pain. He gasped even though his lungs couldn't work, not in the pool...

But they were working. There was air! He sucked in the precious oxygen with deep gulps. His hands came up to cup the item covering his mouth and nose. An oxygen mask? Haru fought to open his eyes and saw Dorf using his teeth and claws to shred through the fibers of the chrysalis forming over him. He wasn't wearing a space suit. Then how was he breathing?

The answer was that he wasn't, because he'd pressed his own oxygen mask to Haru's face.

Part Two

Chapter Seventeen

Haru's brain felt foggy, but instinctually, he fought against the restraints that prevented him from moving. All the while, Dorf ripped at the caul covering his body. They were both wet and while Haru naturally stayed afloat, Dorf kept sinking and jerking himself back up.

He needs oxygen! Haru tried to reach for the oxygen mask covering his mouth, but his hands were still bound by the chrysalis.

"Dorf..." he called weakly past the mask. "Take the mask..."

But he didn't. The little Japoxillian was holding his breath, biting and scratching at the chrysalis until soon he was just flailing in the water.

Why—?

And then Haru understood. The chrysalis had crept around the oxygen mask, adhering it to his face! It was trying to keep him alive while sacrificing Dorf, and Dorf was clawing at the chrysalis to detach it.

"Dorf!" he screamed. "Get back to your ship!" But he knew it wasn't possible. The little guy's eyes were taking on a distant look as the fight began to leave him.

Haru inhaled one long and deep breath and then he forced all the energy from his body, spreading his scales, extending his arms, legs, even his fingers and toes. But it was his tail exploding through the chrysalis and as Dorf began to sink to the bottom of the Galatian pool, Haru's tail wrapped around him and drew him into the chrysalis just as it began to reseal the break.

Fine. At least he had use of his hands and he jerked the tiny mask free from his face and placed it on Dorf's.

Dorf just lay limply against his body.

Wake the fuck up! Haru screamed internally. Haru was no longer worried about his own lack of oxygen. He'd sucked up a great amount and could hold that air for several minutes. But Dorf had inhaled water...

He thumped him on the back as hard as he dared, keeping in mind that he was many times stronger than his friend. When Dorf didn't move, he quickly turned him and pressed the heel of his hand into Dorf's solar plexus. Immediately, water flew from his mouth and into the mask.

Dorf weakly tried to push the mask away as he gasped for air, but Haru held it in place. Haru didn't even realize he was quietly thanking the Great Guardian over and over. Dorf's eyes opened wide, and he turned to look up at Haru.

Haru! You're alive.

Haru turned pink. Thanks to you.

Dorf was pressed tightly against Haru, but he managed to look around. **Uh…Am I molting with you?**

Yes, it appears so.

Dorf pushed against the chrysalis and then used one of his sharp nails to slice at it. It instantly resealed itself.

Can you contact Rafe? Haru asked. **Because it is not safe for you in here.**

Dorf didn't ask questions. He reached out to Rafe. **Rafe, I'm here with Haru and he is okay, but we have a predicament.**

Dorf! We followed your transmission and we are nearly there. What predicament?

Well, it appears I somehow managed to be trapped in the chrysalis with Haru. We have an oxygen tank to share between us. Dorf remembered his friend hadn't had a breath in a while and he detached the mask and placed it against Haru's face, who took several long, deep breaths before indicating he'd had enough.

Wait. Did you just say you are *in* Haru's chrysalis?

Yes, that is what I said.

You need to get out of there, Dorf.

No shit. Dorf looked around and while there wasn't complete darkness, he could see nothing allowing him to reopen the impenetrable fiber.

Haru's injured body seemed to crave time to heal, and he began to drift tiredly to sleep, despite his strong desire to stay awake. Dorf wiggled a bit as his confinement became smaller.

"You're squeezing me a little tight, buddy," Dorf spoke using his mouth.

"I'm not. The chrysalis is trying to absorb you."

"Huh?"

"Right now, you are the best source of nutrition..."

Dorf's eyes widened. **RAFE!**

We are nearly there, Dorf.

I'm being absorbed by Haru!

I know. Hang on!

Hang on?

Ciprio followed the little girl, walking fast to keep up with her despite the fact "Wait!" he called. She didn't. "If you're going back to the villa, you can't go that way."

M finally stopped and turned to look at the boy.

Why? That's the way we came.

Ciprio stopped abruptly and then moved nervously from one foot to the other under the girl's withering look.

"Well, if you want to get in undetected by the guards and cameras, you'll have to go in a different direction. I can...show you."

M just gave him a long look before nodding once.

Happily, Ciprio led the way which seemed much further away. But Ciprio kept looking over at her excitedly. He had so many questions about all the things he'd seen her do. But he had to admit he was still a little afraid of her, especially after the way she had knocked down Germany. And he was a big teenager!

If you are playing a trick on me, I will hurt you, M said coldly when she noticed him looking at her.

"No! I wouldn't do that!" She studied the boy and trusted her instincts that he wasn't trying something underhanded. He seemed nice, but sometimes people hid their true intentions behind niceness because you can get more flies with honey than vinegar—at least that's what granny used to tell her.

But she'd seen how those bigger kids had treated him and how eager he seemed for their attention. She decided for now she would trust him a little, despite the fact he'd been trying to tell their family's secrets to others.

"Did you say your name is M? Like the letter?" The boy asked. M nodded. "What does it stand for?"

M glanced at him as they walked towards a grove of trees. **Why do you want to know? So you can go back and tell those kids?**

She was satisfied when he blushed bright red.

"W-what? But how do you know? You weren't even around."

The same way I knew those times you were watching me.

Poor Ciprio's eyes widened in shock. "You are magical. They say people from Earth are different."

This time, it was M who looked at him curiously. **It is strange**

to hear you call me an Earthling. We're just human beings.

"But Earth is bad. Everyone is corrupt and the poor eat each other. Everyone says after the war, they left millions of dead bodies on the streets until the ground is made of bones. And no one lives in houses, but in underground caves because of the radiation. Some people have turned into mutants!"

Half of M's mouth was turned up in a smile. **Are you talking about movies? That's not real. Those are just actors.**

"No, I know that! They are acting out what really happened!"

She gave him a narrowed-eye look. **Did those kids back there tell you those stories? You know they aren't your friends, right?**

Ciprio looked ahead and didn't answer. M felt a little bad. She was just about to tell him it was better not to have friends at all than to have fake ones. She'd had her fair share of fake friends back when Granny was living. They were fake because they promised Granny they would take care of her, but when it was all said and done, they were ready to ship her off to the whorehouse. She was right to run away.

But before she could speak, Ciprio spoke. "I know they aren't my friends. But sometimes the vacation kids let me hang out with them."

Vacation kids?

"Yeah. The only kids around here are Elites—or Vacation kids. The working class live closer to the town where all the factories and farms are. They only come out here to maintain the rental properties for the vacationers.

"My grandma and grandpa used to work for the Maychesters, so they were allowed to live in the house—for like thirty years, but after the old man and old lady died, Mr. Constantine took over the property and set it out for rent. He told my grandma and grandpa they had to move into the cottage outback and could live there for free as long as they took care of the property and guests."

That's not fair, M said while making a face. She'd seen the old couple. The woman never smiled and looked as if she didn't like anyone. The old man just nodded his head whenever he saw them as if he was afraid they were going to complain about something. If they worked in this beautiful property for three decades, they should at least be able to enjoy living in it.

Ciprio gave her a confused look. "Why is it not fair? Many working-class don't make enough to afford food and housing. My grandparents are very fortunate. We have all the food we could ever want, and our cottage is very comfortable." He pointed to a fence. "There. There is where we cross to get back onto the property."

There was a tall electrical fence visible from between tall clumps of purple and brown grass and weeds. Very clearly was a sign reading: DANGER: ELECTRICAL FENCE.

The fence is broken? She asked while eying it.

"No." He continued to walk towards it while her steps were slowed. "It will probably kill you if you touch it." He looked back and smiled at her. "But I bet it wouldn't kill you because you have superpowers!"

She blinked at him.

Justina sat out on the balcony, gazing at the ocean and enjoying the breeze. Never had she ever been able to enjoy the sun on her skin. As a child, she was told she would freckle and turn brown. She would see the servant children running and playing, but she always had to practice; practice her cooking skills, etiquette, *tripenangle* and voice lessons, posture, balance, and dance. The lessons never ended.

And then when she was sent to the consort school, it only got worse. No Mama or Papa, brothers or sisters, just strict teachers, impossible tasks with frightening results. The only bright spot had been Jayne.

After having her reproductive organs removed, she had cried and lain curled in her bed clutching at her empty belly, still unsure if she someday might want a baby, but completely positive that it was a choice that should have been hers and no one else's!

Jayne had kissed away her tears and promised it wouldn't be scary because they would do everything together. They'd find mates, live next door to each other, and if things got too tough, they'd go to the other for comfort.

It was a plan that never panned out when Jayne saw Karma had more than she had. She allowed greed, prejudice, and jealousy to get her kicked off the Exchange. Leaving Justina to figure out this life on her own.

But somehow, she had. Somehow, she'd grown and matured and figured it out all on her own. And in doing so, she'd found a contentment she never knew was possible. She loved her new friends—the males as well as the females. And if they got their way, then she could live the rest of her life in peace without having to 'service' anyone.

There was a knock on her door. She got up, wondering if it was Maddie or Karma with news about Haru and the men. She knew it wouldn't be Daya. That girl was still a little skittish around her even after she'd made it plain she didn't want Paris.

Well, to be fair, she would be the same if she got an opportunity to be with someone who made her blood race and her heart pound.

Adrian Kelly's face popped into mind, and a soft smile tugged at her lips. Not saying she would, but if she did want to approach the soldier? How would that be done in a place like this? First, she'd have to figure out a way to even see them again! Eden wasn't a planet as big as Earth, but they could be stationed anywhere.

The knock on the door came again. "Coming." She quickened her steps and opened the door, prepared to ask if there was any news. Her mouth just formed a big, surprised "O."

Adrian Kelly was standing on the other side of her door as if her thoughts had conjured them.

Adrian took off their hat. "Hello, ma'am. I hope I'm not

disturbing you. I just wanted you to know I have been assigned as your personal bodyguard."

"Wait...*what?*"

Adrian removed their cap, allowing wavy black bangs to brush inky black eyebrows. They stood at ease with hands behind their backs and legs slightly parted. They wore a black sleeveless shirt that showed off sunburnished skin and wiry muscles. Form-fitting black fatigue pants defined a slender but muscular set of thighs and calves.

"I am your bodyguard, ma'am."

"Stop calling me ma'am! Why are you my bodyguard? Do the others have bodyguards?" Justina asked suspiciously. "I mean...what are you doing *here?*"

Adrian's eyes stared deeply into hers before they answered. "I am here because there are those who want to kill you and the other women here. They have mates and, it is my understanding that you..."

Justina blew out a long breath. "...I don't."

"Yes, ma'am—Justina. I was assigned by Lt. Washington to protect you. You are now my Protectee."

She gave Adrian an embarrassed look. "I'm sorry. I don't know why I-"

Adrian suddenly smiled and relaxed. "It's good to be suspicious and question all motives." Justina noted Adrian seemed proud of her over-reaction.

"Well, I still feel bad." She stepped aside to allow the soldier in. "Come inside. Let me get you a drink."

"My gear is being delivered, so I have to decline."

"Oh," Justina said in embarrassment.

"For now," Adrian completed while staring into her eyes. "I'll be next door and maybe later we can synch our communicators and discuss things?"

Justina could barely tear her eyes away from Adrian's gray ones so she simply nodded.

"Okay." Adrian turned to leave but then turned back in time to catch Justine checking them out. Adrian lifted their hand to wave and Justina waved back. Once Adrian disappeared around the corner, Justina slowly closed the door and then rested her back against it as a broad smile covered her face.

"Thank you Kendrick!" she whispered.

Haru? Are you asleep?

Hm? Haru's eyes opened. **Dorf! Are you okay? Something strange is happening…**

Haru chastised himself for falling asleep! How could he when he was probably consuming his brother! He reached down to run his hands over Dorf's wet fur to check him, but instead, he came across something strange.

There was a second chrysalis, and this one was forming around Dorf.

Dorf! He called.

I'm here, Dorf replied quietly. **But I don't understand.**

Dorf, you're…molting.

Haru felt a soft chuckle against him.

How is that possible? I can't shed my old skin, Dorf replied.

But there is a chrysalis forming around you. Are you in pain?

No, Haru. This is a wonderful feeling. It's like

flying. I feel so…so comfortable. I am once again in my mother's womb.

Ai. Haru agreed as his own brain, once again, began to drift. **This *is* like a womb. Dorf, I do not believe my chrysalis intends to feed you to me. I think it is…protecting you.**

Oh, that is good to know. Dorf sighed as if that news really meant nothing. Perhaps he would not have minded being absorbed into his friend like that old movie where a man and a fly were merged after one of his experiments went awry. If that happened, would he and Haru create a new thing like *Dorafu?* Or would he be an extension of Haru like a strange conjoined twin where his head would be attached to Haru's shoulders?

Haru chuckled. **Or maybe your fluffy little tail would grow out of my armpit.**

Dorf laughed, picturing the image Haru had conjured. **Wait. You can see what I imagine and I can see what you imagine.**

Ai. Strange…

Dorf imagined them soaring through the air, the world beneath them going a thousand miles a minute. When he looked to the side of him, Haru was there, a surprised energy coloring his scales.

Is this what it's like to fly?

This is better! Watch! And then Dorf rolled himself into a ball and shot himself through the air like a bullet from a gun. Haru was right beside him and he too began to roll and torpedo himself. As they flew, Dorf began to chant the words to an old song about echoes and voices inside your head. And the weird thing is that as he flew, he heard the music of that old tune. When he looked at Haru, they were both chanting the same thing over and again.

Voices inside my head
Echoes of things you said,
Voices inside my head
Echoes of things you said…

M stopped walking as Ciprio continued towards the electrified fence.

How many times have you done what you are about to do?

Ciprio turned to look at her. "Well, I don't have to sneak back in, so...not in a while. But it's okay. I dug a tunnel beneath one section of fence and I was smart." He gave her a crooked smile. "I covered it with leaves so no one can find it."

Ciprio. It's not even that important. Let's just go back the way we came.

He looked at her as if she was being silly. "But we're already here. You might as well take a look and see it's not dangerous at all."

She gave him a doubtful look, but he just waved her forward and then headed the short distance towards the fence. With a shake of her head, M followed.

After a while, Dorf slowed and they began to hover, looking around at the strange and colorful world he had conjured.

This is all in my mind, he said in awe.

Am I in your head? Haru asked.

Dorf grinned. **Yes. But this is more real than anything my imagination has ever shown me. It is like I have conjured a new reality. Let me try something.**

Dorf was suddenly holding an electric guitar while wearing a worn leather jacket. He even had the tiniest pair of motorcycle boots on his back paws. Haru was watching him standing on a small stage, and then Dorf began playing the guitar, his cat paws moving at incredible speed as they strummed up and down the frets.

But more importantly, was the sound! The sound of Dorf's guitar playing filled the entire world as if it were an echo chamber! The wind whipped and blew around him causing his fur and feathers to blow in the wind as the rock music thrashed loudly around them.

Haru watched in awe as Dorf rocked out.

It didn't take long before he wanted to join, but he had a different idea.

Just as suddenly as Dorf had appeared on the stage, they were in a deserted feudal village dressed in traditional Japanese attire. Side by side, the two went through a very detailed *aikido* martial arts routine. Soft Japanese strings played around them as the two moved in synch.

Dorf was enjoying the movements and chants a great deal. He had never moved so lithely in his life! No wonder the Galatians took molting in stride. He wished he could do this twice a year, too! He was so engrossed in this new experience he didn't notice that he and Haru were no longer alone.

Rafe had run to the pool the moment they entered the ship. He jumped in and swam to the large chrysalis. He wanted to rip through it, but he was wearing an atmosphere suit due to the lack of oxygen and didn't have access to his claws or tail.

He lifted the chrysalis and quickly waded out of the water with it where Tam was waiting, anxiously pacing. He gently lay the chrysalis on the floor while Paris ran a medical wand over it. Everyone watched the 3D monitor, expecting the worst.

Tam knelt on the floor and placed her hand on the head of it, where she knew by the shadows that Haru's head was located. There was a pulsating light there, an internal glow showing a soft movement as if he floated—not in a pool, but in a womb.

"Hm," Paris said. "Do you see this?"

The men were still standing, watching the monitor.

"Is that a double chrysalis?" Kendrick asked.

"Guardian," Rafe said in awe.

Tam looked up at them. "Are they alright?"

"Yes," Paris replied. "Their vitals are strong thanks to that oxygen tank."

"Let's get them back to the ship," Kendrick stated. "We can open it before it fully matures."

Paris looked at them. "I don't think we should open it. Dorf isn't being absorbed by the chrysalis—he is being enhanced by it."

Tam was still stroking the head of the chrysalis. She placed a hand on an odd lump, which was Dorf. He moved responsively, but gently. "Wow. I had no idea something like this was possible."

Rafe looked at her. "This has never been done."

"What?" When she looked up, it was to see them each staring down at her.

"There have been living organisms that have been caught inside during the molting process such as aquatics, insects, even the occasional reptile," Rafe continued. "That is common. But they are always absorbed by the host. Always."

"What about pregnant Galatians?" she asked.

"Queens don't molt after the first trimester—not until after the infant is born. It has been said that a child born inside of a chrysalis would be lost; killed."

No one spoke as they realized history was re-writing itself right before their eyes.

"Let's get out of here," Kendrick said. "Luck has been on our side so far. But a warship can eventually trace our wake."

"Yes," Rafe jumped into action and lifted his hibernating friends. "And I don't want that tank running out of oxygen before we can get them into our ship."

They wasted no more time and quickly returned.

Once they were back on their ship, Rafe contacted Karma.

"Is he okay?" was the first thing she asked as she hurried to Maddie's room. Drago was already calling her, as was Paris, who called Daya. It was Kendrick who contacted Kemistry. She should be present to hear this.

There were many questions, but none the Galatians could ask. Kemistry's was most important:

How would Dorf be changed? And obviously, there was no answer to that question.

Rafe stood by the pool as they navigated home.

Dorf? Can you hear me? He used their connection through the symbiot belt to try to break through his coma.

It wasn't just Dorf that heard Rafe's distant voice, But Haru as well. Their *kata* ended, evaporating so the two once more floated in starlight.

Rafe! Dorf exclaimed. **Are you here?**

Here?

Dorf remembered the symbiot belt, and he touched it. **Here.**

And just like that, Rafe appeared, floating with them.

Haru grinned, the most vibrant pink imaginable. **Brother! I have not seen you for longer than I want to think about.**

Haru? Dorf? Rafe looked around. **Where in the hell...?**

How is this working for him?! Haru laughed in awe.

I don't know. I don't know. Dorf touched his belt. **This allowed me to bring him into this world of imagination.**

What the fuck... Rafe spun and soared, feeling his fingers, stretching his limbs. He had removed his suit back on the ship and although back there he wore his normal skirt, boots, and harness, here, in this world, he was naked as the day he was born. Naked, free, flying with his two friends.

Watch this! Dorf said.

A moment later, they appeared to be in a beautiful world filled with tropical trees and plants. Instead of three naked beings, they were now dressed in strange loin clothes. Haru and Rafe had bold tattoo markings covering their bodies—something impossible for Galatians to do with their ever-shedding scales.

There was a loud, rhythmic drumbeat in the background of the world, although there was no one else present.

Suddenly they were performing a *Māori haka*, legs bent and hands slapping thick thighs as they shouted, with tongues protruding and eyes bulging fiercely. They slapped their chests, and thighs and made arm gestures as they marched forward shouting their *haka*.

Rafe was amazed he felt it, knew what to do, and that each of them did it all at once.

And then suddenly Rafe disappeared.

His head was pounding and something heavy covered him. Drago was lying across him and he was back on the ship, fully clothed, while Paris was running a medical monitor over him.

"What are you doing?" Rafe asked groggily.

Tam was watching with her fingers pressed to her mouth in surprise and fear.

"Are you okay, brother?" Drago asked as he slowly got up. "You were having a fit." Rafe scrubbed his hands across his face.

"You were yelling and sticking out your tongue, stomping around," Paris said. He scanned Rafe's eyes. "You looked like you were having some strange seizure."

He stood on shaky legs. "No. I was with Haru and Dorf—inside their minds." He turned to look back at the chrysalis. "I'm not sure what happened…"

"It wasn't a seizure," Tam said. "I've seen it before. You were dancing."

Rafe shook his head and explained what he, Haru and Dorf were doing. The others listened quietly, intrigued by the idea of being drawn into another's lucid dream.

"This can't be possible!" Kendrick said. "How is something like this possible?"

Rafe contemplated the chrysalis. "No one wearing a symbiot belt has ever gone into a chrysalis. I believe only a Japoxillian can make this happen. I'm going back in!"

Drago, Kendrick, and Paris were at a loss for words. But Tam clapped her hands.

"Tell Haru I'm here. I'm here and I won't leave him."
Rafe nodded once.
Dorf. Haru. I'm back.

Chapter Nineteen

The electrical fence was tall. Across the top was razor wire and warning signs were spaced every few feet. M was used to seeing them. They were everywhere in the slums and always littered with dead birds. Sometimes in winter the street people would use the fence to start a small fire so sometimes there were blackened areas—not that the fences ever burned down. No, but the sight to M was the sign of oppression. She always considered herself to be on the wrong side of fences like these.

"They don't need cameras here," Ciprio said as he walked a few feet from the fence's base, searching for something on the ground. "Not when they have a fence like this."

M wanted to tell the boy to be careful, but she knew he wanted to prove something, more than he wanted to get her home. "Here!" He dropped to his knees and began moving aside loose dirt and leaves. He looked behind him a M who just watched warily. "Come on," he invited. "Careful of the dead birds. I guess they still can't read the signs."

M went over to the crazy boy and saw a shallow tunnel becoming visible—shallow being the operative word. Ciprio sat back on his haunches and studied the two-foot valley which ran beneath the deadly fence.

"Hmmm, that used to be bigger..."

M looked around the way they had come. **I'm going back the other way. The less deadly way.**

Ciprio shrugged. "Fine, but I'm going through. I'll show you it's okay."

Don't.

He laughed boyishly. "It's fine, M!"

After speaking to Rafe, Karma felt so much relief. Lately, it seemed as if they had been getting hit after hit and it was great to get one in favor for their team.

Justina had opened a bottle of wine and they were preparing to celebrate. She looked down at Runnar, who was just content to be held in her arms and in the company of his aunties.

"No, I'm still nursing. I'm going to have some of that delicious grapefruit juice."

"Man, why is the fruit so good here? The grapefruit juice tastes like lemonade."

Karma headed out of the room. "I'll be back. I have to tell M the good news!" She hurried from the room and out to the large courtyard.

"M?" she called. It was beautiful out here. She inhaled the clean air and felt a smile cross her face. Hour by hour, her depression lessened. Of course, it would, despite everything she was in paradise.

She walked down to the garden but didn't see her daughter there, either. Mrs. Bianchi was there picking vegetables, probably for tonight's dinner. She wanted to explore the crops, maybe cook a meal for her family, but old Mrs. Bianchi had given her the evil eye and she knew when she was encroaching into someone's territory. When she had been a domestic, she hated when the homeowner heard the staff talking or laughing and just had to come into the room to find out if they were conspiring.

She sighed, happy those days were over. "Excuse me. Mrs. Bianchi, have you seen my daughter playing?"

The old grey-haired woman shook her head while giving her an accusatory look. "I no watch children."

"No," Karma assured her. "I didn't expect you to keep an eye on her." Karma moved over to one of the stone patios. She'd napped there once, and it had been amazing, looking at the ocean with the sound of the sea.

M wasn't there either. She had probably gone back to her room, but this property was too big to be traipsing around looking for a little girl. She used her communicator to contact her.

M answered but didn't initiate the holograph feature.

"Hey, baby, where are you?"

I'm with...a new friend.

Karma's brow moved up. "You made a friend? That's good. But where are you?"

M swallowed and looked around.

"M, put your communicator on hologram," Karma said.

She did, and Ciprio suddenly ran to her side.

"Hi, Miss. I was showing M around the property," he said. "My grandparents are caretakers for the villa. I'm Ciprio. Ciprio Bianchi."

Karma moved her own image, so she wasn't showing herself or Runnar—especially not Runnar.

"Oh, I just saw your grandma. I didn't realize they had any grand-children. They don't talk much, so-"

"No, ma'am. My grandma says not to bother the Elites." Karma hesitated at that info, never considering herself in those terms. Ideas like that are why Earth was in shambles. Rafe had made it seem as if it wasn't much different here.

"Well, it's time for M to come home. Your Uncle Haru will be arriving soon."

M's face lit up. **He's coming here?! I'm coming, Mama!**

"Mhm..." Karma said while tapping her foot. She wouldn't embarrass her in front of her new little friend, but she was about to be grounded. Rafe was right, they didn't like restricting their daughter, but she had to follow the rules; the spoken as well as the unspoken ones.

Haru, Rafe, and Dorf were flying through the air—well, in the air created by Dorf's imagination.

How are we doing this? He asked. **This feels very real...** Haru flew ahead until he was ahead of Rafe and then turned to face him, flying at a frightening speed backward.

You just imagine it, and it happens. More than that, it uses your memories—like the *Haka*. I have seen it done, but I would have never remembered the steps and chants. But here, it becomes real.

Try it, Dorf said.

Rafe gave his friends doubtful looks. The next moment they were no longer floating in the air but in a luxury home—his old penthouse apartment. Rafe was dancing, dance moves he had never in life performed. And yet he moved as if he had spent weeks being choreographed. Best was Haru and Dorf were behind him, mimicking the moves exactly.

Suddenly Rafe began singing.

Cause this is thriller, thriller night
And no one's gonna save you from the beast about to strike...

I knew it! Dorf said. **All those times you sat there watching us dancing, I knew you wanted to join us!**

Rafe just laughed, not allowing himself to be too embarrassed to give in to one of his biggest desires. It was fun to sing and dance to the old popular song. But it would be better if M and Karma were here dancing, too—laughing, freestyling, each doing their own thing.

And then he remembered there were a lot of important things to consider and the music faded and the trio's dance ended. He turned to Haru who was laughing, his face doing the near impossible: Smiling.

Haru, Tamsyn is here. She is holding you in her arms and has asked me to relay to you how much she loves you.

Haru's eyes widened. He suddenly faded away. Dorf sighed.

That is what you did when you woke up. Are we safe?

Safe enough. No one has pursued us, but I saw the condition of Haru and Mizpaki's ship. They had definitely been under attack.

Dorf nodded. **I saw Mizpaki. He was still in his chair, as if he had used his last breath to get them here.**

Rafe nodded once. **He was a good ally and a good friend.**

M turned and stomped back the way she had come.

"Wait!" Ciprio had to scurry to catch up with her. "What's wrong?"

Didn't you hear my Mama say *mhm?*

"Yes."

It means I'm in trouble!

"No. I told her it was my fault. Plus, if you go back that way, you will run into the guards-"

She spun to look at him. **The guards don't worry me more than my Mama and Papa!**

Ciprio continued to keep up with the little girl, happier than he'd been in a long time. He had a friend! That's what she had told her mother. She was his friend, and she was mysterious, powerful and an Elite.

Haru jerked in his chrysalis. Tamsyn was sitting in the pool, along the safe edge where the water was tepid. She had shed her clothes until she was just in underwear and was holding onto the chrysalis.

"Tam?" Came Haru's faint voice.

"Haru! I'm here!" She placed her ear to the fibrous material that encased the man she loved.

"I love you, too. Always. It's always you. Everything for you..." His voice began to fade.

"I love you." Tears filled her eyes.

"Soon I will sleep too deeply to awaken. But I have never loved like this. Be safe, *okusan*, for if anything should happen to you, I will destroy this world to find the culprit!"

She chuckled past her tears. "Don't do that, my love. Our friends will still need a place to live." She kissed the cocoon, knowing he had drifted back into hibernation.

When Haru reappeared to Dorf and Rafe, he was sitting on a rock looking as stony-faced as the object he sat upon. They gathered around him.

Your molting will pass more swiftly for you than for those that await your return. Rafe reminded him. He conjured a stone boulder for himself and sat. Dorf did the same, although his boulder was topped with a nest of smooth branches and turquoise feathers and down.

It is always at the most inopportune time! Haru stated but then calmed. **But thank the Guardian it was here for Dorf and me to protect us.**

Yes, my daughter just had surgery and I've left

Kemistry alone to look after our children—although I am pleased to have been here to find you.

You saved my life, Dorf.

Dorf nodded once.

What happened? Your ship was shot and why didn't you contact us? Rafe asked.

Haru's eyes lit up. **Ah. Everything was ruined before it even began. But humans have a saying about lemons into lemonade.**

~Haru's story~

When I arrived in Galatia, I expected to be interviewed by Amalia and her council. That interrogation lasted days, but they could not get what they truly wanted. Just as you instructed, Rafe, I fed them the information you permitted me to disclose. It was a good idea to have a fake plan and then for you to change it once I was no longer privy to the information. I told them everything—repeatedly; your plans to attract former and current Galatian Guards and how you intended to do so. Your plans to threaten to leave the Interplanetary Collective unless they support your endeavors, and most importantly, your desire to replace the Queens with humans.

The latter had the most impact—especially when I professed that I would never agree with replacing the Queens or to seek a subservient role for them. You were right that I would need to feed truth with misdirection. None of my responses were lies because it *is* true that I would never seek the demise of the Galatian Queens. Just as it is true that I would never replace them with human mates. You know my stance—each man should be free to love whomever they wish to love.

And then after they were satisfied with the information I supplied, they finally released me to return to Caeda. And this is when things turned sideways.

Chapter Twenty

M didn't have much to say to Ciprio despite his constant chatter.

"Is the air black with pollution on Earth?"

"Is it true everyone is forced to carry a gun?"

"My friends say it gets so hot that if you're caught outside your eyes can pop in your head, and so cold during winter that if you breathed the air, your lungs would freeze!"

"Why won't you talk? I don't mind that you speak through that thing on your wrist."

M had spun around at his rudeness. **You ask too many questions. You don't have manners. And I don't trust you! Now go away!**

The boy's steps faltered and then slowed until he just watched her disappear into the distance. M didn't care. She had her own neck to worry about! Because she'd been worried about how much he'd seen and who he was going to tell it to, she'd broken Mama's rule about staying in the courtyard.

She didn't mean to be bad, but sometimes she reacted before

thinking things through. But danger was around every corner and she had to be vigilant because sometimes big people didn't see it coming —even if you warned them.

But she didn't want Mama and Papa to be mad at her. But she didn't know how to explain that she wasn't just being a brat. Although...she probably was. They probably wished they had never adopted her.

One of the guards finally reached her just as she was about to cross back onto the property. He gave her a stern look as if she was more trouble than she was worth.

"Miss. You are not supposed to leave the grounds." She nodded her understanding. "You could have been kidnapped. And the Lieutenant would have had all of our bal—heads."

I'm sorry.

He led her back to the house, probably looking forward to telling her Mama and Papa about her. Ha, they already knew. Mama might be mad at her, but she wouldn't like some soldier telling her that her daughter was misbehaving when she already knew it.

"My bound mate was very pleased at my return. But she is no fool. I would never have agreed to accept her as a bound mate if she were foolish. She tested me in many ways—ways I would not want my Tamsyn to ever learn about. We mated at every opportunity, and once she was satisfied that I truly desired her, she began asking me questions that mattered most to her.

"'Did I love the human?' To which I answered it is my duty to love and care for my ward. 'Is that not what I am meant to do?' But then I explained that a consort is not a Queen; and could never be my bound mate.

"Hmph, how others long to hear what they want to hear. I am grateful Tam is not a Queen as it is the Queen's nature to want her workers to do nothing but what she commands. And to be a bound mate is equivalent to being a prisoner bound to his oppressor. Tam is mine and I am hers and no other title is necessary. In this way, it is easy to be evasive."

Rafe and Dorf nodded without interrupting.

"I believed any doubts between us were resolved. I went about working a new job; as a consultant to Amalia. I was used to supplying intel to determine your next moves. I was also tasked with training the members of the war council. How ironic I was to teach them hand-to-hand combat techniques that would save their lives if they ever came up against us in battle."

Haru chuckled mirthlessly. "I did not dare hold back, although I gave them nothing concerning our advanced weaponry. They are still in the dark ages using demolition bombs instead of thermobaric devices."

"That is a dangerous game, brother. There are Guardian among them who side with the Queens. Any of them can reveal that information."

"But strangely, they have not. Those Guards who do not agree with us have also chosen not to support the Queens."

Rafe listened with interest at that. "And Commander Einar?"

"Especially Commander Einar. I have seen him in conference with the Queen's council and he hasn't disclosed much more than I have. The Commander may not be on our side, but he is not on the side of the Queens."

"He is a spy. I would not trust him," Dorf stated, "Not until one of our Japoxillian gets their teeth into him."

"Perhaps. But as I began to relax and provide information to our contact, I learned I was being watched. There were spies in the household—and they weren't just Queens. The males that had never had the opportunity to leave Galatia were in the pockets of the Queens.

"One such individual was Honoree. He is an elder who maintained the electronics in Caeda's home. He has known her since she was a child. There are others, a physician, a groundskeeper, the attaché, and an ex-lover...or current lover. I do not know, nor do I care which.

"I was eventually contacted by an unlikely ally — one who would risk her freedom, her status, and her life just to get a message out to our team. Filene—Titus's bound mate. She acted on behalf of your mother."

Rafe came to his feet. "My mother!"

"I could not tell you at the time, Rafe. I could not risk anyone ever finding out—for her safety. And, fortunately, I did not because I learned many things after our meeting. Her message to you is that she supports you, Rafe. But just as importantly, she loved the idea of having a grandchild and would not have cared what breed his mother was.

"When she learned that your child had been murdered, your mother vowed she would never see another child killed just because they were hybrid. She went against Amalia and the council, and she wasn't alone. Paris's mother is also a vocal supporter. I believe that all of our parents support our cause."

Rafe could not believe what he was hearing. His head was reeling with the news. He had come to terms that his mother and all Queens were more interested in upholding tradition than loving their child. But why would he think anything different when it was their mothers who raised him to be submissive to the Queens? Rafe turned his attention back to Haru.

"Jadorith even held a gathering for those who did not want to see their loved ones murdered in war, and the number was large! Not all were necessarily supporters of our cause, but they had questions—that is until Amalia put a stop to it and had her placed under lock and key.

"Amalia locked up my mother?" he asked in alarm.

"Your mother is safe. It was just for a day. Amalia meant to send a message. Jadorith's status as an elder with two living offspring is too important. Your mother's status is her protection."

Rafe paced while rubbing his chin. "But Amalia's way is that of assassination." Haru just nodded once. "Our mother's support could mean their deaths..."

"Your mother is a wise woman. She is no longer as vocal and is aware she is being watched. But Amalia cannot watch everyone. Not only are our parents allies, Filene appears to be a sympathizer, and Leolo is on our side, as well, even though he has relinquished his consort and position. I cannot say how large our numbers are, but what I know is Amalia has not moved forward with calling for war because she does not know if she could prevail in the event of a war.

"This is fantastic news!" Rafe exclaimed. "Perhaps we can avoid a war. If The Collective knows this, then they wouldn't dare risk being on the losing side of a war where they would lose the support of their Guardians!"

Dorf nodded in agreement, but Haru looked at them grimly.

"There is more. I did not know my mother was one of our supporters until she visited me before the parley. Part of me thought it was a setup, but I listened to her.

"I had not seen her since my arrival in Galatia. I assumed my family was ashamed of me. I initially did not seek them out and when they paid me no visit, I decided it was done; I was no longer my mother's son.

"And then, the day before the parley, I fell ill. The cook had placed a small amount of ***iktai*** into my meal and I had to travel to the pool for a prolonged visit. Yes, it turns out that Caeda's cook was also a sympathizer.

But once I arrived at the pool, I smelled my mother's scent and followed it to the top of a mountain where she was waiting for me. She promptly made me remove my communicator and leave it there. She then touched my face and said I was not to trust anyone or anything and bid me to follow her to a distant location where we would watch that mountaintop.

"I did not know what to make of that, but I listened without responding. Which is when she told me about the supporters that numbered among the Queens. She told me not to trust any electronic devices, for they had been bugged and trackers had been placed in all vehicles that I had access to. She also told me about the bombs placed in Caeda's space pods—just waiting for me to steal one of them in the event that I was a spy.

"A red anger crept along his scales.

"Caeda would rather see me dead; blown up in an explosion than to allow my freedom! Rafe. Dorf. I remained calm, but I was shaken by that news. I wanted to trust my mother, but in this place, trust is not anything you should easily give. Luckily, my communications with our allies had all been done using written symbols only known to us, and never spoken aloud.

"My mother went on to explain that should I ever need to escape this place, there was a large transport fueled, weaponized, and free of tracking devices, and then she gave me its location. She named each of the people who had been set to spy on me and where I could locate the hidden monitors and listening devices. And finally, I saw what she wanted me to see. Old Honoree and Caeda's lover had arrived on the mountain top right where I had left my communicator. My mother had known they would come looking for me. While communicators are trackers, it was now obvious that they were using it to actively keep tabs on me.

And now they knew I had figured out that they were actively following me.

"I thanked my mother and when I returned to Caeda's home; I explained I had gone for a run and, due to being ill, I had taken a fall and lost my communicator. I wasn't believed, but it didn't matter. I was just counting the hours until I could leave, only thankful my mother had been able to warn me not to use any of Caeda's pods to make my escape.

"That is why I was unable to contact you. I didn't trust any communication devices that Caeda had access to.

"But why was your ship under attack?" Dorf asked. "How did they know you would make your escape during the parley? Our meeting interests everyone in Galatia. I know Amalia made the parlay into a public broadcast so everyone on the planet should have been watching it."

"Indeed. I will tell you how I came to be chased and under attack by the Queen's War Council."

Chapter Twenty-One

"Caeda and I had a conversation in which I voiced my desire to attend the meeting. But just as I predicted, she did not think that was a good idea.

"Since my return, Caeda had made extra strides to be...equitable. She made suggestions instead of demands. She made her best attempts to satisfy me sexually, but as Queens don't find favor in facing one another during intercourse, there can never be a level of intimacy as we have experienced with our chosen ones."

Haru was quiet for a time before he inhaled and continued. I allowed Caeda to believe it was her idea I not attend the meeting. She voiced concerns others might mistrust my motives—as if that hadn't been the case for the entirety of my stay.

"Of course, I argued I had more of an investment in the meeting than anyone since I'd turned on my friends and brothers. But the more we discussed it, the more I realized she feared you would change my mind. Which is how we left it; with me assuring her I was where I wanted to be. Not a lie. I wanted to be there gathering the information I needed to help our cause.

"Everyone in the household left to attend a gathering where the meeting was being broadcast—everyone except Honoree, who complained he didn't like crowds, and the cook who wanted to prepare a beast for dinner. Of course, Honoree only stayed behind to watch me. I turned on the broadcast like a good little captive.

"And just as he was settling down to watch and make his usual disparaging comments against our team, I put that old bastard in a stranglehold, sealed his mouth shut, removed his communicator—which I kept right there by the visualizer, and then I dragged him to the back of the cavern. I knew the cook was an ally, and I didn't want to do anything that would place her under suspicion. Then I was on my way!

"I left the communicator sitting right there in the same area with Honoree's and I pretended to make my way to the pool in case anyone was watching. Of course, others were watching. I just didn't know it.

"The original plan was for me to meet Mizpaki at a pre-ordained point. But obviously, we could no longer use that plan. I had to contact him, though. And there was only one way for me to do that—by using my communicator. Which is how they knew of our plan. It was now a matter of out-racing them. Thankfully, while those who were watching me knew of our plan, they didn't have Mizpaki's identity.

Haru looked at Dorf and Rafe. He spoke the question for which he already knew the answer.

"Mizpaki is lost to us, yes?" Both men nodded once. "Eh," Haru continued. "He died a hero's death."

All present knew Haru did not simply mean he died during battle, because any inept individual could be killed due to their own ignorance. No. To die an honorable death meant to die during battle painfully, prolonged, or both. While suffocating in outer space, Mizpaki had certainly achieved both.

"Thankfully, the transport was left in a place where I could easily travel by foot. It was a good model, and I was able to race to the desti-nation. Even without a tracker on me, I had a difficult time keeping ahead of my pursuers. My neighbors were watching me, the neighbor's groundskeepers were keeping tabs on me, even the human offspring of the neighbors! But I am a Galatian Guard and I outraced them while the majority of the populace was enthralled with hopes of outwitting you!"

Rafe realized Haru had no idea what had occurred during the parley. He'd been too busy racing for his life.

"By the time I reached Mizpaki, an order had been given to fire upon us. I had to lower the shields in order to engage the transport, which is when we took a direct hit to our engines. We lost fuel and air but managed to leave Galatia."

"They didn't chase you into space?" Dorf asked.

"No. They weren't properly outfitted for space travel. But they did enough damage."

There was a prolonged quiet. "We will get word to Mizpaki's bound mate... although, she may not want to hear from us," Rafe stated.

"I can attest to that. Mizpaki stated that while she wasn't suspicious of him, she was very entuned to his every move. That is important, but just as important is the safety of our parents." Rafe's eyes flashed. "The parents of the Galatian Guards are certainly under a great deal of suspicion right now."

"Haru, Dorf, I have to leave you. I am pleased we are not being pursued, but we are far from being safe—especially our mothers." And with that, Rafe disappeared.

After he returned to his ship, Rafe looked at his crew—including Tamsyn. He was still sitting in his chair at the command and was pleased he wasn't sitting on the floor somewhere babbling like a fool. He gave them each grim looks.

"We don't need to worry about being pursued. But we have to figure out a way to save our mothers." He stood and relayed the story Haru had told him.

When M got back to the house, the soldier who escorted her knocked firmly on the door. The room was empty. The other women had quietly left after overhearing the conversation between Karma and M. Anyone could tell that things were going to get tense just based on Karma's expression alone.

"Mistress," the soldier bowed his head respectfully. "I found your daughter outside of the boundary. I wanted to personally escort her back since we don't know if the surrounding area is hostile."

Karma's eyes moved from M to the soldier. "Thank you. Come inside, M." M stepped inside, but before Karma could close the door, the soldier continued.

"Oh," he said quickly. "I hope the young Miss understands the importance of staying within the designated areas. The soldiers are spread very thin handling our military requirements without having to also be engaged in babysitting duties." He gave her a polite but somewhat condescending smile, and then another short nod of his head. "Mistress," he said before turning.

"How did she get out?" Karma asked before the soldier had fully turned to leave. He stopped and then turned back to look at her again before answering. "I do not know, Mistress-"

"Your military duties are to protect this family. That's the reason you're on this planet with us, is it not?"

"Well-"

"You're a soldier whose only purpose for being brought to this planet is to protect this family. And yet, you don't know how this child was able to leave your secured boundaries undetected?" The soldier's face turned red. His mouth parted to speak—likely in order to say the wrong thing...again. But Karma leaned in and spoke softly but distinctly.

"Instead of you making assumptions about what this child knows or doesn't know, you should be focused on why a child was able to breach your security undetected."

The soldier licked his lips. "Yes, Mistress." Karma closed the door and looked down at M, dismissing the soldier.

"Why did you leave the courtyard? Don't you understand why I told you to only play on the premises? The reason I need to know where you are at all times?" M was nodding but couldn't answer because Mama kept asking more questions. "Especially now, M, with that insane Ragna on the loose and Rafe on a mission and all of your uncles gone? The soldiers can only do so much. *I* can only do so much!" Karma swept her hand over her face to calm her emotions. When she spoke again, it was in a much calmer voice.

"You cannot just go wandering around-"

I didn't, Mama.

Karma paused as she second-guessed everything she had thought about raising this little girl. She loved her with her *entire* soul, but did she truly understand what it was to be a protector of a girl like M, of a girl exactly like *herself*?

The first time she'd seen M she'd seen herself, barely surviving a world that wanted to eat you up, disrespect you, hate you, just because you were born a brown child. But what if she'd been all wrong about what M needed...

"M, please tell me why you completely disregarded my directions?" she asked quietly.

I'm sorry, Mama, but I had to follow the boy. He was spying on me and Bain while we were playing. Mama, he was on our property watching us and he was going to tell other people. What if he told about Runnar? Or that you were consorts? Then everyone would know who you are!

Karma frowned. "What boy? The one who was on the communicator with you?"

M nodded. **I heard him, Mama. He was going to tell the others just so he could have friends!**

"Don't worry about that boy," Karma said dismissively. "I will handle that boy. What I want to know is why didn't you just come and get me, or one of the soldiers?"

I-I don't know. But she did know. She just didn't have the words to express herself, and it had nothing to do with the fact that she was mute and spoke through a mechanical device on her wrist.

Karma shook her head in disappointment at M's mediocre excuse. "M, when your father wanted to punish you for breaking out of your sleep chamber in order to kill a dangerous being, I stood up for you and told him to look at things from all sides. That's because I understand you are not the typical child. You have seen the dirt that lies beneath the surfaces and all the monsters that lurk in the darkness. I see in your eyes you will do whatever it takes to protect yourself from them, but also protect those you love."

M said nothing as she stared into her mother's sad eyes.

"You're not wrong for doing that. You are supposed to do whatever it takes to survive. The problem is, that at nine or ten years old, you shouldn't have to know about being attacked by Black Masks, being hunted by aliens that are trying to kill your mom and brother. You shouldn't have to feel the need to protect secrets that are well above your years." Karma sighed. "I swear all I ever wanted was to shield you from the worst of Earth. Instead, I exposed you to even more danger. But how in the world am I supposed to *unteach* you everything you're supposed to know about how to survive?!"

At the sight of the unshed tears in Karma's eyes, the words M had fought so desperately to find finally came to her.

When I went after Ciprio, I didn't know he was just a little boy running to tell tales to other kids who didn't even like him. I thought someone had to see where the attack would come from. Someone had to see their faces, where they lived, who Papa and uncles would have to hunt down when they...came to hurt us.

I followed a person who might have told our secrets. But all he turned out to be was a little boy who wanted some friends.

Karma placed her palms on the little girl's cheeks. M's eyes filled with tears as she covered Karma's precious touch with her small hands.

Mama. I don't know how old I am. Two fat tears spilled from her eyes and she sniffed them back, her voice making a terrible croak. **But Mama, I don't feel like a kid. I don't think I ever have.**

Karma went to her knees and pulled the little girl into a hug. They stayed that way, hugging for a long time before Karma pulled back. She wiped the tears from M's face and then from her own.

"When I was about your age, my childhood was ripped away from me. Having structure and safety and regular meals didn't bring my childhood back. At St. Aloysius, it was like when rich people put clothes on their dogs as if they were people instead of dogs wearing little sweaters."

M understood exactly what she was saying. She still had a lot to learn, but she hoped her mother would stop trying to squeeze her into little sweaters.

Chapter Twenty-Two

Karma walked into the kitchen where she knew Mrs. Bianchi would be preparing dinner. As expected, the older woman was stirring something bubbling in a large pot which filled the room with the aroma of deliciousness.

"Mrs. Bianchi. May I have a word, please?"

The woman's back was so crooked she had to turn bodily to look at Karma. Her ruddy face sagged with what Karma took to be a perpetual expression of discontent. She was tiny at barely five feet, although her bent form and height should not fool a person into thinking of weakness. Karma had seen her carrying a side of lamb over one bent shoulder!

With silver hair which she pulled back into a bun and covered by a scarf whenever in the kitchen, Karma thought she was easily in her mid-seventies. Still, she was a seventy-year-old who could probably whup the ass of someone half her age.

"Yes, Mistress?"

"It's about your grandson."

Mrs. Bianchi's brow lifted. "Ciprio. What about him? Has he misbehaved?"

Karma, who had been standing at the entrance, walked into the kitchen, thinking how sad it was this was her first response. But maybe she knew her grandson and his penchant for spying on the guests. Still, she hoped that would never be her first response if someone should mention her children.

"My daughter told me your son has been spying on her, and while I understand that children will be children, we require anonymity and discretion—two things my-" She was about to say husband when she caught herself. Here she wasn't an ex-consort but a group of women who were being guarded by Galatians. "...*we* were assured we would receive that here."

Mrs. Bianchi didn't take her eyes off Karma, but she put the large wooden spoon down on the stovetop and moved to the back door.

"Ciprio!" she yelled in a surprisingly strong voice. She addressed Karma again, who noticed a thick Italian accent. "Your daughter, you say?"

"Yeah, I can get her-" Karma gestured to the entrance.

"CIPRIO!" The woman bellowed louder than Karma could have expected from such a small woman.

"I just wanted you to please remind him not to spread our business amongst his friends."

But Mrs. Bianchi's sour expression had grown even more unpleasant. "I will get to the bottom of this!" She craned her neck to look out the door. "Where's that boy? Ah! There! You come here right now!"

Karma raised her communicator to her mouth and summoned M to the kitchen. She didn't want a situation of "he said, she said".

When the boy hurried into the kitchen, his eyes widened at the sight of the guest. "Have you been spying on these people?" The older woman asked sternly.

Ciprio's face seemed to pale. He opened his mouth, closed it, and when he reopened it, his grandmother grabbed his ear and gave him a shake.

"Don't you like to me!"

Karma reached out as if she wanted to save the boy but stopped herself. "Uh...I just wanted him to know not to speak about what we do-"

The grandmother paid Karma no mind. "Well, boy? Did you tell anyone about the alien baby with the human face?"

Ciprio was obviously in pain, but he looked at his grandmother in confusion. "No, ma'am."

"What about the Galatian men that sleep in this villa?"

"Ow, grandmother! No!"

Karma stared at the old busybody. Mhm...she had her picture. That old lady probably knew more about them than the little boy ever would.

"Well! What stories have you been telling?" She gave the ear another twist and the poor kid made another pained cry and nearly dropped to his knees.

M entered the kitchen then, and Karma hated her to see the boy being abused like this. She placed an arm over M's shoulders as Ciprio cried out what he had told his friends.

"I just said I saw the little girl playing with a ghost boy, grandmother! OW! And I said she had a robot voice!"

Mrs. Bianchi dragged her grandson over to a fireplace, where she grabbed a slender piece of a branch from a small bin of wood. When Karma saw he was about to get a switching, she could no longer hold her tongue.

"Mrs. Bianchi! Please don't. I just wanted to make sure our family was free of gossip."

The old lady paused to look at Karma. "Mistress, I can assure you if others gossip about your family, then we are not the source of it! Now, begging your pardon, I will attend to my grandchild."

Karma looked at the poor kid, still stooped in an awkward position to relieve the pain of having his ear wrenched. When the old lady began whupping him with her switch, she turned.

"Let's go, M."

M hastily followed her mother but craned her head to catch the last glimpses of Ciprio's grandmother tanning his hide as he hopped around, trying to protect his backside.

When they were safely out of the kitchen, Karma gently lifted M's face. She could see the shock that was plastered over it, just as she knew hers was probably filled with shock *and* guilt.

"I did not intend for that to happen, and I don't condone causing physical pain to children! But," she sighed. "I won't lie, my own Mama whupped me with a switch once or twice."

M's eyes widened in shock. But Karma just smiled.

"Yeah, I remember I was playing one of my Mama's vinyl albums without permission, and I scratched it. I didn't tell her but later she found the scratch. I got spanked for being sneaky and for doing something I wasn't supposed to be doing."

Did your papa ever spank you?

This time, Karma's eyes widened. "No! My dad would never lay his hands on me or my mother." She smiled grimly and looked off into the distance before sighing, pushing back old memories. She placed her hands on M's shoulders. People needed to touch more. It was the one thing she missed once she lost her parents—not having anyone to hug or just touch her with kindness. It was something she swore never to deprive her children of, and she knew Rafe felt the same. He always held their hands, enjoying the feel of human skin.

"Anyway, I didn't want you to think I wanted Ciprio to get a whupping."

I feel bad for him. He must feel pretty bad getting whupped in front of us.

"Yeah, baby. The next time you see Ciprio, be sure to be nice to him. It seems like he's got it bad."

I will Mama, M quickly assured, remembering how hard he had tried to be friendly and how she'd coldly shot down his attempts. She promised herself she would apologize for the first opportunity she had.

Rafe and crew returned home at the break of dawn. Rafe had sent out a party to collect the broken-down ship Haru had escaped in. The decision was made to move Haru and Dorf to one of the larger Galatian pools onboard the spacecraft that had been used to bring them to Eden.

A physician was called in to monitor their health, and Tam set up a pallet on the floor and informed everyone she was going to stay there. Rafe did not object. He wanted nothing more than to go home and spend time with his family before brainstorming about how to rescue their mothers.

Everyone needed time with their families except Kendrick, who opted to stay on the ship for Haru and Dorf. Well, in honesty, he had no immediate family to be with. That didn't sit well with him today. He didn't miss Auras, but he did miss having someone who paid attention to his needs and wants.

He walked to the command center of the ship, distracted by his troubling thoughts. If not for this, he would have recognized that rapid footsteps had been following his movements for far too long.

Without slowing, Kendrick used his tail to view who was shadowing him. The ship had been settled in Eden for days but it was still bustling with activity as the crew monitored safety levels on both land and in space while providing a workstation for the numerous military forces that had no place in Eden; such as aliens who were so strange it would disrupt the Edenites.

Although no longer Earthlings, the Edenites were still human and still considered a 'protected' species.

Therefore, certain areas of the docked ship were very busy. But not so busy that a six-foot-tall human woman wouldn't stand out. Further, he recognized this particular woman. He'd bumped into her while also on the ship when he'd recruited Adrian Kelly.

He rounded the next corner and then pressed himself against the wall in the small alcove. He didn't have to wait long. The tall woman appeared and when she saw that she had been discovered, instead of becoming flustered, the woman just looked up at him. Her expression was decidedly not subservient.

"You're following me. Why?" he growled.

The woman didn't immediately respond but took time to simply stare into his eyes. She finally spoke.

"Because I want to fuck you. Sir."

He blinked in surprise. Of the many possible responses that he could have expected, *that* was not one of them. "I...beg your pardon?"

The woman licked unpainted lips that were still very pink despite her complete lack of makeup. Her skin, mottled with brown freckles, gave her a strange cast, as well as the red hair that was pulled back into a military bun which was tight but not tight enough to tame the red curls that framed her face.

"Sir, my name is Sgt. Marisol Mckenna," she replied respectfully, but still without coming to attention. Strangely, her brazenness didn't bother him. He was distracted by everything about her. He thought her voice was unique, with a deep country accent that reminded him of the dialect of those from the southern states of North America. The North American province was his favorite place in the entire universe—specifically the southern states.

"I have been a member of the Special Forces for several years," she continued. "And have kept to myself. Since serving, I have never been involved in any romantic or sexual encounters. And even before being recruited, I kept mainly to myself.

"But I know how big your prick is, Sir and I've been fucked by big country boys. I can take it." She smirked. "I prefer it."

Kendrick was struck completely dumb. Something he could not say happened very often, but his prick surged.

"Uh..." he tried to find his words. "Why would you want to do that... with me? A Galatian? Are you often attracted to sex with aliens, Sargent McKenna?"

The soldier wasn't intimidated by his response as she continued to stare into his eyes. And in that way, Kendrick knew she was being authentic; there was no lie in her breathing or heartbeat.

"When you first came to the compound, I saw the way you connected with us humans. Most of the Galatians barely speak to us unless it is to give a command. But everyone knows you really seem to be more human than alien, just like all the scientists always taught us.

"I hope you don't take any of that as an insult, Sir, because I happen to think highly of both races. I've always been strong and, therefore, I have no choice but to admire the strength of Galatians. And just because I'm human doesn't mean I don't have a craving to fuck." For the first time, she allowed her eyes to drop to his skirts, which didn't lie as flat as it normally would. She licked her lips again.

Chapter Twenty-Three

Rafe knew the small pod would likely attract attention and he should just use one of the trucks, but to hell with it! He would arrive in a fraction of the time and he missed his woman and children. Drago and Paris felt the same.

"Karma," he spoke into the communicator. She didn't give him time to continue.

"How long before you get home?" she asked in excitement. He smiled.

"I will be there within minutes. We have used one pod."

"Oh? Where will you land? Don't even think about landing on the Villa's grounds. The Bianchis are sticklers about maintaining this yard!"

"Hm. We can land on the beach and run up the cliffside."

"I can't wait to see you. I missed you!"

He chuckled. "I have been gone for just a day. How are the children? Did Runnar learn any new skills and has M been practicing her movements?"

Karma had thought about how she would address M leaving the grounds. She wouldn't keep anything from Rafe—besides, it wasn't wise since that soldier knew about it. But she wanted him to understand why she had second thoughts about punishing her. They would need to talk about it.

"The children are fine and they miss you, too. I haven't told M about Dorf being in stasis—I don't really understand it myself. But she's ecstatic to see Haru."

"Eh. Well, I see the beach ahead. I'll be home shortly. I suppose there is no chance we can slip away for a quicky? I regret not making love the other night, and now I'm extremely horny."

Karma laughed. "Oh my goodness! With you, my love, there is no such thing as a quicky! I will make the wait worth your while."

He growled. "I'm sure you will. See you soon."

Karma scooped up Runnar, who was on his sensory mat playing with objects that were supposed to stimulate his motor skills. Not that he needed the items on the mat. He was nearly four months old but had the skills of a baby twice that. He could pull himself up into a sitting position and scoot to any number of items so he could place them in his mouth.

When his mom picked him up, he instantly went for her hair and pulled it into his mouth, gnawing and cooing happily.

Karma was headed to Daya and Paris's quarters to get M. Daya had kindly offered to continue giving M, Bain, and Kelsie their lessons. The other two children attended the schooling via hologram, which was the best way to keep the three of them attentive.

By the time Karma got to the living room, Daya was already arriving with M by her side.

Mama! Papa's coming!

"Yep. Let's meet them in the courtyard."

Maddie and Justina were already there. Rex was bouncing excitedly in Maddie's arms. "Dada! Dada!"

"Whoa," Karma exclaimed. "He just said Dada."

"He's been saying it ever since Drago left. I can't wait for him to hear it! He's going to freak!"

Justina stroked the baby's fine black hair. "You are such a cutie," she said wistfully.

Adrian, who was standing a few steps away, trying to stay unobtrusive, took note of the longing on her pretty face. Adrian had always just considered consorts as vapid and out of touch. But that was before being recruited into the special services. Now it was plain to see they were just as much victims as the poor and desolate—it was just their prisons were gilded cages.

It wasn't long before the sound of the ocean was joined by swift movement along the cliffs. The first to appear was Paris. He had no boots on but was still wearing his other rigging. Daya stepped forward, but Paris closed the space of a few yards in seconds. By all outward appearances, he was about to bowl the poor woman over, but she simply raised her head and he stopped cold inches from her, looking down to meet her brown eyes exposed in a form that was otherwise concealed by thin veils and scarves.

He placed a gentle kiss on her forehead without touching any other part of her body.

Next appeared Rafe and half a step after him was Drago.

Papa! M yelled. She darted across the courtyard and went flying into the air into her father's waiting arms. He immediately caught her and spun her around. Karma strolled a little more calmly, even though Runnar was doing everything possible to leap out of her arms.

Rafe rescued the baby from an imminent fall by plucking him up. The baby seemed to wrap himself around Rafe's forearm. His tail looped his wrist while his claws settled against his father's scales for purchase. They were still soft and not capable of damaging him and Runnar seemed to intuitively understand this, just as he knew his claws hurt others with soft skin.

With a child in both arms, Rafe drew his wife close to him, using his tail. The two kissed briefly while his children climbed up his body.

As far as Drago, his homecoming was completely different. Rex saw his son kick and struggle out of his mother's surprised arms, but when he hit the ground, he immediately began crawling to where his uncles had appeared.

Maddie had nearly panicked when she'd dropped her son, but it immediately morphed into surprise when she saw the way he rapidly crawled forward, completely unhurt and happily calling Dada.

Drago came to a complete stop. Neither he nor Maddie moved as they watched the baby speed crawl. Previously, he had rocked and scooted, but hadn't done much in the way of crawling. Maddie knew that even with the enhancement surgery, her son might not meet his milestones. But at eight months old, he now appeared to be surpassing them!

Drago bent low. "Rex. Did you just say Dada?"

"Yeah!" Rex gurgled happily. Drago couldn't wait for him any longer and picked him up.

Maddie was at their side. "Did he just say yeah?"

"Yeah!" Rex shouted again. It was mostly baby gurgle, but that word was easily heard.

Drago hugged him and laughed. "My big boy!" He reached for Maddie and hugged her, spinning her around once before settling her back on her feet.

"Our son is talking!" she exclaimed.

"Did you see how fast he crawled?" Drago asked excitedly.

Maddie stroked her son's cheek. "We're going to have to call you Rex the Racer!"

Everyone had turned to watch, equally in awe.

Justina looked around. "Where's Kendrick?"

"He and Tamsyn will stay aboard the ship to watch Haru and Dorf," Rafe replied.

Dorf? M looked up at her father. **Is something wrong with Uncle Dorf?**

"No, little one." Everyone gathered around them. "Haru went into stasis and when Dorf went to check on him, something miraculous and unexpected happened. He was closed into the chrysalis with Haru, which formed a second cocoon with him inside."

Will he be okay? M's expression was filled with fear.

"There is no need to worry. The chrysalis is sustaining him and he has an oxygen tank which will last for several days."

Bain and Kelsie-? Why hadn't they told her?

"Bain and Kelsie don't know," Karma interrupted. "Their mother plans to sit them down to explain along with the physicians onboard. In the meantime, guess who will be arriving to Eden?"

M's eyes lit up. **They're coming?!**

Karma smiled. "Kelsie's doctors say she is travel ready and Kemistry wants to be close to Dorf."

When Mama?! M whooped happily.

"It depends on whether they go into warp speed, and that's based on how healthy Kelsie is."

M jumped down from her father's arms and leaped happily.

Mama, can I call them?

Give their Mama time to talk to them. They'll call you when it's done."

It was a happy gathering in the courtyard. The soldiers that guarded the villa were relieved their bosses were happy. Mrs. Bianchi, who was in the garden, tried her best to ignore the hoopla. She was a Guard-fearing woman and did not want to set eyes upon the evil that she knew took place under the roof she'd worked at for most of her life; aliens and humans fornicating.

She knew that sort of thing occurred in other places of the world, but she never in a million years thought she'd ever be a witness to it!

The woman wanted to chastise her grandson to keep their disgusting secrets and while her family was known for their loyalty and discretion; it wasn't the only reason Lydia Bianchi wouldn't speak of the unholy things that happened in this home—it was because she was too much of a God-fearing woman to do so.

Kendrick's eyes had narrowed as he looked at Marisol. The woman didn't flinch. He inhaled and found the aroma in the air to be pleasing. This woman was aroused, which did more to trigger him than his lengthy abstinence. Correction. Not just her growing arousal, but her arousal for *him*.

Kendrick nodded once and then turned his back and began heading for the elevator.

Marisol followed at a distance. She understood the ways of the Galatian; their short, curt attitudes that could easily be misconstrued as arrogance or anger.

The truth is, Marisol was used to this of type reaction. As the textbook redheaded stepchild, Marisol had grown up ignored and shunned. No one was allowed to be kind to her and yet they often showed her kindness. And in that way, she saw beyond the surface responses. If your mother ignored you, shouted at you, or cursed you; she would later come back with an extra piece of cake.

If her brothers and sisters taunted her and threw rocks at her for fun, they would kick ass the minute someone else did it. Even Daddy —or the man she called Daddy — would work her like a mule, but he always made sure she had enough to eat and extra blankets whenever the barn got too cold.

She knew there was warmth, even in coldness. She followed Lt. Washington into the elevator. She'd had her share of clandestine meetings when she lived on the farm, so she knew how to act. Big farm hands who didn't mind that she was unattractive often met her in the cornfield for a triste, even though being caught would mean them getting fired and losing their season's wages. She never took an offer from the wiry ones—even though skinny boys often had the biggest pricks. But the way she rode a man could easily damage them. She only accepted offers from the big men with big pricks, and she always made them show her what they were working with before she gave them a second thought.

Marisol was used to hearing that she didn't fuck like a pretty girl, but like an animal. It didn't offend her. She liked fucking, and they liked her—or they wouldn't keep coming back. So she followed Lt. Washington from the elevator and to his quarters, making sure to keep at a distance in case anyone was watching. Others always watched whenever the Galatian commanders were around, but they always watched her, too, because she was almost always bigger than them.

She discreetly signaled for the door to his quarters to open and it did as he had kept it unlocked for her.

"I-" she began. But Lt. Washington lifted her into the air with hands planted firmly on her hips. When his face was inches from hers, he stared at her.

"Do you give your consent?"

"I give my consent, sir."

After a moment, he lowered her back to her feet. Her heart was pounding with excitement. Even the big cornfed country boys couldn't do that to her!

"Then when we're together, I am not, sir. You can call me whatever pleases you, but not sir. I am not your master."

"May I see you now?" she asked, accepting his request without a need to acquiesce.

He felt disappointed but undid his belt and then unwrapped his skirt. It always came down to the size of Galatian pricks. Magazines and pornographic movies always portrayed them as sexually dominant beasts when nothing could be further from the truth.

Sex had the power to dominate *them*.

Marisol's eyes lit up. It was green! His prick was hard and straining out towards her just like any other man's prick—albeit two or three times as big as a normal human prick. Otherwise, it looked no different; hard throbbing shaft lined with thick veins, a glistening mushroom-shaped head, and testicles that hung low and heavy as if ready to fill some lucky individual with a shit ton of cum!

She reached out to take him in her hand, only to stop and look at him in question.

He nodded, giving his consent.

Oh, fuck yeah! Her pussy throbbed so hard it caused her to ache. She'd never seen anything so beautiful in her life. She gripped him in both hands and then dropped to her knees in front of him.

Her lips immediately went around the head of his prick. He tasted like magic! She greedily slurped and licked the precum dribbling from the small hole that tipped him.

Kendrick threw back his head and groaned loudly. He grabbed the base of his penis, and Marisol quickly remembered she was not just here to please herself. She fisted his shaft, marveling how her fingers didn't make it completely around. She worked him slowly but firmly.

Kendrick's knees began to weaken. He wanted badly to cum but knew that not even last a minute would prove to her that Galatian men were just talk. It took nearly every bit of strength he had, but he pulled her up by her shoulders, hearing his prickhead release from her lips with a soft 'pop'.

*Fuck...*he silently cursed. But if she kept doing what she did, he wouldn't last even another ten seconds!

He had selected quarters that had a real bed. Unlike the majority of Galatians, he enjoyed sleeping on a mattress and having soft things touch his body. He carried her to the bed and tossed her upon it, and before she stopped bouncing, he was unfastening her pants and dragging them down her legs. Her panties were saturated! Kendrick nearly came again at the sight and smell of her. Marisol saw the look he gave her and spread her pale freckled thighs showcasing her wet crotch.

Crawling between her legs, Kendrick gripped the top of the black material with his teeth while his clawed fingers hooked at the sides and pulled them down. Her heat blasted his face, and he drooled. He drooled right on her pussy! Her panties weren't even halfway down her thighs. He could only get them past her ass before he began tonguing the cleft that hid her bud.

"Oh, shit!" At least she had muffled the loud cry into the duvet. She looked down as she thrust into his mouth, only to see the top of his head. His scales had colored from green to blue, red, and yellow. He was a kaleidoscope of revolving colors and her mind began to comprehend something she had never thought about when fucking a human;

I can see inside of him...

Marisol came within a minute of Kendrick going down on her. He hadn't even gotten to play with her clit before she was bucking wildly beneath him.

Kendrick backed off even though he wasn't ready to. She was swollen and would surely be sore. He knew this from Auras. Another thing he knew from Auras was to get behind her and while her body was wracked with the after-math of her orgasm, he held her against him, his arms protectively around her in a position humans called spooning, but what he knew to be a show of gratitude for the gift she had given by showing her he would protect her while she was at her most vulnerable.

Marisol turned to face him. She drew close and for a moment Kendrick thought they would share a kiss. Instead, she reached for his prick and held it firmly. He closed his eyes, throbbing in her grip.

"I never came so hard and so fast in my life," she said in her deep country accent. "You have a talented tongue."

Kendrick just hummed as she stroked him. Marisol moved down the bed, her fingers and lips tracing a trail down his torso and over his muscled pecs. When she reached his toned and flat stomach, she nipped him gently.

That was cute, he thought. A human might have liked it more. For him to appreciate such a gesture, she would need much sharper teeth. But he couldn't deny how much he enjoyed the contact, especially when her lips once again found his prick head.

Kendrick's hips swirled with pleasure. "Your tongue is quite talented, too," he groaned.

Marisol sat up and quickly swept off her top. With it came a sports bra, releasing heavy freckled breasts with pink nipples.

Kendrick cupped them easily within his big palms. Before he could sit up to take her breasts into his mouth, she straddled his hips.

"If you like my mouth, just wait and see what this pussy can do."

Kendrick easily plucked her off his lap. Once she was kneeling on the bed, he came up on his knees, his erection as heavy and hard as it had ever been. But he wasn't tempted. She watched him, perplexed, and he explained.

"There cannot be intercourse."

Marisol's eyes widened. "But why? You won't hurt me."

He was shaking his head. Once upon a time, he would have said it was forbidden. But now he didn't believe in that. He was fighting so no one would ever set such rules for him. No, he didn't stop her because it was forbidden.

"I stopped you because I cannot take a chance that you will get with child."

Marisol heard him, but she wasn't listening. She was very nearly drunk with desire. She looked hungrily at his prick. Yes, she'd just had an amazing orgasm. But oral didn't satisfy the deep need that came with penetration. She was under no delusion that she could take all of his length. But what she craved was his girth. He would feel amazing pushing into her tight canal; stretching her to her limits, seeking a shared rhythm, coaxing another orgasm from her depths.

Her pussy clenched and quivered as she lightly bit her lips. "Not even just the tip?" But even as she asked this question, she watched as precum pumped from his opening to ooze down his thick shaft.

"No. As long as your uterus is intact, my semen cannot be near it. I will take no chances."

She met his eyes. "I could get on birth control. And there is always the day-after pill-"

A shadow crossed his face. "Marisol, Galatians do not use contraception. Ever. A child—a pregnancy is much too important to us. Which means if I ever did something that could create a pregnancy, I would never stop it—not even if it meant I would have to battle all the Black Masks in Galatia."

He moved to get off the bed, but Marisol gently gripped his wrist.

"Lieu—I mean, Kendrick. It's okay. I understand. It's just been such a long time since I felt a man inside of me."

He allowed himself to be pulled back, and then he drew her close, his arms resting around her hips. "You can still feel this man inside of you. It just won't be my prick. Just allow me to cum first, and I will show you all the ways I am willing to be inside you."

She licked her lips hungrily. "Okay," She reached for his prick again but he quickly turned her, and once her back was to his front, he lay them down, returning to the spoon position.

Once again, Marisol was amazed at how strong he was. He moved her as if she was a pillow! And while she had witnessed many amazing Galatian feats; things most humans would never be privy to, having him lift her so effortlessly truly impressed her.

Once he had her in the desired position, he parted her leg slightly and then slipped his prick between her thighs. It jutted out and upward so the head was facing her belly.

Marisol looked down at it in amazement. Slowly, he glided in and out of the crevice so that his hard shaft parted and then grazed her labia and clitoris. Once his pelvis was against her ass, she felt his heavy balls pressing and grinding into her.

He repeated the move, thrusting in and out of her crevice, his precum plentiful enough to lubricate the motion. And then the slap of his balls against her ass.

Oh shit...

No one had ever done anything like this to her!

He thrust harder and faster, creating the perfect amount of friction. Marisol cried out in pleasure. She gripped him in one fist that was soon wet from thick streams of precum. The moment she fisted him, his movements became staccato and his breathing burst from him harshly. He pulled her hips closer as he pounded against her. With an uncontrolled curse, Kendrick ejaculated, sending an eruption of semen into the air.

Marisol wrapped her sopping wet hand around the head so she

could feel the cum shooting rhythmically into her fist. It was enough to send her over as well. The two moaned and gasped in unison. She nearly blacked out when he reached up and captured a thick pink nipple between sharp nails—gently, but not too gently.

Dinner at the villa was a festive occasion, despite the serious implications of the Galatian mothers being left in a hostile environment. Still, Haru was safe and Dorf was changing history. Not to mention the fact that Kemistry and the children would be joining them soon and their family would be reunited.

Daya had stepped out of her comfort zone by requesting a shipment of some of Paris's favorite side dishes from the ship. Luckily, it wasn't anything that needed to be cooked as it was the creepy, crawling, living variety. She didn't think Mrs. Bianchi would appreciate having her kitchen commandeered, and with (what humans called) vermin.

The men exclaimed happily at the sight and grabbed fistfuls of the 'spider-bugs', shoving them into their mouths while munching happily. Whenever one tried to get away, dashing across the table, M made sport of it by capturing it and popping it into her mouth.

The ex-consorts weren't phased by the variety of 'bugs' that squirmed and made low, disturbing scratching sounds within the large bucket-sized bowls. But none of them had a desire to eat them, with the exception of Daya. When she saw M would rather eat them than the smashed fruit she described as looking like zombie brains, Daya decided it was time for her to try one.

Paris watched her curiously. "Be careful not to choke. It can be tricky when they are this lively. You can stun it by holding it by one leg and flicking it in the head."

Daya looked at him in surprise as she held onto one smallish creature by a furry leg. "I'll just eat it quickly."

It's good, Miss Porter. See. And then M popped another one into her mouth. She allowed a squirming leg to peek out from the corner of her mouth, hoping to gross someone out.

"Don't play with your food," Karma said while offering Runnar a spoonful of zombie brains.

Daya popped the creature into her mouth and quickly chewed as if she was eating the world's hottest pepper and didn't want it to touch her tongue. At one point, a chill of disgust actually ran up her body when the insides flooded her mouth. But a second later, she frowned and actually allowed herself to taste it.

"Mmm." She peeked at M. "Beef jerky?"

It's good, isn't it? M asked happily.

Daya looked at Paris. "Why didn't you tell me these were so delicious?" She popped a bigger one into her mouth.

"When you learn to cook Galatian cuisine, you will find many items to your liking," he replied.

Justina just shook her head slightly. To each his own, she thought. Maddie and even Tam probably thought the same thing. But to Karma, Daya, and M, eating 'exotic' Galatian cuisine wasn't a stretch, not when each of them had, at one point or another, dined from trash cans.

As the night wore on, people began to drift from the table, claiming fatigue—although that was not always the case.

Paris and Daya went to their quarters, and he slipped off her silken robes. He kissed every inch of her body, from her unburned toes to her bald and scarred head, and then she did the same to him.

Maddie and Drago went to their rooms while coaxing their son to crawl, scoot, or maybe even take his first steps. But the distance was too far and before long he sat on his butt and whined to be lifted. Of course, Drago swooped down to lift the baby and sat him in the crook of his arms.

They repeatedly asked him to speak; 'Say Mama.' 'Say Daddy.' 'Say nose. Say mouth. Say eyes.'

Rex just grinned happily but didn't say a word.

Karma and Rafe supervised M's bath and then got her tucked into bed. Nurse wordlessly took Runnar leaving Karma and Rafe some alone time.

All evening, Karma had looked at her husband; the cut of his muscular body in the leather harness, the way the pleated leather skirt hung on narrow hips. When Karma looked at Rafe, she didn't see an alien. She didn't see a lizard man. She didn't even think about his scales, or forked tongue, or the talon-like nails that seemed to shred the sheets at least two or three times a week.

She saw a man who excited her, physically, mentally, even emotionally.

She ran a hot bath and while he wanted to bathe her; she refused and used his wire brush to scrub his body. He moaned in appreciation as he reclined in the oversized bath. It wasn't a Galatian pool, but it felt wonderful.

After the scrubbing, she polished his scales—some of them, however, he was so aroused that her touch was just torture. They made love painlessly, his erection buried deeply into her depths the way she had long fantasized. Afterward, he ran her a bath and washed, then lotioned her body before they both fell into an exhausted sleep.

Even Justina had a satisfying night. She sat out on her veranda with the glow of the stars and the sound of the ocean surrounding her. Soft music from a local station played in the background and she drank cool wine. Her security guard sat opposite her. While they wouldn't accept a drink as they were still on duty, the two enjoyed a long and intimate conversation that revealed more about themselves.

For the first time, Justina talked about wanting to be with a woman and finding that being intimate with a man was much more disturbing than the idea of being intimate with an alien—however, combining the two was just more than words could describe.

Adrian listened sympathetically, recalling a time when they had been unable to express their own desires and had to conform to the ideas of their parents and even some friends. Adrian was just happy they were where they wanted to be.

Adrian's eyes lingered on her, and Justina smiled.

Chapter Twenty-Five

I've been waiting for you to call! Mama said I had to wait for you to call me!

"We're on our way to Eden!" Bain shouted.

Shh. It's super late here.

"Oh, that's right. I keep forgetting."

"You heard about our dad?" Kelsie asked, her face etched with concern.

They were using the hologram, and it was easy for M to see they were both worried.

Papa said he talked to your dad while he was in the chrysalis. He said your dad was flying through the air and singing concerts.

Kelsie laughed. "That sounds just like Dad."

Bain nodded with a big smile. "Dad likes music."

"Dad's *life* is music," Kelsie corrected.

When will you get here?

"Mom's not sure," Kelsie replied. "It depends on whether we can go into warp speed."

M looked around at the room where Kelsie and Bain were in. **How long have you been on the spaceship?**

"We just got to our room," Bain said. "We would have called earlier, but Mom said we had to hurry up and get all the things we wanted to take with us because we might not be back for a real long time."

"Eden sounds pretty," Kelsie said, her face once again filled with worry. "But it's an alien world and I don't know if I'll like it. Earth is ugly in a lot of ways, but it's still home."

M grinned. **You'll like it, Kelsie. I promise. My mom showed me where you'll be living. It's one of the outbuildings with a loft for your Mama and Papa but real rooms for you and Bain.**

"Our dad can't live in the loft," Bain said softly. "He can't fly anymore."

"He can use a latter!" Kelsie said quickly, not wanting to think about her dad's limitations.

M just smiled. **Papa said the chrysalis was repairing his wing. He already has a little baby one growing.**

Kelsie's brow lifted in surprise. "Dad said that growing another wing wasn't like growing a new set of lungs. Mine will work automatically, but he said it would take many years for him to learn to fly evenly. He said it just wasn't worth the time and energy."

The children were quiet as they contemplated that.

"Wings that don't work well are better than no wings at all," Bain finally said, and everyone agreed.

"Children?" Kemistry came into the room and smiled when she saw M. "Hi M. Did the children wake you up?"

Hi Aunt, Kemistry. I was waiting for them to call.

"Well, we have to go into stasis now. The doctor gave his okay. It shouldn't be too long before we arrive. Good night, Little one. Get some sleep. Tomorrow is going to be a busy day."

Okay, Auntie. Bye Bain. Bye Kelsie.

After everyone said their goodnights, M jumped back into bed.

She was so excited she thought she'd never sleep. But that wasn't true. She fell asleep counting her blessings—although she didn't really understand that was what she was doing.

Not only were her very best friends in the entire world arriving, but Kelsie would be healthy, and now so would Dorf. Bad things happened but all in all, life was good!

Kendrick sauntered into the sickbay. He didn't realize he walked differently, lighter on his feet, maybe. But others took a second look. There was something different about him.

Tam was sipping coffee and sitting on the edge of the pool. "Why are you so happy?"

"What?" Kendrick paused and looked down. He didn't even realize he was bright pink. He immediately toned it down. "Nothing," he lied, and quickly changed topics. "Any change?"

She gazed back at the large chrysalis and allowed her fingers to swirl into the water. There was a responsive sway. "He knows I'm here. But hasn't spoken."

"Yes," Kendrick confirmed while stripping out of his clothing. "We're aware, but it's best to not be drawn completely out of the hibernation." He dived into the pool, not conscious of his nudity. Tam admired it, but not in a sexual way. Haru was the only person with the ability to elicit a sexual response from her.

Kendrick swam around his friends, did his morning business, and then placed a hand on the chrysalis, allowing them to feel his presence. There was a responsive swaying.

"Tam has been here by your side." He looked over at her. "She refuses to leave until Kemistry arrives, even though things are well taken care of."

Tam stood and stretched, hiding her smirk. "My accommodations are much better here than at that Rebel compound. I use the medbed, I ring for food, and I use the pool when I... well you know..." she blushed a little despite having long ago changed from the introverted consort everyone had first known. "Besides, I've been telling Haru everything that happened while we were apart."

"Ai," Kendrick acknowledged. "She's pretty badass," Kendrick whispered, using the English vernacular easily. "I have information about Kemistry and your children, Dorf." This time he spoke louder so Tam could hear.

"The onboard physician confirmed warp speed would not adversely affect your daughter's lungs—in fact, they said that the prolonged stasis would help her lungs heal even faster. Like father, like daughter.

"So, they should arrive later today and they are very anxious, although they know you aren't in any danger." There was a flipping movement, and Kendrick laughed. "Okay, calm down, little buddy. You won't leave stasis until the chrysalis thinks you're healed. Sleep, Dorf. We'll likely be starting a new mission and we need you."

Immediately, the chrysalis calmed. Kendrick checked them again and then left the pool and slipped on his rigging. He didn't care if he was wet because the material close to his scales was all made to withstand it.

"I'm going to head back to the villa. Rafe may have a meeting, but I suppose you'll just attend via communicator?"

"Yep."

"Okay. Later." He left, and Tam cocked her head at his easy attitude.

Drago, Paris, and Rafe hurried to the compound's Galatian pool before their spouses awakened, which meant it was well before the crack of dawn. While not the heaviest populated area, it was still a very healthy Galatian pool utilized by approximately twelve to twenty individuals at any given time.

The Galatian population stationed in this province of EX-112 numbered less than one hundred, but Rafe still wanted to rally them for their cause. Many of them had fought alongside Rafe and his crew in battle and while he was not directly their commander, they still gave him the respect of a Senior member of the Galatian Guard. Drago had even set up a parley with the Galatian commander of this region. Unfortunately, life's misadventures had gotten in the way.

The trio ran the short few miles to their destination, slowed only because they wore their skirts—luckily exposing their clawed feet was acceptable, albeit controversial. Still, they left their boots behind. Galatian nudity was strictly prohibited here, as it was on Earth, although the Edenites were well aware of their enhanced endowments, just as Earthlings were.

Unlike most lifeforms, humans had a way of sexualizing nudity which made it difficult for Galatians to be at their best—hence the leather, pleated skirts and combat boots.

They raced each other, Paris doing leaps and flips while Drago and Rafe used the power of their thighs to drive them forward. When the pool was in sight, Rafe used his tail to shoot him forward and, with one final acrobatic flip, he landed in a crouch right at the pool. Paris was a split second behind him and Drago, who didn't stop running, just dived into the pool with his skirt on.

Galatians looked on in annoyance before realizing who they were. Drago just laughed along with his companions. The pool was not a place to frolic but a necessary part of their hygiene and well-being. A Galatian could live without a pool, they just wouldn't thrive without one.

"What will we do about our mothers'?" Drago asked after they had relaxed in the hot springs."

"I don't know," he hated to admit. But he was honest. "We need allies for this, which will be difficult when the dust has yet to settle after Haru's escape."

"Perhaps we can utilize Filene," Paris said.

"Filene may be against a war while still being against us," Drago replied.

Paris settled into a floating position, his eyes closing contentedly. "She will be the safest means to get a message to our mothers."

"Then we have a plan." Rafe noted the way two Galatians were looking at them while consulting one of their communicators.

Rafe's caution rose. They might have allies in Eden, but not everyone agreed with them. Still, he didn't believe a Galatian Guard would ever betray them. It went against their code of honor and an active Guard would live and die by honor.

One of the Galatians approached. "Lieutenants."

"Eh?" Rafe replied. His brothers watched with equal caution.

"Sir..." The Galatian hesitated. "There is a galaxy-wide alert. Sir, the Inter-planetary Collection has issued a warrant for your immediate capture and...arrest."

Rafe blinked. "For what reason?" Of course, his first thought was of Haru. But rescuing his teammate—even a teammate accused of spying on the Queens, was not a reason for arrest.

"Sir, the report says you are responsible for the kidnapping and murder of your bound-mate; Ragna of __." Rafe's blood ran cold.

Drago was on his communicator, monitoring the information. Paris made a fist.

"This has already been addressed!" Paris growled, turning fiery red. "That *itchnol* Amalia is just pissed because they no longer have Haru!"

The Galatian relaying the information, looked uncomfortable with the disrespectful description of their leader. Still, he didn't dare speak about it.

"What did they have to do to get Mayva Heath to side with them after being thrown up under a bus's wheels?" Rafe speculated.

"By releasing her. That's all it would take," Drago said while turning his attention from his communicator back to his brothers. "The information is correct. It was released not even an hour ago. Not only are you wanted, but they've placed a bounty on your capture."

"A bounty?!" Rafe roared. "They put a target on me?"

"I'm contacting the Japoxillian delegates," Drago interrupted. "We need to get back to the ship. The Collective has summoned the rest of us—likely to give up your whereabouts."

The trio quickly climbed out of the pool. Rafe and Paris didn't worry about dressing but headed at a dead run to their ship. Now that dawn was approaching, there were a few humans out and about, but those who saw the streaking Galatians would never quite believe their eyes.

Mayva had taken a hot shower and now was soaking in a luxury spa bath. She had been quiet while three human servants had removed the vermin from her hair, taking great care to detangle it without cutting it.

She didn't care if they did. They could shave her head for all she cared.

"Madam? Would you like more hot water?"

It took Mayva a few moments to hear. She finally shook her head and stood. A white cotton robe was slipped over her shoulders. She was happy not to have to see her own nudity. She was skin and bones.

When she'd first been released, a physician had been forced to give her an intravenous feeding. What she really needed was a hospital stay and time to heal from her recent imprisonment. Instead, Queen Amalia had quickly whisked her away to Galatia for 'safe-keeping' after learning she had passed her interviews without a hint of a lie detected.

Mayva wasn't even sure if she was surprised. She'd had to say what she had to say in order to save herself.

Her attendants had dressed her in cotton lounging pajamas and then offered her another meal to fatten her up. She ate without complaint despite the fact that her severely starved body had a difficult time with the rapid intake of food. But she didn't dare get sick.

Don't make waves. Don't make waves. Because I have a very special trait...

Chapter Twenty-Six

Her mind drifted back to the cold concrete cell, the gruel that she hadn't been able to digest and would always vomit up the discolored water, and the taunts from the others-

Mayva squeezed her eyes closed.

She is severely confused, but she knows what she saw, the Queen's attaché had reported after her most recent interview. He was human, attractive, and very confident—the way she had once been.

The Japoxillian are guilty of abuse of a prisoner! He'd said while pointing at her. *She is to be released immediately!*

Afterward, things moved quickly. The human attaché spoke almost too rapidly for her to understand as he whisked her to an awaiting transport.

You have a unique trait, Miss Heath; a trait that allows you to do something not many people can do. You can lie with conviction. I don't want it to scare you. Humans are guilty of giving those with your —disposition a bad rap. In any case, in this matter, it is very beneficial.

She was in a luxury space pod; her release was orchestrated by her benefactor; Queen Amalia. However, her luxury pod could not be appreciated when she sat in urine-soaked pants and had fleas crawling all over her head. She rotated her behind against the soft seat without a sense of impropriety or embarrassment while the lawyer looked at her in surprise. She didn't care—not about her looks, not about her smell, only about the terrible burning itch. The crack of her ass itched from her own shit because when she'd been forced to squat in the hole situated in the center of her cell, she had refused to run the shit-caked rope that had been used by previous prisoners between her ass cheeks to clean herself.

She didn't fail to see that the man leaned back, away from her as he spoke in his too-fast voice. The crux of his words came to one thing: her freedom would be determined by how successful she was in remaining in the good graces of the Queens—in Amalia's good graces.

And there was the silent, unspoken threat. Continue to lie for them, or be returned to prison—which might even be worse than the last...

Mayva finished eating the food even though it took nearly half an hour. And then she crawled into bed. She placed the thick duvet over her head and once any hidden cameras were out of sight, her eyes narrowed. She would have clenched her teeth, but she'd lost a few of them due to malnutrition and they had yet to be replaced.

You fucked with the wrong human...

Mayva had never been on the Queen's side. The only side she knew was her own; the only person she'd ever been loyal to was herself. But now she counted the Galatian Queens—especially Amalia as one of her enemies—and that was a place she hadn't even placed Karma and the other consorts.

The attaché had described her as having Anti Social Personality Disorder. ASPD. It was the fancy way of saying that she was a psychopath. The title didn't even bother her. She might even agree with it. She'd killed others who she hadn't even hated. But hate was what she felt for Amalia and what she intended to do to that inhuman lizard-bitch would be a million times worse than what had been done to her.

Kill you. Kill you. Kill you...

She mentally chanted this until she fell into a dreamless sleep.

The order to deploy had sent everyone rushing within the large ship. Cheryl Frost and her lackey Kendra hurried to their station. As team leaders, they would be the first face of command for their team of twenty to thirty soldiers.

Downtime on Eden had been nice, but this is what they were made for; battle. And space battle was even better than hand-to-hand. She was good, better than many of the men, but when it came to flying a ship, the odds were even and she excelled.

Despite this, she hadn't been selected for the previous mission to hunt down the traitor who had kidnapped their 'asset'. No one dared to speak her actual name, but they all knew who the asset was and what she represented to their commanders. She was the baby murderer who started this all.

No, Sgt. Cheryl Frost didn't care about a human's right to have a Galatian baby. She didn't actually care if the Galatians were ever free of their tyrannical rule by the Galatian Queens. Somebody ruled everybody, and that's just the way things were. A smart person found a way to place themselves at the top of the pecking order, which is something Cheryl Frost had done.

And now she had her sights on locating Dr. Garry Brookstone and bringing him back to the commanders to be reckoned with. The asset could finally be dispatched, and she hoped as one of the top-performing Sergeants, she would be a witness to it.

"I hope this isn't another training exercise," Kendra said as they rushed down the corridor with their gear propped over one shoulder.

"Not this time," Cheryl hinted. She wouldn't say more while in this crowded corridor, but The Interplanetary Collective had put out a warrant for Lt. Sigur. Kendra looked at her hungrily, waiting for more. She would eventually tell the girl. Having important knowledge was another thing setting her apart, and how would it benefit her if she kept it to herself? Soon everyone would know, but for now, Cheryl was only one of a very few people who had received the outside information, which was only because she'd befriended several members of the telecommunications team.

"Hey…" Kendra said while slowing in her tracks.

Distracted, Cheryl was about to bark an order for her to hurry up, but she spotted what Kendra was looking at.

The big red bitch was up ahead, already decked out in her deployment gear. She was also a team leader, although Marisol's was one of the largest, with fifty men. Generally, seeing the larger-than-life woman only annoyed Cheryl, but this time, she was shocked.

Lt. Washington had just hurried past to catch up to her. With Galatian speed, he made this an easy task, not to mention the fact that he had much longer legs than the majority of individuals.

Once he caught up to her, he leaned into her and said something which stopped the tall redhead. The hard look of concentration she perpetually wore on her ugly face disappeared and she smiled. She smiled! Lt. Washington continued walking until he quickly disappeared. The exchange had lasted no more than two or three seconds and most would not have thought much of it except Kendrick Washington had turned bright fucking pink!

"What did I just see…" Kendra spoke in awe.

"They're fucking!" Cheryl hissed.

Kendra looked quickly at her friend. "No fucking way!"

"Come on," she demanded. "I'm getting to the bottom of this!" Not waiting for Kendra to follow, Cheryl ran past the throng of people who were bustling about. She had to sprint the last few feet in order to reach the tall redhead, almost knocking into several smaller aliens.

"Yo, Marisol. Wait up!"

Marisol looked around and slowed her steps, but didn't stop walking. "What's up?" she acknowledged with an uptick of her head.

"Yo. Did I just see you talking to Lt. Washington?"

Marisol's light eyes rested on the smaller yet muscled woman. She saw the suspicion in the other woman's eyes. Hmph. She easily saw all the thoughts swirling in Cheryl's mind; *did she actually fuck a Galatian? What was it like? How had she done it?*

Marisol decided that if they *had* made a bet about who could fuck a Galatian first, then she would be the winner. But none of it made her no never mind. She didn't need any person's validation—not since waiting in vain for her family's acceptance.

So instead of answering, she just smirked at the competitive woman and turned away, leaving Cheryl gawking after her. Which was answer enough to Cheryl.

"No, bitch, no!" Cheryl growled—not quite under her breath.

"What did she say?" Kendra asked once she had caught up.

"Shut the fuck up!"

"I have to find Ragna and the doctor." Rafe stood at the port window, staring out at the map of space. One of his men had silently brought him and Paris skirts.

Drago pointed to the map. "This is where we were when he stole the pod. We have been able to follow the EE path. However, as you know, we can't follow exotic energy into a wormhole and there were two."

Exotic energy was the waste left behind once a ship went into hyper warp, which changed the energy density. Under normal circumstances, it could be followed with complete accuracy—at least until space matter caused it to dissipate. But circumstances had not been normal.

"How many available hands do we have to explore?"

"Five thousand available," Drago replied. "...and ready to deploy."

"What about our families?" Paris asked. "I trust our crew and team not to disclose our location, but the Edenites should be considered hostile."

Rafe shook his head. "This is a closed world. They've lost contact with Earth one hundred years ago."

"True but the merchant importers are another matter."

"Eh," Kendrick rubbed his chin. "By now, we must consider our large ship has garnered much attention from the importers. I will contact the region's Galatian Commander to determine how many drop-offs have been made since our arrival."

"Eh. I'm in contact with him to parley about joining forces," Drago replied. "He seems to agree with many of our concerns. I will contact him." He walked away to use his communicator.

"Which still leaves the matter of our families," Paris stated.

Rafe ran a hand over his face. "I cannot continuously disrupt the lives of my wife, my children, your families!" He sighed. "I'm going to give myself up to The Collective."

Everyone turned swiftly to look at him, including Drago, who was speaking to the Region's Galatian Commander. He quickly ended the call.

"You can't be serious! You know what they will do to you once they have you in their hands! They can turn anything you say and do against you!"

"Alternatively, I once again rip my family from this place—a place where they are comfortable and happy. And I am *not* sending them running with me along the galaxy! Haru and Dorf are here. Dorf's family will be here shortly. The Collective will use any excuse to question our women—detain them and we all know the poor accommodations they provide! I am *not* a wanted man and I won't behave as such! I didn't get the pleasure of killing that *itchnol* and I will not be taken down as if I did!"

The men paced but could not argue Rafe's point. They all had to run or Rafe had to sacrifice himself.

Chapter Twenty-Seven

By the time Karma woke up, all hell had broken loose. Soldiers had converged on the villa's grounds. M had jumped on her bed, waking her from a happy sleep. Last night, she'd spent a wonderful time with her husband and things seem to be looking up.

Mama! The soldiers are all over!

Karma's eyes popped open, and she quickly looked around, expecting to see Rafe beside her. When she didn't, she jumped out of bed and hurried into the nursery where the nurse and the baby were sound asleep. Relieved, she closed the door quietly and then hurried to the French doors.

It was light enough to see the grounds were hectic with movement, even though the soldiers were in stealth mode and moving as silently as mice. She looked at M, knowing her enhanced hearing had once again placed her in a role above that of the average child.

Karma quickly closed the door and drew the sheers. "Come away from the window, baby, until I find out what's going on."

She called Rafe, who answered with a grim cast to his expressionless face.

"What in the hell is going on, Rafe?"

"I was just sending an escort for you and the family. There is a... situation. I'll explain when you get here."

Karma shook her head. "Tell me now or I won't be able to relax."

Rafe sighed and nodded. "The Collective has placed a bounty on my head; courtesy of Amalia and her Queen's council. I am to be questioned in the disappearance of Ragna."

She gasped, but before she could speak, there was a rapid knock at the door.

"Mrs. Sigur. It's Sgt. Adrian Kelly. I've been asked by your husband to collect you and the ladies and escort you to the ship."

Karma's wide eyes moved back to Rafe's hologram. He nodded. "Go. There is no danger to you but speed is of an essence."

M didn't wait for another word. She hurried to her room to collect her essentials. Karma quickly opened the door for the soldier, only to see Justina was already there, her hair rumpled as if she had been pulled from sleep seconds before.

Sgt. Kelly looked at their monitor before turning to look at Karma. "Sorry ma'am, but we have to leave now-"

"Yeah!" Karma jumped into action and went back to the nursery where she roused Nanny. The older woman didn't ask questions. She quickly grabbed a pre-packed bag for both her and Runnar and Karma realized she'd allowed herself to become too complacent after the success of the parley. How could she ever think they'd get a minute's reprieve?

Sgt. Kelly quickly escorted them to a waiting transport where Daya, Justina, and Maddie were already seated. Rex was nestled in her arms, sucking on his pacifier while calmly watching the action. Runnar seemed to also understand something important was happening as he sat quietly in his nanny's arms without making a peep.

Maddie reached for Karma's hand and drew her to the seat next to her and the others. "Oh, Karma! Drago called me and told me what's happening with Rafe!"

M's ears perked. She'd heard her Mama and Papa's conversation but knew to remain quiet if she wanted more information. The word bounty had been enough to scare her, though.

Nobody liked bounty hunters. In some ways, they were worse than the police. At least the police had rules they were supposed to follow. But anybody could be a bounty hunter as long as they could afford the licenses. And once you got permission to act like you were the law, then you could do almost anything you wanted, even tearing apart entire shanty towns while looking for one single criminal.

Their bounties always picked on the poor, because who were they going to tell?

"Rafe just told me about a bounty they put on him!" Karma explained.

"What?!" Justina said in alarm. As the only ex-consort who didn't have a mate, she hadn't received the inside information. Adrian had just suddenly appeared over her bed like a lovely dream—only they were stern-faced and demanding she quickly get dressed.

Karma quickly ran down the information she knew as the truck drove them to the ship. Unfortunately, there wasn't much more to tell. Daya then repeated exactly what Paris had told her, which is that the Queens had formally accused Rafe of kidnapping and murdering Ragna and were bringing charges against him with The Inter-planetary Collective.

"This was resolved!" Karma exclaimed. Runnar didn't seem to like the tone of his mom and aunties and his face screwed up to let out a loud yell. But M handed him her communicator—something no one ever let him touch due to his penchant for biting with sharp teeth. She had put it on a simple game and immediately his focus went to the flashing lights and soft tings of the mechanical device.

There was more Karma wanted to say. Instead, she reached for her baby and held him close, stroking his dark curls while he drooled and tried to eat the communicator.

"Nanny, when we get to the ship, would you mind taking M for a while? Maybe you can take her to the simulator and let her work on her combat until Bain and Kelsie arrive?"

M made a face.

"Certainly, ma'am. I can take Rex, too."

Maddie readily accepted the offer. Rex was very easygoing and easy to parent, but she knew he'd be more comfortable with the nurse-turned-nanny than in a tense meeting.

They arrived in no time at all. The ship was in a state of havoc. A humanoid droid led them to one of the council chambers where Rafe and the others were waiting. Karma immediately hurried to Rafe, who pulled her close while she buried her head against his strong chest.

"How is this happening? It's obvious Amalia is grasping at straws!"

Drago pulled up a 3-D screen. "There's another development." He ran through several channels until he reached a dedicated Earth news station.

"Our telecommunications team has been monitoring the various news channels. Rafe's arrest warrant is trending news." Drago looked at Karma. "And if Rafe is trending news, *you* are trending news."

Karma threw up her hands. "I don't care about trending! They're trying to lock up my husband so they can put a stop to our demands!"

On the screen was a large demonstration in front of the North American consulate. Several people were holding signs and shouting, many even held the American flag, which had become controversial since the end of government rule.

Where is Karma! Where is Karma!" a crowd of hundreds were chanting.

Karma blinked in awe at the large crowd of people marching and chanting. A reporter was seen interviewing one young white man who looked like a government worker—a very unlikely ally, but ally is what he was.

"We want the whereabouts of Karma Sigur disclosed! We know the aliens are holding her!"

"Which aliens, sir?" The reporter asked.

"The ones who run The Collective! The ones running this world. Humans have been asleep for far too long and it's time to wake up! Where is Karma! Where is Karma!" He began chanting again.

The female reporter turned back to the camera. "There it is. Many are questioning the productivity of having non-humans operate on Earth. Many are saying the Interplanetary Collective rules humans, while others support the guidance provided by those with advanced knowledge.

"What we can say is that while this began in the North American Province, the outcry has spread around the world. Where is Karma Sigur? Why has no one heard from her since her explosive interview one week ago? Back to you, Jerry."

Drago turned off the broadcast.

"Oh my Guardian…" Daya said softly. "Karma! Remember when we were talking about you becoming a human delegate on the Collective? I think we really need to consider it."

Rafe frowned. "A delegate? Do you understand the corruption that exists within The Collective? Very little happening there is about right or wrong, but about who stands to benefit." He shook his head. "No. I don't want you anywhere near them!"

Paris whipped around to glare at Rafe. "And we don't want you anywhere near them, either!" Paris snapped. "Tell her your plan, Rafe."

Karma looked at Rafe in fear. He rubbed her shoulders. "If I turn myself in, then they won't have to hunt me down-"

"Rafe, no! Are you insane?! You know what they'll do to you once-"

"No, my love. Truth is on my side. I have nothing to hide."

Karma was shaking with emotion. "Baby, you have a lot to hide! You have a hybrid child! If they get you alone, what's to stop them from finding out about Runnar?"

"And," Kendrick added, "You won't be able to deny that you physically had Ragna in your custody. All they need to do is ask you what your intent was in holding her and it will be the gallows for you, Rafe."

Rafe released Karma and paced. "We can't keep running."

Karma grabbed his forearms. "When I told you I would fight by your side, I meant it! I will run to the ends of the universe with you!"

Drago looked at Maddie, who nodded her consent at the unspoken question. He looked at his friend and commander. "We will fight, not run. We cannot trust The Collective."

"What we need to do is find that doctor who took Ragna!" Justina said.

"He's probably killed her by now," Karma was now pacing. "And he's hiding because he knows his ass is dead when we find him. By now, he is a needle in a haystack."

"Not necessarily," Drago said calmly. "We can trace the path of his ship by doing a reverse search. Once we locate it, then determining where he's gone will be a lot simpler."

"Then why haven't we found him?" Karma asked.

"Two wormholes. To put it in layman's terms, the trail of his pod would have been tossed around as if in one of Earth's tornadoes. Our initial exploratory ships have made great strides and with enough pilots, we can and will find that trail. We have nearly five thousand able bodies at the ready."

Rafe huffed. "Five thousand able bodies that should be ready to fight our war and not out searching for two beings that aren't worth the air they breathe."

Paris's eyes lit up. "That's it! Narrow the search to star systems with breathable air. Brookstone is a mercenary. He knows the star charts and would have used them to his benefit!"

Drago moved with lightning speed to exit the room.

After he was gone, Karma looked at Rafe. "I want you to consider me becoming a human delegate within the Collective."

Rafe was turning red with anger. "I know the delegates. I know what they think of humans and, more so, what they think of consorts. It would not be safe."

"He is right," Kendrick said. "The Collective doesn't see humans as equals. Plus, the law would need to be changed in order to move man from the ranking of a lesser being." Karma opened her mouth to protest, but Kendrick held up a finger in an oddly human gesture.

"However, since we are fighting for change, maybe Karma is right that this change has to begin at the very top. Besides, we've already pissed them off by having a rising number of humans question their authority. Which is how worlds are overthrown. Having human delegates could be the answer to their problems.

Paris cocked his head in agreement. "Yes. And if they have Karma on their side, it means they think they will have humans in their pockets."

"Well, I won't serve as a delegate to be in someone's pocket!" Karma exclaimed.

Kendrick shrugged. "But they don't know that."

Rafe held up his hands as if asking for everyone to shut up. "First thing is first! We need to find out what happened to Ragna!"

Drago's hologram appeared just then. His normally calm face was filled with excitement. "We triangulated the only possible courses from the two wormholes and there is only one location with breathable air. Our closest explorer was able to lock in on his EE. Rafe. We know where Brookside's ship landed."

"How soon can we be there?"

"From the wormhole, it will take 5.5 hours. We can take a small pod which should allow us to arrive in less than two days."

"Prepare a pod," Rafe said, while heading for the exit.

"I'm going with you," Karma said. Rafe nearly stumbled to a stop. "But... the children-"

"Which is precisely why I am coming; my children's future. We have a village to watch our children."

Daya nodded. Justina looked at Maddie and then Karma. "I'll care for your babies as if they were my own."

Rafe didn't bother to argue. He nodded once and the men plus Karma hurried out of the room.

Chapter Twenty-Eight

"M, I'm going with your Papa to get Ragna and the doctor," Karma spoke into her communicator while she hurried after Rafe. He wasn't slowing just because she was following. Her coming along on this mission meant she would have to be tough and not slow them down despite not being in her best health since... well since the day her baby was killed.

"I'll keep in touch, but you know how it works; we will be in stealth mode-"

Mama! Don't go without me!

Karma glanced down at the monitor to see the small picture of M's distraught face. She bit her lip.

"You know I can't do that."

Mama, don't leave me again!

Oh Guardian. Karma's heart dropped in her chest and her eyes welled with tears. She nearly walked into Rafe's back. He had slowed and was reaching for her spare hand. Karma blinked back her tears and doubled her pace.

"Let's go," she said brusquely while pulling her husband forward.

She looked at the monitor on her wrist where her strong and brave little girl was crying like she'd never seen her cry before.

"Listen, baby girl. Hush now and listen. I need you." Even though the little girl's tears continued to fall, Karma could tell she was listening. "You can do something no one else can do, M. You can defeat anyone that underestimates you.

"I have to go in order to take care of the Galatians. You have to stay in order to take care of everyone else."

M's face calmed. Her dark eyes seemed to clear despite the unshed tears glistening in them.

Karma knew Galatians were technically intelligent, but they also had difficulty tapping into their emotions. It is why their link was so beneficial. The Queens had taught the men the best part of them was their loyalty and fighting skills, while she knew the best part of them just needed to be coaxed out of them; which is their hearts were bigger than anyone knew.

"Do you understand, baby girl? Do you understand what you need to do?"

M nodded. **Take care of everybody.** When she spoke, it was without hesitation.

"That's right."

Okay Mama. M was the one who disconnected the call.

Rafe gently squeezed her hand as they walked. She looked at him.

"You did good, my love. Our daughter responds well to protecting others."

"I wasn't gaslighting her. If something goes sideways, then M will go into kick-ass mode."

"Hm. That is what worries me."

The fastest weaponized pod only held accommodations for Rafe and his team, along with fifteen crew members. Karma was the only human among them, which meant she was the only one going into a sleep chamber while they navigated warp speed.

Rafe was staring at her as he placed the final probe onto her temple. "What did you mean when you said you needed to take care of the Galatians?"

She gave him a grim smile. "Half of our target is human, which means at least one human should be present—and there is no other person invested more than I am."

"We're killing the human..."

Karma shook her head. "Fine, but what if we need to negotiate? Galatians aren't known for their communication skills."

"The only thing we need to negotiate is how many ways I will hurt the doctor," he growled.

"And Ragna?" she asked while studying his color more than listening for his verbal response.

He took a moment before answering—enough time to control his emotions. "We need her alive, but I cannot promise she won't receive a bit of damage."

"We need her alive." Karma reached for his hand and squeezed it tight. "It's unfair, but I don't intend to sacrifice my husband for that piece of shit."

He closed his eyes briefly. "Ai." Rafe leaned forward and kissed his wife's lips. He stared into her eyes again, mere inches from her face. "I love and respect you, my wife, my lover, the mother of my children. I have heard you."

He closed the glass chamber and before she had time to respond, Karma was falling into an artificial sleep. But it didn't happen too quickly for her to know his truthful words masked an unspoken lie. She just hadn't had an opportunity to figure out which parts he was trying to hide from her. And then at the last moment, a spark shot through her consciousness.

Damnit...you don't intend to pull me out of the sleep chamber...

"She will be very angry with you," Kendrick said when Rafe returned to the bridge. Rafe sat in his Command chair with a short nod.

"My wife is untrained and despite trying to hide her slow rehabilitation from me, I know she is still physically recovering. I've made the decision that I must. Despite her anger, at least she will remain among the living."

Paris kept his mouth shut on the matter. Rafe would learn in his own way, just as he'd had to learn; regardless of whether they are right or wrong, never mute the voice of the human who loves you.

With the help of the full team back on EX-112, Rafe and his team followed the trail of breadcrumbs from the wormhole to a planet that had been long shut down due to humanoid violations by Trinchian slave traders.

"Yet another reason my woman could not come along," Rafe said as if trying to convince himself of his reason for keeping Karma away from the extraction. "We don't have a suitable space unit to prevent acid burns."

"Ai," Drago said as he coordinated an extraction point. The planet contained corporeal life forms rumored to be those of human escapees, mutated and driven mad by long-term imprisonment and torture. Roving sects of these 'mutants' were scattered about. But there was one spot showing a significant expulsion of energy; the top of a mountain where there was an unlimited view of all approaching crafts.

"If it is him," Paris said, "then he cannot run far. He surely would have expended most of his fuel keeping his pod running."

Rafe shook his head. "I don't like it. Why would he do that knowing that by running the pod he could be tracked? It is not as if he needs breathable air. The oxygen levels can sustain human life." Rafe shook his head. "Let's go."

Drago stepped in front of him. "Wait. Bring Karma."

"What?" Rafe frowned, appalled his friend would speak on this personal matter. They might be friends—brothers even, but that was crossing the line. Before Rafe could roar, Drago continued in a calm, reasonable voice.

"If you do this, she will continue to love you, but she will never trust you again. Never." Drago turned and left the room.

Rafe's mouth parted to explain that her life was more important. But the truth is he would rather die than lose her again and if that meant placing her on a high shelf where she would always stay protected, then so be it. He could tolerate her anger more than her injury.

But there was the flip side of the coin. Karma was more than his mate, a mother, a humanitarian. She was a warrior just waiting to emerge, and she needed someone to encourage her growth instead of stifling it.

Rafe left the bridge while speaking into his communicator. "Drago, take the lead while I get my wife."

A short time later, Karma's eyes opened. The first thing she saw was Rafe watching her as if she had only just shut her eyes. She tried to sit up and Rafe reached to help her. She pulled her hand back, avoiding his touch.

"So, how did the mission go without me?" Karma snapped bitterly as she sat up.

"It hasn't happened yet. Come." He held out his hand to her again. "We must hurry before Drago acts without the benefit of your wisdom."

Karma looked at him in surprise. She leaped into his arms and gave him a deep hug before quickly releasing him. "Where's my space suit?"

"You won't need one, just a pair of Galatian boots. Still, you'll want to avoid stepping into any acid pools—even the small ones."

"Uh..." She followed him with lots of unanswered questions—but the most important one concerned one individual and one individual only; Ragna.

Dr. Garry Brookstone sat on an outcropping of smooth rocks. His normally neat white hair fell into his colorless eyes and his beard had become thick and itchy.

If not for the world having a strange orange cast, he would have thought he was sitting on the Yunam Peak in India, taking one of his many lonesome sabbaticals. Although, at the time, he didn't realize he was lonesome.

He stared down at the land below him. He'd seen the ship, obviously, but there was no way to outrun a Galatian fighter ship—not when his small space pod wasn't even weaponized.

He heard stirring from inside the pod as *she* had evidently completed her swim. She'd emerged from her chrysalis only two days ago with a ravenous appetite. Unfortunately, nutritional biscuits weren't sufficient.

So, he'd gone out and hunted, bringing down something that resembled a deer with just a slingshot and then finishing with his hunting knife. She was too weak to do much more than eat. He'd forced her to wait long enough for him to at least boil the meat in the sauna portion of the pool. The air was safe enough, but he couldn't be sure about the bacteria and parasites living in the animals on this planet.

He could have laughed at the irony of what amounted to a septic tank being cleaner than the animals that lived on this planet. But the waters of Galatia and the antibodies within their plentiful pools did wonders.

He was a witness to that.

When he saw the first Galatian, Garry pulled himself to his feet and held up his hands in surrender. It was Paris. Garry recognized his tall, lean form immediately. Drago was behind him, and then a small army of soldiers who had weapons pointing at him.

"Where is she?" Paris growled.

Garry gestured with his head. "Inside."

Paris studied the man he once considered a friend. "You didn't kill her, did you?"

"No," Garry confirmed. "I've been-"

Paris punched him, and Garry's face broke. He didn't know because he was knocked out cold.

Drago gestured for his men to get into formation and checked for Karma and Rafe's ETA. Five minutes. He cursed internally. There was no time to wait around because there was no telling what plans Ragna had.

Paris had locks placed around Garry's wrists and ankles and set two Galatians to guard his unconscious body.

Kendrick and Drago were the first to force their way into the pod, swarming with quick movements over the walls as their soldiers fell in afterward with weapons trained in every direction.

But there was no need for it. Ragna sat calmly on the edge of the pool. She had no weapons, no clothes, and she was radiant.

The Galatians froze, and then each slowly lowered their weapons, including Kendrick, Drago, and Paris. They just stared at her in awe.

Minutes later, Rafe pushed past the soldiers to enter the pod. Karma had done a good job of keeping up, but she took the blame because they hadn't been in the lead. Her heart was racing now as adrenaline filled her. Memories of hate, anger, and fear made it difficult for her not to shake with the desire to...

She ran into Rafe's back as he came to an abrupt stop. Karma finally realized no one was shooting, fighting, or taking anyone into custody. And there *it* was—the individual who had taken the lives of so many just to end her and her baby.

It was the first time Karma had seen her without her injuries. But Karma hadn't expected her to look this different.

When she'd first seen her, it was while she wore the black mask and body suit meant to conceal her identity and smell. The only thing visible had been dark amber eyes. Those same eyes had been filled with pain the last time she'd seen them.

And now, she looked nothing like the rare photos that existed of Galatian females. Her scales weren't a muddy brown or burnt and bleeding. Ragna was a vibrant bronze with scales of varying tones of green.

Rafe wasn't moving and Karma had to wonder if they had the wrong woman, but not the way the creature's large amber eyes locked onto her. And those were the same eyes Karma saw in all of her nightmares.

Not wanting to take her eyes away from the creature, she forced herself to do so in order to look up at Rafe questioningly.

"What? It's Ragna, right?"

"It is," Rafe replied.

"Then what are we waiting for?"

Ragna tilted her head as she watched Karma. "They don't move against me because I am with child. Galatians can do no harm to a Queen Mother."

Part Three

Chapter Twenty-Nine

"What the ...?" Karma looked at Rafe again. "With child? She's pregnant?"

"She is."

"But it's only been a week-"

Ragna was the one to respond. "For Galatians, our bodies change at the moment of conception-"

Karma swung around and pointed at her. "I didn't ask you, bitch!"

Rafe rubbed his hands over his head. "What she says is correct. Galatian Queens go through a...metamorphosis or something close to it once they become pregnant."

Rafe stormed towards Ragna. She just looked at him, safe with the knowledge that her pregnancy was her protection from any Galatian male. It was Karma she had to now worry about.

He grabbed Ragna by her wrist and yanked her to her feet. He slapped wrist bindings on both wrists and yanked them tight. He pulled her forward, and she stumbled. When he looked down, he saw she was missing a foot right above the ankle. Her tail was little more than a stub, so she couldn't use it to help her walk.

He looked at one of the Galatians included in the mission. "Carry her!" he commanded. He couldn't stand the idea of her being close to him.

The Galatian quickly came forward and gently lifted the pregnant female. Rafe watched them step out of the pod and Karma took hold of Rafe's wrist and hissed.

"What in the hell did Brookstone do? Did he...?"

"Oh, I intend to find out!" Rafe turned to Kendrick. "Check the fuel levels and then fly this pod back to the starship."

"Ai," Kendrick replied.

Rafe stormed outside, where Garry was moaning in pain. Half his face was swollen and his jaw was misshapen. Rafe lifted him from the ground by his throat. "You got her pregnant?"

Garry just made guttural sounds.

"I don't think he can breathe," Drago said. He went behind the dangling man and lifted him under his arms. Rafe released him with a frustrated grunt. Garry rubbed his neck, gasping for breath.

"Jaw... broke," Garry managed.

"It's not the only thing that's going to be broken," Paris growled.

Garry held up his hands in supplication. "Hard...hard to speak. Will tell you."

Rafe stared at him, weighing what he wanted more, the man's death or his story. "Take him back to the ship. And I want his jaw fixed by the time we return to Eden."

As the team moved back to the ship, Rafe and Karma stood side by side watching.

"I know she is your get-out-of-jail-free card, but I want that fucking bitch dead."

He gave her a perplexed look. "Get out of jail free card?"

She shook her head. "Sorry, it's from an old American board game called Monopoly. It just recently came back in popularity, but it basically means that they can no longer accuse you of murder."

"They can accuse me of kidnapping. And based on the truce set forth by The Collective, it is still a punishable crime."

"This is just... unbelievable," Karma sighed. "Let's go home."

It was the next day before they reached Eden. Karma went into her sleeping chamber, wondering if she would ever wake up. For the first time, she didn't completely trust the Galatian crew members—except for her brothers, of course. She'd seen the other's reverence at the sight of the pregnant Galatian. What if Ragna got to them?

She made Rafe promise to only allow Paris or Drago as her guard and to not allow another Galatian to even look at her. Oh, and he had to promise not to kill Dr. Brookstone—at least not while she was asleep.

He promised to follow her orders, kissed her, and set her to sleep for the long trek home. When she awakened, everything was as she left it; Ragna was still alive and still pregnant, and Dr. Brookstone's broken bones had been set and rapidly healing within his sleep chamber. By the time they touched down inside the larger spacecraft, Garry Brookstone only had minor swelling and could speak.

He had been moved to an interrogation room, while Ragna had been sent to a secure Galatian cell. The cell was ugly to the eyes of a human, with its dark cavern-like appearance and small Galatian pool, but to the Galatians, it was comfortable and cozy. Again, Paris was her initial guard until they got a team of experts to watch her. But she remained quiet and made no fuss and just sank into her pool.

"I want the interrogation filmed," Karma stated as she and Rafe headed to the interrogation room.

"You want evidence? It may not sway The Collective, as surely he will speak on our plans to torture Ragna."

"I want it recorded." Karma reiterated. She lifted her monitor and made a call. "Hi baby girl."

Are you back, Mama?!

"I sure am. Papa and I just got back a few minutes ago. And guess what?"

What? M asked in her robotic voice, despite the animation in her face.

"We got the doctor, and we got Ragna."

And they're both alive?

Rafe leaned to the side to be seen by the monitor. "Yes, and little one, you are forbidden to do anything to change that!"

I won't Papa. I promise.

Rafe felt a smile at the sight of her big, brown, sincere eyes. "Just so you know, the female has permanently lost her foot and even more of her tail. It does not appear able to regenerate."

Oh. Are you going to let her go, Papa?

"We do not have to let her go to prove she is alive."

Karma looked at him. This must have been an idea he came up with while she was asleep because it was the first she'd heard of it.

"We will see you as soon as we can. Are you taking care of baby brother?"

Yes. I took him to swim in one of the pools. The Galatians were surprised we both could swim in it. She laughed.

Karma smiled. "They are going to learn." Karma said her good-byes, because they had reached the interrogation room.

Garry was sitting in a chair in front of a table. There were two seats opposite him, and Karma supposed they were there for her and Rafe. But she didn't think she would be here long enough to sit down.

Garry looked at them warily.

Kendrick had returned, and he and Drago flanked the door. But it wasn't as if he was in any condition to escape. One wrist was cuffed to the chair, and he was thin and unkempt.

"I know you think my actions are unforgivable—and they are. I stole your prisoner out of a sense of humanity-"

Karma lunged forward and slapped him in the face. "Shut up! Just shut up! You have no idea what your actions meant to us—how it affected our entire family! Your idea of humanitarianism is screwed because you either raped that monster in there or you allowed your-self to be seduced!"

Garry held his sore jaw with his free hand, but then his colorless eyes grew large at her words."

"I didn't have sex with her!"

Karma calmed. "Then who got her pregnant? And don't say it happened before she was taken because she didn't look like that when we had her!"

Garry nodded. "Can I just start from the beginning?"

Rafe touched his wife's wrist when it appeared as if she was going to yell at him again.

"Tell your story, doctor."

~Garry's story~

"When we left the spaceship, I had Ragna's chrysalis placed into the pool. It was a way for her to continue to get nutrients while I monitored her. As you well know, there are only a few things able to penetrate a chrysalis. And of course, I could have used any of those things to kill her while she was in stasis. It was my intent to give her a pain-free death. Sawing her open as if she was in a tin can would have been no different from what you wanted to do to her.

"So, I ran with her, to give her a chance to be reborn, at which time I would give her an injection of a substance that would stop her heart instantly. There would be a small amount of pain, but only for a short time. My intent was to return her body to you and face the consequences of my actions. I had no intentions of running for the rest of my life—however short it might be after my actions.

"I know her crimes. I know it is your right to seek vengeance. But when I was placed in a position to heal the enemy, my own moral values got in the way. So, I made a plan to give her a quick death— one such as your daughter intended. Although, electricity probably would have resulted in a prolonged death considering her resistance to the current that placed her in danger.

"With my head start, I headed for the wormhole we created while leaving Earth. I knew it would take time before you could track me. I had hoped to have the matter done with before it got to that.

"I found a location with breathable air, although considered a hostile environment—not that I intended to leave the craft. There was enough food and water to last several weeks.

"When I arrived, I was exhausted and my adrenaline had crashed. I got into the pool knowing whatever nutrients I left behind would only be beneficial. The first time, I fell into an exhausted sleep. It couldn't have lasted long, but I realized I was rocking in a soothing wave. I woke up alarmed and got out of the pool. I monitored my patient and saw her vitals had improved greatly, and wondered at the rocking of the water.

"I surmised that she might awaken within a week. I prepared the injection and waited. While I waited, I went over my old case files and anything that could keep my mind active. I couldn't risk listening to any transmissions for fear they could be tracked.

"I used the pool liberally, again, knowing I was only adding to the nutrients that would help the patient... the *prisoner* to heal and to shed the chrysalis. No, I did not develop an affinity towards her. Her actions were deplorable and disgusting and my only purpose in taking her was to give her a swift death.

"One night, after many hours of studying my old cases, I decided to take a swim in the pool. Again, I fell asleep without realizing it was happening. I dreamed. I dreamed about... well about someone I had loved. It was a very long time since she and I parted, but in that dream, it felt like we never had. Just holding her in my arms was a dream come true.

"I woke when I realized I'd... well I'd had a nocturnal emission. I'm not an overly sexual person, but the dream felt so real, and the rocking of the water was so rhythmic. It was like I was actually in the moment. Once I realized what had happened, I immediately got out of the pool.

"I saw her rocking the water, and she was floating in the aftermath of my semen. She rocked the chrysalis in my semen!

"I was disgusted but didn't realize the extent of those actions. I studied and when I got bored, I went outdoors and explored. I stopped using the pool to relieve myself and found a place outdoors. But then I noticed a change in her monitors. At first, I didn't understand. I went over everything over and over, thinking she had developed a type of cancer. Finally, I did a pregnancy test and, in horror, I realized she had become pregnant because of what I'd done in the pool.

"I did not have sex with her. But I feel as if her actions were calculated. A being in a chrysalis can think just as sharply as if they weren't in one. Instead of using the time to hibernate, she used that time to calculate."

"No, Karma. I do not believe she planned to become pregnant. I believe she planned to seduce and then ingratiate herself to me. She thought my actions of rescuing her meant that I intended to save her. But I would only discover that once she awakened."

Chapter Thirty

~Garry's story pt. 2~

"**I** saw the chrysalis was breaking apart only two days ago. I didn't know what to expect. I trained my laser on her and had the injection prepared, and then I waited. When she emerged, she was weak. But I didn't trust that. A weakened Galatian was still stronger than a healthy human male, and I wasn't at my optimum strength.

"'Dr. Garry Brookstone'," she said. It was her first words. I asked her how she knew my name. She told me she remembered from when she was in sick bay. Then she looked down at herself. She even seemed amazed at the way she looked.

"There is some type of... reaction that comes from a pregnancy. I'm not referring to her physical transformation in colors or the shape of her body, but to how I sensed her. When I looked at her, I knew I wanted to protect her. Quickly. I felt as if it was some type of pheromone, but to me, she was suddenly beautiful.

"I knew the damage she'd done, but I also knew she was growing a child within her body—*my* child within her body.

"I asked her if she'd done it on purpose. "You know you are pregnant! Did you do that on purpose, thinking I wouldn't kill you?!"

"Her emotions went haywire. She turned so many colors it appeared she was a kaleidoscope!

"'You lie!' she accused. 'Not by a human!' I left the monitor for her to look at the truth. She stared at it for a long time, still going from red, black, purple, but finally a tinge of pink.

"'What do you have to be happy about?' I snapped. And she said to me, 'Our kind has tried everything imaginable to become pregnant and all of this time the remedy was in the species we created so many hundreds of thousands of years before.'"

"So, I told her I didn't believe Galatian women didn't try having offspring with other species, and she glared at me with the first sign of hatred. She told me no Galatian female would ever allow herself to be defiled by a human. Mating was out of the question because our penis could never come close to filling them, and a hybrid could never be a Galatian, so it was pointless.

"I still didn't believe her. In all the experiments their scientists had done to find out the root of their infertility, no one had thought to explore using the semen of other life forms. Again, she was insulted but explained their scientist were tasked with resolving why Galatians couldn't procreate with each other. The fact remained that saving their species meant they had to remain pure.

"Their racism was so deeply embedded because of so many years of their separatist ideology, that the Galatian females would rather go barren than allow themselves to breed hybrid children. And with that is a jealousy at the ease of humans to procreate. In time, that turned into a deep-set hatred.

"I didn't learn all of this the first day we talked. It took Ragna time to accept the fact of her pregnancy. It was a time I should have used to kill her. But...I don't share her hatred of hybrid children and I didn't hate the child growing inside of her; because it was *my* child she carried, and I knew I could no longer take her life.

"We talked when we could do so without malice and accusations.

And she admitted she listened to my routine and knew when I worked and when I slept. So, when I got into the pool, she knew if she rocked the waters, I would sleep. She listened to the rhythm of my heartbeat and could sense when I was aroused, which she used to her benefit. She rocked the waters more rapidly, enhancing my...pleasure, I guess. And after I ejaculated, she used the semen for nourishment, not knowing what the results would be.

"She admitted she thought I would protect her if I felt a sexual connection to her. But that would not have worked. I was repulsed by my actions and before her pregnancy, not at all physically attracted to her species. She wasn't insulted by my admission. She found most humans to be hideous...except for me, who she found intriguing because of my albinism.

"But finding myself attracted to her disgusted me. I knew I was being manipulated—whether intentionally, into feeling protective of her. I found myself trying to spend more time outdoors trying to break the connection. But when I returned, I still found her beautiful and desired to care for her.

"She finally asked me the question I guess we were both waiting for; what my intentions were. I told her I didn't know because a pregnant Galatian and a man with albinism weren't something easy to hide. But make no mistakes. She wanted us to flee—but strangely, not to Galatia. She wanted no part of that world. She never did tell me why, but taking her there was the only place I knew I could safely leave her. I was still thinking about it when you arrived. And that is the entire truth."

Rafe huffed. "Do you know why she refused to be returned to Galatia? Because they would have done to her what she did to our child. Which tells me Ragna wants this pregnancy."

Drago was listening to his monitor, and he quickly looked up. "You have to see this! There's a recent development!"

Karma's stomach dropped. "Not another one…Is Ragna still in lockdown?"

"Yes, but it is not her." Drago brought up a large window for them all to see.

"This latest development has rocked the entire world!" A newscaster was reporting.

"We just received the first recording less than half an hour ago and since then, the recording has been verified."

The picture changed to a grainy recording. **"Is this the vile creature you've been looking for?"**

Karma's hands moved to her mouth. She recognized that voice. It was the voice of her father!

Suddenly, the grainy picture showed a Galatian female leaving a building. Moments later, there was something flung at her and she dropped as an electrical net enclosed her. Within seconds, she convulsed. Several humans dressed in military gear with blacked-out face masks surrounded her. They had lasers trained on her as she writhed on the ground.

"Once again, The Interplanetary Collective and the scum controlling them have tried to manipulate the story. They accuse Rafe Sigur of kidnapping and murdering the Galatian cunt known as Ragna! But we are the ones who took her. And who are we? We are a new rebellion, one that has joined forces with other insurgent groups. You can call us the Human Rights Initiative. My name is James Chambers. Look me up. I, as well as hundreds of other humans, were captured and tortured by the Tybernees. But instead of being rescued by The Interplanetary Collective, we were traded into slavery!

"I watched my wife die in front of my eyes at the hands of the Tybernees while my daughter was left to be raised on the streets! And the Tybernees are allowed

to sit on the council as delegates! Now you all will rue the day you ever fucked with the humans—and especially against the Chambers family!"

As the broadcast ended, the newscaster returned to the screen.

"You have heard it here first. A force has taken credit for the disappearance of Ragna of Galatia—the Black Mask that sparked the impending civil war among Galatians, as Rafe Sigur seeks freedom from the tyrannical rule of the Galatian Queens. All across the world, there has been a cry of Justice for Karma; Justice for humans, Justice for equal rights among humans."

"Breaking news!" The newscaster interrupted their own broadcast. "The Interplanetary Collective has issued a statement in response to the Human Rights Initiative."

A Tybernees individual was suddenly seen on the screen. Karma took a step back as if she was being transported in time to them, climbing into the window of her home and kidnapping her father.

Rafe's tail formed a protective circle around her.

The Tybernees could not form human words and had a mechanical translator who tried to mimic the human voice.

"I am an Interplanetary delegate for the Tybernees and I am here to address the heinous rumors spread by these despicable kidnappers. For many years, before Earth was placed under the protection of the IPC, humans were routinely traded for cheap labor by several intergalactic species.

"Your Earth was in virtual ruins and your people were close to complete annihilation. It was the Galatians who spoke on your behalf and who allowed you to find protection within our Collective. Since then, we have done our very best to return your world to one you can be proud of—in a way you have not been proud of before our arrival. We have put an end to wars. We have put an end to inequity. We have made your land greater than it has ever been before!

"There are a handful of ragtag rebellion groups seeking to thwart your happiness and your safety. Yes! I say your safety is now in danger! They want to drag you into a war you could never win; a war between humans and the entire Interplanetary Collective. Think about it, humans. Should we remove our protection, you would once again face alien invasions, slavery, and more.

"We protect you and will continue to listen to reasonable inquiries. But we will not be threatened, nor will we tolerate others under our protection being threatened. Those responsible for the kidnapping of Ragna will be dealt with under penalty of death! Do not think you will hide from us! We have allegiances in places you wouldn't know, and as we speak, we are tracking down those involved in this Human Rights Initiative. They will be treated as traitors and instantly killed—which goes for anyone found giving them aid."

There was a quick shot of human rebellions being beheaded by aliens wearing official Interplanetary Collective insignias. Karma gasped and looked away. Rafe pulled her into his arms protectively.

"We take these accusations seriously. We know who James Chambers is. He is the father of Karma Sigur-Chambers and out of a misguided need for justice, he took it upon himself to hunt Ragna down and capture her, instead of allowing the ICP to handle our investigations. This will not be tolerated. Vengeance is no justification for what we saw done to Ragna.

"At this time, we have removed the bounty from Rafe Sigur and he and his team are free to go about their lives lawfully. In the meantime, there will be a bounty placed on James Chambers and his rebel group

that is going by the name; of The Human Rights Initiative. That is all."

The broadcast ended, and the newscaster seemed pale. **"That from a delegate of the Interplanetary Collective. They have...um... indicated they will strike against rebels. We saw the heinous killing of human-"**

The broadcast was suddenly cut short as if someone had pulled a plug.

Everyone looked at each other in shock, including Dr. Garry.

This is the end of the world as we know it," he said.

"Uncuff him," Karma said sternly. "And follow me!"

Kendrick didn't even look at Rafe for affirmation before he unlocked the cuffs from the doctor. Following the demands of an authoritative female was so ingrained in him he didn't question them.

Garry looked surprised, as did Rafe and Drago, but they followed Karma. Before long, they realized where she was headed; to the cell Ragna was confined.

When the door opened, Paris looked surprised. He hadn't been made aware of the broadcast, nor had he been made aware they were coming.

Ragna was in her pool. When she saw the doctor, her breathing came easier despite the hostility coming from the human female.

They hadn't killed him. It must mean something. Humans had such soft hearts when it came to babies-

Karma grabbed Rafe's laser gun and shot Ragna in the head before she even had a chance to finish that thought. Her head separated from her body and fell into the pool even before her body dropped.

Chapter Thirty-One

Rafe spun to look at Karma. "What did you do...?"

Karma turned calmly to Garry, who had covered his mouth in horror. He cringed when he saw her looking at him.

"How long do you have to get that baby out of her belly before it dies?"

Garry looked at her, stunned, before turning to the bloody pool.

"I-I... I need a scalpel! I need to get her to sickbay!"

Karma turned to Paris, whose eyes were as big as saucers. He was in complete and total shock.

"Pick her up and get her to sickbay. And leave the head. She won't need it. Be quick."

Paris moved quickly with near superhuman speed. Within seconds he was gone, leaving behind a wet trail of blood and Galatian water on the floor. Garry had to sprint to catch up with him. Kendrick followed while Drago looked from Karma and then out the door before he followed the others, obviously deciding he would leave the two to their discussion in private.

Once there was only Rafe and herself in the room, Karma hyperventilated. "She's gone. She's gone. She's gone."

Rafe grabbed her shoulders. "You killed her-"

"So! She deserved to die! But that baby deserves a chance. You spliced my embryos and saved our unborn babies. He should be able to do something similar to save his baby."

"But... we may not have the equipment-"

"Then he better freeze it until we get it! That unborn baby is being given more of a chance than mine ever was!" She made a fist for emphasis, her eyes cold—as cold as what so many others would describe as an unfeeling Galatian.

He had only to look into them for a split second to know there was no more to be said. "Okay. It is done."

"My father gave us a way out. He has taken the blame upon himself."

"Well, it was his fault, after all."

"Rafe," she said simply.

"He took it upon himself to kidnap her and then I was blamed for her disappearance."

"He did it so I could kill her. I've finally accepted the gift he gave me."

Rafe closed his eyes. "It was a good gift." He looked at her again. "And a quick death."

"I learned sometimes that's the best way."

This time, when he placed his hands on her shoulders, it was to give her a comforting touch. "And how do you feel?"

"I don't know. Cold. Almost as if I don't remember how to feel. I'm just glad it's over. That *she's* over." He hugged her, waiting for her trembles and then her emotions to go into overdrive. But they didn't. She didn't cry. And when she eventually pulled back, she looked up at him.

"Rafe, that Tybernees never denied they had something to do with enslaving humans even after we entered The Collective. My father accused the Collective of knowing about it, and even supporting it. And we're serving them! We're allowing them to rule us!"

"But Karma, the alternative, is too dire to even consider. The Galatian Guards are mighty, but we cannot protect the entire Earth alone."

Karma nodded. "I know. But we don't have to remake the wheel."

"What?" he asked in confusion.

"I just mean all we need to do is clean house."

"I am unsure of your meaning?" he asked, still as confused.

"Oh, gosh, honey. I'm sorry. I'm saying we need to fix the Collective. How can they hope to rule us when they don't even understand us? They think threats will keep us in hiding? Not for long. Fear only turns into anger. The only thing they've achieved is to garner us more support. Rafe, I need to speak to the people!"

Rafe rubbed her arms. "Yes. We both do."

"Together?"

"Together. But no mention of Ragna. None."

Karma nodded. "Okay. Let's talk to Drago about a broadcast. Man, I can't wait to tell everybody about the Queen's treachery! And about that lying bitch, Mayva. I want her ass next."

"Okay," he blinked. "What did you do with my mild-mannered wife?" He tried to joke.

She set him into her cold sights. "She went bye-bye." Her words sent a shiver down his body.

Mayva had listened to the broadcast. Amalia had immediately sent for her, wanting her to make an announcement. But the moment she saw the condition the human was in, Amalia knew there was no way Mayva could be the voice of The Collective. She looked as if she had been tortured—which, in essence, she had been.

Amalia once again put her aside until she could be of some use. Meanwhile, Mayva knew Galatia was in turmoil. Her Galatian servants were jumpy and fearful. And Alma had been anxious when she'd visited, demanding Mayva fix herself, to which Mayva drooled.

Amalia said several curse words in Galatian before leaving the room. Mayva was just happy she hadn't been instantly killed or had her television set removed. She supposed the rationale for her even having one in the first place was to keep up on current events should she ever be returned to her role as a spokesperson.

But based on the way things were looking, that ship had sailed. Mayva climbed back into bed and then beneath the sheets and comforters which had become her refuge. *Go humans, go. Get those dirty Galatians!*

"Do you think it was wise to just kill Ragna without considering...?" Drago stopped talking when Karma glared at him. They had gathered the ex-consorts and Rafe's team into an impromptu meeting.

Maddie placed a hand over Drago's. "You did more to the people who intended to hurt Rex. And he wasn't even our son, yet." Drago nodded and looked away—not in shame he had incinerated the humans capable of such atrocities, but he had questioned someone as fair as Karma.

"I'm sorry," he said.

"The developments on Earth are dire," Karma said. "They are killing the Resistance, the people that are trying to fight for us! We cannot just sit on that!"

Tam nodded in agreement. She had left Haru for the first time to attend this meeting.

Kemistry was present, having just arrived several hours before. "I know Dorf would agree that we have to take action now!" she said.

Paris looked around the table. "I am ready to fight! No more talking! No more waiting for the Council to decide on a punishment for the Black Masks! They have no intentions of siding with the humans, which means they have no intentions of siding with us!"

Kendrick slammed his tail against the floor, causing everyone to look at him. "I will fight a war, but I want our mother's safe! That won't happen if they know they can use them against us."

"He is right," Rafe stated.

"Maybe we can negotiate for the freedom of your mothers?" Daya stated softly. "They're afraid. Putting those Tybernees on air only proves it, or they would know that was absolutely the wrong thing to do."

"True," Justina said. "What do we have to negotiate, though? We have only demands."

"What they want, we can't give," Karma stated. "They want us to return to blindly following them!"

"Let's face it," Tam said. "It's hard to negotiate when all parties aren't present. We need to have a dialogue with The Collective."

"I don't want Amalia involved. She is sneaky and thinks too highly of herself," Rafe stated.

"Agreed," Karma stated. They looked at each other. Karma took his hand. "I'm ready to do this."

Rafe kissed the back of her hand and then looked at Drago. "Can we do this while masking our whereabouts? Before, during the parley, we were in outer space."

"We can scramble the origins or we can make it appear as if we're broadcasting from a specific area—Galatia, even."

"Hm," Rafe thought. "It matters not to me as long as it's not this planet or Earth."

"Ai." Drago got up to prepare for the broadcast.

The others got up to leave as well. "You got this, Karma," Daya stated. "You, more than most, understand all we have lost under the rule of The Collective." Karma nodded, knowing Daya meant that, unlike the other mates, they hadn't been raised under the protection of the consort school. They'd had to scratch and scrape to make ends meet.

"Thanks, Daya." Paris waited and led his mate out.

"Are you sure about this?"

"It's make or break time," she replied.

"Which means you are certain," he stated.

Karma smiled. "You will need to learn American slang. But yes. I am sure about this. We can offer them an out and they have to take it."

"What do you mean?"

"Think about it, Rafe. If they allow humans as delegates in the Collective, then they will get a false sense of control. But they don't understand; They. Cannot. Control. Me."

"No. They don't know you. And you would have friends and allies there."

"And I can negotiate—wait, what? Did you just agree?"

"I did. If I was on the outside looking in, then I would recognize the viability of your idea. It's only the fact that I love you which gives me resistance. But I know you are intelligent and you are fearless. And I won't put my fear on you."

She took his hands. "Thank you, baby. I love you and I am afraid. But I'm more afraid of what will happen if I don't do this."

He leaned forward and kissed her, and then tilted her head and stared into her eyes. "You are more than my wife. You are a leader, Karma Sigur. I won't hold you back any longer. I'll be at your side for your battle, just as you will be at my side for mine."

She nodded. "What exactly are we going to say?"

"Everything you want, my love."

When Kelsie and Bain entered the simulation room where the nanny was babysitting, M leaped to her feet. The three friends sprinted to each other but then stopped before they collided and looked at each other in embarrassment. Kelsie suddenly moved forward and pulled M into a hug. M hugged her back happily and then Bain was suddenly there, turning it into a three-person hug. The friends laughed and hugged until M touched Kelsie's backpack.

Is this how you breathe?

"Yes. Until my lungs are fully formed."

Where is Aunt Kemistry?

"She's visiting dad."

Nanny came over to them with both babies in tow, each in their own hover carriage.

"Hi, children. I told your mom I'd keep an eye on you, but I have my hands busy with these little tykes. I take it you will be on your best behavior?"

"Yes, nanny," Bain and Kelsie said in unison.

Runnar was sleeping while Rex was lifting his hands, indicating he wanted out.

"Look how big Rex is." Kelsie said. She reached for him to lift him out of his basket, but Bain swooped in to pick up the baby.

"Mom said not to exert yourself and he looks heavy." Rex grabbed Bain's face and gave him a big, slobbery kiss. Bain laughed. "I missed you, too, buddy. But wow, you're big."

He can crawl now, M announced.

The kids promised to watch him for a while so nanny could catch up on her reading.

"There is always something new in the medical world," she muttered with a sigh. It was easy to forget that before she took on the task as Runnar's nurse, she had assisted Dr. Sanjay and was studying the hybrid baby to document his progress.

The children played with Runnar for a while until he got tired and cranky and Nanny gave him a bottle and put him to sleep.

"I can't wait to have my own kids," Kelsie said wistfully.

"Ew. Not me," Bain said while studying the controls to the simulator. "Want to play rocket attack? We don't have to run and can just use blasters."

Yeah! M was so happy to have her friends back. None of them had any idea that the world they knew was changing right beneath their noses.

Chapter Thirty-Two

Drago was setting up for the broadcast, and Rafe led his wife to a small simulator room for them to pick out the background that would be shown to the world.

Karma was thinking about what to say. She still hadn't absorbed all that had happened. She was so deep in thought she didn't see Rafe press the keypad, locking the door. She barely noticed the cameras were disappearing.

What she knew was that Rafe came up behind her and lifted her in the air so her feet were dangling a foot from the floor. She twisted her head to look at him and saw his eyes were burning with a fire she recognized.

His green-slitted eyes locked into hers as he carried her to a platform that quickly appeared in the middle of the room. She covered his powerful hands on her hips—not to remove them, but to feel the rough strength he possessed.

The smooth platform had barely rezzed before he bent her over it. Karma pressed her palms against the smooth stone, even more surprised he planned to take her from behind. The simulated stone was hard and unyielding, just like Rafe's movements when he pulled her pants down over her ass and hips, not completely removing them, leaving her bare brown buttocks exposed to him.

She felt a rough caress as he palmed her ass cheeks. When he spread them, it surprised her yet again, especially when she felt his thumb stroke the puckered entrance. Karma's breathing came fast, almost as fast as his sexual attack. Karma had never thought much about the many different entry points a man could take, but she decided she liked the way it felt when he stroked her hole.

She looked behind her again and saw him unbuckling his skirts, which fell heavily to the floor. Her eyes widened. Was he going to—?

His big green prick bounced upward, already throbbing and seeping. Her eyes glazed as his hands gave it a few perfunctory strokes to lube it with the generous precum streaming down its sides. She felt her clit swell and unconsciously she rubbed her hips slightly against the smooth rim of the platform.

Rafe placed a firm hold on her thigh, stopping her movements. "All mine," he growled. "I want none of your essence wasted on the platform."

Karma's pussy clenched and she nodded and stopped grinding her hips while he continued to prep his prick.

She suddenly felt the pad of his forefinger lightly push past the folds of her pussy and she gasped and nearly began grinding again before remembering to remain still.

"Mmm," he said after removing his finger. When she looked over her shoulder again, his finger was in his mouth, savoring the taste of her. He saw her looking. "You're drenching wet. I know something about you, Karma Sigur..."

Her brow moved up to respond with something sexy, but swiftly his prick was at the opening of her vagina with the head slipping into her pussy—and thankfully not her asshole.

He intended to take her with one straight shot all the way to her very guts with no interruption from her cervix! Karma quickly tightened her grip on the edge of the platform, knowing what was about to happen. They'd been gentle in the months since her coma and sex surgery. He'd been so cautious. He'd taken it slowly and eased his length into her to get her accustomed to his considerable size.

But not today.

Karma knew he was about to give her a hard pounding! And no sooner had she gripped the edge of the simulated stone platform then she felt herself being spread mercilessly by his hard, hot prick! He pushed forward in one easy movement until he had reached the end of her vagina and had entered the new canal that had been surgically created by opening and then tilting her cervix.

She gasped as her canal widened and widened until she felt as if there was no more she could give. And then her man was buried deep into her body, his heavy balls pressed against her mound.

Karma groaned in pain-laced pleasure as her pussy surged to life and then throbbed around him. Rafe rocked his prick against her, grinding as if he wanted to go even further before he pulled back and slammed roughly into her.

Karma shouted something; a moan, a groan, a sigh — she wasn't sure which. But then he did it again, faster, and again even faster. She'd heard about men pistoning into their lovers, but no one could do it with more precision and more speed than a Galatian. He fucked her so fast and so hard but with amazing care.

Karma clung to the platform as she wailed out her pleasure. They'd never done this. They'd never fucked so hard with him, completely bottoming her out. She realized it wasn't just her crying out in ecstasy, but Rafe's animal cries also filled the room—sounds that seemed mixed with Galatian so she didn't know which were his moans and which was the alien language.

Karma's body rocketed forward with each rapid thrust. She'd never been fucked like this before! Her toes curled in her shoes as her engorged clitoris was being pounded by his rapid thrusts.

A muscle she wasn't familiar with tightened in her gut. Rafe's movements became staccato. *What was that?* It happened again, and he shouted and slumped over her back, his normally rhythmic thrusts faltering.

Karma knew she was gripping him from deep within her belly and it was taking him out! In awe of this ability, Karma was brought back when his hands burrowed beneath her and slipped between her legs. The pad of his middle digit pressed and stroked her as if to say 'two can play that game'.

Losing control, Karma's body writhed beneath him.

"I'm going to cum so deep in you-" Rafe couldn't even finish the sentence before he was making it happen. Karma felt the warmth of his seed filling her belly.

More! Give me all of you, Rafe! Karma wasn't sure if she thought this or screamed it, but Rafe didn't exit her body until he'd deposited every drop of his seed inside of her.

"Is there time for a shower?" she asked lazily. She lay in his arms, still dressed from the waist up, his powerful arms now offering her a cushion from the hard stone platform.

"We will make time." He stood and walked to the control panel where he rezzed a shower with actual working water.

Karma hopped down from the platform and quickly stripped out of her clothes. This type of technology had been around for ages, but it was still new to her, as it was primarily used by the military. Even the very rich couldn't afford their own simulators. Just using one cost an arm and a leg. Whenever a movie star wanted clout, they were always sure to film themselves inside of one.

To her, it was just strange, real water, real materials, but they would break down ready to rebuild themselves utilizing the prompts of the user.

Rafe stripped down, too, and stepped into the shower. He washed her with lavender soap, being careful not to wet her hair. He had learned that long ago.

"Okay," she looked at him. "So, is this real soap?"

He chuckled as he gently ran a soapy hand over her legs. "This is real soap and real water. But all the things used to turn it into soap will return to its original composition and the water will become water vapors again."

"But we can't eat the food?"

He looked at her. "People have been known to do it once and only once. It will taste like sawdust."

She picked up the loofah brush and scrubbed the top of his head, neck, and back while he was stooped at her legs. Karma didn't want to stay in the shower too long because she couldn't quite make herself believe the soap or any of it could be real.

Once they were dressed and ready to leave the small simulator, Karma remembered something Rafe had said when they were in the heat of passion. She stopped him before they could leave the room.

"You said you knew something I liked. What did you mean because I'm not sure about anal play..."

He shook his head. "No. It wasn't that." He turned bodily to face her instead of just turning his head. He crossed his arms as if expecting an argument.

"You enjoyed killing Ragna."

She scowled. "Well, yeah. Of course, I would-"

He shook his head. "That is not what I mean. You weren't afraid to end another being's life. It can be traumatizing even when it is well-warranted. And after it was done, I could sense your disgust; at her, at yourself, at the act—I'm not sure which. Nonetheless, when that ended, you became empowered as if her death transported her life force into you." He made a soft vibrating noise that lilted up and then down.

"That is what we call it when you become stronger instead of weaker after taking a life. Your panties became wet and your nipples hardened and I was intoxicated by your smell. If I could, I would have taken you then and there," he sighed.

He wasn't trying to turn her on, but his words made her breasts feel heavy and her nipples sensitized. How is this normal? How is it normal to become aroused after killing someone you despise?

She nodded in understanding at his words. "Maybe I am just a stone-cold killer. Or maybe finally killing Ragna brought me back to life."

Rafe opened the door. "I think there will be many other opportunities to determine which it is."

When the unannounced broadcast interrupted what was already a chaotic transmission day, the shockwaves had already extended throughout the entire world. There was an uproar in the streets as protestors demonstrated the human beheadings and the threatening language of the Tybernees.

In the North American province where normally protests occurred between classes, there seemed to be a wave of unity as the common enemy became The Interplanetary Collective. Province-wide curfews were enacted, but the police force was easily overwhelmed by the massive number of civilians.

Not even the conservative ruling class could influence the crowds with threats of job termination or incarceration, and they were soon forced to flee the pelting of rocks or catcalls during public speeches.

Soon, business owners were forced to lock down their businesses and stores as the poor rioted with celebrity encouragement. Movie and singing stars had joined forces with the common men and women to make public announcements opposing government control. Some of the most bold and popular stars even called for an end to the control of The Collective.

When Rafe and Karma's broadcast appeared, televised in homes, shops, and public squares, the arguing and fighting seemed to instantly stop.

"People of the world," Karma began. She wore a serious expression on her otherwise beautiful face. "I have seen the broadcasts made today; first from James Chambers—who is indeed my father. The second from the so-called Tybernees delegates of The Interplanetary Collective. I say-so called because long after Earth entered the Collective, our men were still hunted, kidnapped and then trafficked into slavery by the Tybernees. My father was one of those men.

"Where I lived, everyone knew to keep our men safe—not from muggers. Not from accidents. But from slave traders. I came from the ghettos and projects, which was the hunting ground of the Tybernees.

"When the government announced years of freedom from alien attacks, it was only freedom for some. Not for *us!* Not for the poor and the working class. That freedom was only granted to the rich!"

Karma's piercing dark eyes narrowed as she stared into the camera as if she was looking into the souls of every human person watching her.

Chapter Thirty-Three

"**I** am continuously appalled at the level of disrespect we are expected to endure. Not only do they expect our gratitude for their protection from the very same individuals sitting on their highest council, but they have the gall to have a Tybernees address us—not to apologize, not to explain they have changed, but to further threaten us! And this time, the threat isn't to people like my father; poor, non-government workers—but all of us; rich and poor alike!

"Make no mistake, when The Interplanetary Council executed humans that they call "Rebels", with no trial, it speaks of everything we need to know; which is they don't care about us! They don't care about *you!*"

Rafe's tail touched her leg, and she turned to look at him. After a silent but brief exchange, Rafe looked into the camera."

"As a high-ranking member of the Galatian Guard, I work closely with the Interplanetary Collective and there is a reason they need to categorize humans as lesser species. In this way, you fall outside of the equitable guideline treatment reserved for only those The Interplanetary Collective considers intellectually advanced.

"Many humans refuse to believe that man descended from us. But something that cannot be refuted is only a shared species can propagate. And there is no question that humans and Galatians can interbreed—not after you saw the attack of Ragna against my wife and my unborn child." Rafe paused, his breath coming fast, his color darkening. Karma took his hand and a moment later, he continued.

"Humans. You are not lesser than any alien that serves on The Collective—just as having government positions, and more money doesn't make one human superior to another! Galatians have been guilty of allowing ourselves to be ruled by our female counterparts. For thousands of years, we allowed ourselves to be treated as lesser beings, incapable of thinking and acting for ourselves.

"Therefore, when it came time to assist mankind, we didn't take action to prevent you from being treated in the same manner. When the Galatian Queens made laws making humans subordinate to Galatians as well as other alien species, we did not question it. We did not realize that by taking away your independence, we had taken away your power. We thought by placing other humans in charge while we enforced your laws we were empowering you.

"But how can Galatian men know anything about empowering others when we have been rendered powerless by Galatian Queens? We didn't even know what freedom looked like!

"My wife knows a great deal about mistreatment—just like many of you who were not given an equal opportunity because of the color of your skin, or your race, or your government status. While those who were sworn to protect you failed to recognize your suffering.

"I know too much to go back to being blind! Now that my eyes have been opened, I refuse to be a subordinate to another being! I fight for the rights of the Galatians, but I also fight for your rights. Because as long as The Interplanetary Collective sees you as a lesser being, you will be treated as such."

Karma was amazed at Rafe's words. He sounded like a human! She squeezed his hand tightly. The Queens tried to breed the passion out of their men. But passion was their best attribute. Galatian men loved hard and may the Great Guardian help anyone threatening those who fell under their protection!

Karma leaned forward in her seat as she spoke. "Today I tell The Interplanetary Collective that we humans reject your threats. On the behalf of the humans of Earth, we demand equal status and equal representation on The Interplanetary Collective as human delegates!"

She swallowed without looking at Rafe. "And we demand that one male Galatian sit as a delegate with one Queen to represent all of Galatia.

"These demands are non-negotiable. You have twelve hours to decide, or we wage war on the Queens of Galatia."

Drago and the communications team ended the broadcast. Rafe looked at Karma. One brow quirked up.

"You just waged an entire war, my love."

"I don't think so," Karma said, although she wasn't completely sure. "They may not give a damn about the humans, but I think when it comes down to it, The Collective knows that no Guard will side against you and they don't want their elite force of warriors fighting against them."

He nodded once. "And I suppose you meant for me to be the male delegate to represent Galatia?"

This time she gave him a half smile because he wasn't angry about her actions. After all, she hadn't discussed him serving on the council.

"Who else is better equipped to keep me safe while I'm serving with those backstabbers?"

"True. Come, we should meet with the others. I am certain they have lots to say." He led her out of the room.

Karma and Rafe always garnered attention, but it seemed as if everyone they passed in the corridors had listened to the broadcast and looked at her with newfound respect. They treated her as if she was as important as Rafe, instead of the tragic consort that had been the target of the Black Masks.

But one thing gave Karma pause. A Galatian Guard—one that had probably been on the mission to retrieve the doctor and Ragna took one look at her and looked away. He didn't even acknowledge Rafe the way they normally did.

Karma waited to see if Rafe noticed, but if he did, he didn't react. She thought back to the way the males had regarded Ragna once they realized she was pregnant. It was as if they'd forgotten they were hunting down a baby murderer—

Karma's breath caught in her chest. The Galatian Guards had sided with Rafe—against their mothers and other Queens because the violence done to her and the others just couldn't be ignored. But now that she'd killed a pregnant Galatian, did they see her as no different from Ragna? If that baby died, was she no better than Ragna?

She stopped walking, and Rafe gave her a curious look.

"I need to speak to Dr. Brookstone. I need to find out about the baby—the embryo..." She sighed. "The baby."

"Karma. We had a plan. You carried it out."

"I know. I don't care about Ragna, but I...that baby should have a chance."

Rafe didn't reply, but he took her elbow and led her to the sick bay where two Galatians were standing guard. Neither looked at her, although this time they at least acknowledged Rafe and she knew she was definitely getting the cold shoulder.

Dr. Garry looked like hell. His greasy white hair hung in his eyes and his abnormally white skin was still swollen and red on one side— at least the part that could be seen past his heavy mustache and beard.

He looked up from a scope. His light eyes were wary, but he said nothing—waiting for his life to end or for them to change their minds about the life of the baby.

On one of the examining tables was a tarp obviously concealing a dead body. Blood had pooled on the floor.

Karma didn't feel anything about that, but she took a deep breath as she met the doctor's eyes. "Were you able to save the baby?"

"I was able to place the embryo in cryo-preservation. It is still viable, but I'm unsure for how long."

"I see. What do you need to keep it viable?"

Dr. Garry visibly relaxed once he realized Karma wasn't here to tell him to stop his efforts. "The most important thing is a cryo-stabilizer. The adult human would need to be placed at a much lower temperature than an embryo.

"I believe I can achieve this by making a cryo-bag."

"Then request whatever you need."

"I just...I know human physiology, but for Galatian hybrids, there just isn't much infor-"

"Nanny. Nurse Gayton has worked with Doctor Markheef, who is Galatian and Dr. Sanjay who..." Karma swallowed and looked away before looking at Dr. Garry, "who treated my unborn baby."

"I know Dr. Sanjay Bhatt," Garry said quickly. "Any help from a protégé of his would be of great use."

"Let me speak to her." Karma turned.

"Thank you!" Dr. Garry said. Karma just nodded and left. Rafe glowered at the man before following his wife.

"You don't have to do this, you know."

"You didn't see the way your men looked at me."

"I saw," he said. "But they remain in service. They have not rejected us."

She glanced at him. "Maybe not yet, but if that baby dies..." Karma blinked, "that's not what I mean. I don't want the baby to die."

Rafe just made a grumbling sound. "I hate its mother and its father, but I suppose I would prefer it to live."

Karma didn't realize it was so late. It was dinnertime and the nanny, the ex-consorts, and children were having a meal in the officer's dining hall. Kemistry and Tam had returned to the sick bay to be with Haru and Dorf.

Poor Runnar was curled up asleep in his hover carriage and Karma felt a stroke of guilt for being away from him for so long. Her hands longed to lift him for a cuddle, but it wouldn't be fair to wake him if she wouldn't be staying—and she already knew her work was long from being over.

Mama! Papa!

M got up from the table and ran to them, reaching Karma first. After a big hug from her Mama, she got one from her Papa, who lifted her in his arms.

"Bain, Kelsie, would you like a tour of the ship?" He asked, knowing M knew nothing about Ragna's death, her embryo, or the impending war. All of that would require a very long sit-down. Until then, he didn't want them overhearing Karma's discussion with the nanny.

Karma gave him a grateful look as the children enthusiastically followed Rafe.

Maddie waited for the door to shut behind Rafe before she exclaimed in excitement. "Your broadcast was fantastic!" She bounced Rex up on her hip as he watched and listened with interest.

"Thank you, but a lot is going on." The nurse moved to retreat, but Karma stopped her. "Nanny. Can you stay? This concerns you, too."

Nurse Gayton seemed surprised. "Certainly."

"I want to thank you for all you've done. You're here to study and help with Runnar, but you've become much more than that to me-"

"To all of us," Maddie said. "Rex is never any trouble, but I knew nothing about babies and you've helped me and answered so many questions for me. I don't know what I would have done without you."

The older woman smiled. "Working with children has always

been my passion. Runnar's case is a first, but so is Rex's with his enhanced intelligence. Even M, is one of only a very few children who have received surgical enhancements.

"But just as importantly, I believe in what you are doing. I feel as if I am a part of this. I thank you for your trust."

"Well, you might not feel that way after I ask you for this next favor," Karma said

Karma wasn't surprised the ladies knew about Ragna's death, including her pregnancy. Drago and Paris would have told them, and they would have shared the news with Justina. But Nurse Gayton hadn't known. She'd been busy with the children so she hadn't even watched the day of broadcasts.

She was shocked and speechless at everything Karma revealed from her father's declaration of guilt at capturing Ragna to the threats made by the Tybernees and, finally, her declaration of war.

"Whatever you need me to do to help, considerate done," Nanny said in awe.

"I am going to ask you to help Dr. Garry save the life of his child. He has the embryo cryogenically frozen, but he says he needs to stabilize the temperature and thinks he can do it with a cryo-bag."

Her mouth fell open. "I can help! We can keep the embryo frozen or we can grow it in an artificial womb!" She suddenly paused. "But what about Runnar? I can't monitor him and work with the doctor-"

Justina raised her hand slightly. "I can help." She looked at Karma. "I know you're busy, sis. I would love an opportunity to take care of Runnar. I've known him since he was born and I've watched Nanny and you, so I know what to do! Plus, M can help-"

Karma laughed. "Yes! Justina, yes, I would appreciate it if you would take care of Runnar."

Sgt. Kelly was quietly watching the entire interaction. They hid their smile of approval, happy that Justina was able to do something like care for a child.

"I'll help, too," Daya said. "I work with babies all the time."

"And you know I'll help," Maddie said. Karma held out her arms to hug them all.

"I love you, guys. You are the best family any woman could ask for."

Chapter Thirty-Four

The men, plus Karma, sat in the communications room watching the shocking broadcasts from Earth. Many of the traditional stations had been blacked out, but pop-up broadcasts would appear, providing the world with information about the many demonstrations.

There had been rioting earlier in the day, but after Karma and Rafe made their speech, the majority of people stopped fighting amongst themselves. It seemed as if they knew they might soon have to fight an even bigger foe.

Many people all over the world appeared to join forces dismissing long-standing racial and economic differences. People marched and chanted in the streets, side by side and shoulder to shoulder, some wearing expensive clothing alongside those that had nothing but rags to cover their nudity.

Humans sang of solidarity in one part of the world while others stormed government facilities demanding equal representation within The Collective.

Of course, just because there was no rioting didn't mean there wasn't violence. The military continued to attempt to enforce curfews, to no avail. In London, the police opened fire on a group of youth, injuring and killing hundreds.

Karma's hands were fisted as she watched. "I can't stand sitting here doing nothing! I need to be on Earth fighting with the others!"

Rafe placed a calming hand over hers.

"For many humans, this is the first time they've been able to express their dissatisfaction. They need this. As difficult as it is for us to watch, they need to feel empowered."

She calmed, knowing he was right. "How many hours has it been since we made our ultimatum?"

Drago replied. "Almost six hours."

"You should get some rest," Rafe said. "Things will move fast once The Collective responds." He looked at his men. "We all need rest. Go back to your mates and we can reconvene when there is an answer."

"Ai." Paris rubbed his hands over his sleek head. "I may be getting close to my change." Rafe gave him a wary look.

"How soon?"

"I can put it off a few days."

Rafe nodded. "You and Daya will remain aboard the ship. I suppose she will want to take care of you."

"We've discussed it and she would like to. She's become accustomed to the pool but not so comfortable about others seeing her body. Being aboard the ship will give us some privacy."

Rafe looked at the others. "I believe our families will be more comfortable back at the villa. I am sure our children will be. It is too hectic here. At least there will be peace for them to play out in nature."

Karma nodded in agreement. "Also, we need to have a long talk with M, and I'm sure Kemistry will want to do the same with Bain and Kelsie. I need to touch base with her to find out if she wants to have this discussion together."

"Karma," Rafe chided. "You need rest. You haven't slept in two days."

"I'm too worried to sleep." Immediately after saying that, she yawned deeply. "Okay, you're right. But I want you to get some rest, too."

"I don't need as much sleep as a human, but I will." He leaned forward to accept her kiss as she bid him goodbye. She waved goodbye to everyone else in the room before leaving.

Drago stood. "We should bathe, and then I will see my family."

Rafe stared at him. "Has the head been removed from the pool?"

"It has been incinerated."

"Fine. Then let us visit that pool. I will enjoy bathing in Ragna's blood." Everyone agreed, and they went to the now vacant jail cell where Ragna had been beheaded. The floors and rocks had been cleaned, but they could still smell her blood emanating from the pool.

Rafe's men stripped and entered the pool and Paris closed his eyes and conjured memories of Laylay nagging him about his disposition.

Drago allowed the heat of the sauna waters to steam his scales as he remembered the sound of Titus's thick Scottish brogue and his mastery of the heavy Scottish swords.

Kendrick swam deep within the coldest depths and remembered his friend Pogo guiding him safely through hundreds of missions with the use of the symbiot belt. And he hadn't been there to guide him to the afterlife...He cursed Ragna's memory.

Rafe also cursed her memory but for a different reason. He could not seem to push away thoughts of Ragna running naked through the Galatian forest, trying to hunt the great beast with the adult Queens. Even as a child, she refused to learn a child's place. And as a young adult, she warned that he too would have to be more than what was expected of him if he wanted to be on her level.

It was true. However, her demands backfired because it was due to her constant nagging that he knew he could never be happy with her or the life she wanted.

Rafe swam in the remnants of her blood and thought about a life where he and Karma raised all of their children in total peace—including the one that was no more.

"Are you going to kill the Black Mask?" Bain whispered. They were supposed to be sleeping, but the children weren't tired. Aunt Kemistry had allowed them to have a sleepover in the sick bay with her and Aunt Tam as they watched over Uncle Haru and Uncle Dorf. The women were sleeping with Aunt Kemistry making soft purring noises, just like a cat.

They had wrangled up an extra nest for M, who lay curled up in the softest bed she'd ever experienced.

No, she replied. **I messed it up the last time and I won't have another chance. Mama and Papa know that no more chances can be taken. They will do the right thing.**

"What about Dr. Garry?" Kelsie whispered. "You said you liked him, but he did something real bad."

M took a moment before answering. **Papa said when people die while in battle, it is considered an honorable death —even if they die at the hands of their enemies. Because they died fighting for what they believed in.**

If Dr Garry had to die, at least it would be because he did something he thought was right.

"How do you think they'll do it?" Bain asked.

I don't know, but they should do it fast and get it over with.

"It's gross," Kelsie said. "Let's talk about something else or I'm going to have nightmares."

I can't wait for you to see your new house. It has tall windows so your mom can fly in and out. There's a loft and a kitchen and bedrooms with beds. But maybe your mom will take them out and put nests in them.

"I rather sleep in the nest than a bed," Kelsie replied. "But I won't mind having both."

Your house is near the cook, gardener and their grandson. The cook is mean. She whipped the boy even though he really didn't tell any secrets. She whipped him with a branch.

"You saw it?" Bain asked.

She did it right in front of me and Mama.

"Did he cry?" Kelsie asked, appalled.

He did a lot of hooping and hollering, but I didn't see tears. But I think he's pretty embarrassed. I know I would be if I got whipped in front of someone.

"What did he do the next time you saw him?" Kelsie asked.

I haven't seen him since because we left for here. But I feel bad. She gave them guilty looks. **He wanted to be friends and I wouldn't. I don't think he has any. He tried to be friendly with these elite kids, but they were mean and rude. One boy even tried to beat him up, but I put a stop to it.**

Bain nodded as if he wouldn't have expected any less.

"Why don't you want to be friends with him?"

M shrugged. **I don't know. I guess because I thought I was going to get in trouble for going outside of the boundaries. But it wasn't his fault.**

"We should make friends with him," Kelsie said decisively, and M and Bain agreed.

Kemistry stretched on her perch above the pool. "Kids, it's late. Go to sleep. You can talk in the morning."

"Yes, Mama." Kelsie said. The others chimed something similar before snuggling into their soft bed of feathers and drifting off to sleep.

Justina stared down at the sleeping baby. He was absolutely beautiful. His caramel-colored skin had a few patches of green scale, mostly on his torso and limbs. His face was very human and yet he still looked like a mixture of Rafe and Karma.

Through the baby, Justina could glimpse what Rafe would look like if he was human with skin instead of scales. Even with his dark curls, the baby was obviously a hybrid child. It was evident by the claws on his hands and feet and, although his serpent tongue wasn't currently visible, it routinely showed whenever he babbled, cried, or laughed.

And then, of course, there was his tail which poked through a disposable diaper. Justina had gotten a quick lesson on diaper changing by Nanny, who made it seem very easy, so she was sure it would be okay.

Adrian stood next to her as she stared down at Runnar. "He is certainly a cutie."

"He really looks like Karma and Rafe." She couldn't help but think she'd never know such a thing.

"I wondered..." Adrian began hesitantly. Justina looked at them curiously. "Didn't the consort school save your eggs before they modi-fied you?"

Her lip moved up mirthlessly. "They didn't care about any of that. The Queens had them take our reproductive capabilities out of spite because they couldn't make their own babies. I mean, they sold us the lie that it was to accommodate our mates, but that was just one part of the big lie they fed us."

Adrian rarely touched Justina. It wasn't their place to do so, but they regretted saying anything that caused her pain. So, they reached out and placed a comforting hand over hers.

"I'm sorry that happened to you. It should never ever happen to another little girl."

"Guardian willing, it never will again. They've long ago outlawed genital mutilation of children, but they continue to promote it for the Galatian Exchange."

Justina slowly turned her hand until she could grasp Adrian's. The soldier gently squeezed it. They looked at each other for a few moments before turning their attention back to the sleeping baby.

"Wahhh! Wahhh!" Justina jumped out of bed and hurried over to the hover carriage, where Runnar had pulled himself up into a sitting position, rubbing his eyes and crying.

Adrian had been in the next room sleeping on the couch since they now guarded not only the ex-consort but also the commander's only son.

"Hush, hush, now," Justina said sweetly as she reached to lift him from the carriage. He was probably wet and hungry.

Runnar gave her one look and tried to wrench away, his cries intensifying. He might know her, but she wasn't his Mama, his nanny or sister. Justina could certainly sympathize.

Adrian jumped into action and grabbed the baby pack for one of the bottles. "I can mix his formula if you think he's hungry."

"Yes, please!" Justina stated as she jostled the baby on her hip as he tried to reach for anyone but her. "Oh, it's okay, honey. I know you want your mommy and nurse. But auntie is taking care-"

Runnar turned towards her with his mouth wide and reached for her face with his sharp nails.

"Eeek..." Justina had time to squeak at the sight of the rows of sharp teeth visible in his wide-opened mouth. She had time to think about the bloody scratches and claw marks that used to cover Nanny's face and neck back when he was a bit younger. Even M had the occasional bite mark on her arms and hands.

Justina resigned herself to the attack and squeezed her eyes closed, not even considering she could just drop him.

Adrian could only watch in horror at what was about to happen. They hoped facial reconstruction wouldn't be too painful...

Runnar sank his wet mouth against Justina's cheek and began

suckling it hungrily. He held onto her tight as he drooled down her face and neck.

Justina opened her eyes when she didn't feel his teeth. She looked at Adrian, who quickly jumped into action and quickly finished making up the bottle. The soldier sprinted to her as soon as the formula was mixed, shaking it furiously before handing it off to her as if they were playing football.

Justina slipped the little one into the crook of her arm and quickly replaced her cheek with the bottle. He gripped it frantically and hungrily and began to drink.

Jeez, I feel sorry for Karma's tit...

But she smiled down at the babe and watched as his brown eyes drooped while he continued to gustily drink himself to sleep.

Man, I wish I could have one of you...

Adrian watched the longing in her eyes, and their heart ached. They'd never really thought about having a kid and while the soldier no longer identified as a woman, they still had eggs the military had saved just in case...

Chapter Thirty-Five

Karma felt Rafe's body mold along her back. She inhaled sleepily and reached up to cup his sleek head as he placed a kiss behind her ear.

"It's been twelve hours," he said.

Her eyes opened, remembering the importance of that information. She pulled herself up to a sitting position.

"Has there been any word from The Collective?"

"No. Nothing."

Karma looked down for a moment, and then a resigned expression came over her face. She swung her legs over the edge of the bed and slipped her feet into her shoes.

"Well, that is that."

Rafe made a huffing sound, which equated to the same thing. They left the room together to return to the simulator chamber.

"I have been in talks with the current Lieutenants of the Galatian Guard. They indicated unanimously, that they will follow our lead."

"What does that mean for The Collective?"

His hand was around her waist as they walked, and it moved over her hips in appreciation. "It means they will be too busy fighting for *our* cause to fight for The Collective. It means as soon as we announce our intent to battle the Queens, they will leave their posts to convene with us. In essence, The Interplanetary Collective will be made vulnerable to their many enemies."

Karma's brow arched. "But surely The Collective has other fighters?"

Rafe made a scoffing sound. "They are not warriors in the way Galatians are. They are capable, but they don't excel." He said those words with indifference. He was not one to mince words, and he fully believed there was not a more formidable fighter than male Galatians.

"That is awesome news!" But Rafe did not show the same excitement.

"It is, but we have heard from our allies on Galatia. The males stationed there—whether they be warriors, or under other professions have indicated their reluctance to align themselves with us. It is a bad blow. However, they stated that while they could not fight against their Queens, they also would not fight against us. Therefore, they will not be fighting on behalf of the Queens. It is the next best scenario."

"It is," Karma agreed. "But it's a shame they'll benefit from our fight when we win."

He smiled inwardly. His woman did not doubt their success. For them, there was no other way; it was either fight or die. They would not be permitted to live if they were unsuccessful.

Paris, Kendrick, Drago, and three heavily armed guards were waiting outside the door of the simulator chamber. Each Galatian had a beautiful lavender tint—but as beautiful as it looked, she knew the emotion behind it was displeasure that could easily become anger.

She nodded to them, and they did the same. It was alarming to see such heavy firepower, and more than anything else spoke of their dangerous situation.

"Still nothing from The Collective, although the fighting on Earth has taken a darker turn," Drago said.

Worry lines appeared on Karma's forehead as she listened.

"Various government groups across Earth have begun mass shootings of protestors. It is said The Collective has authorized it. Also, there are reports of the capture and killing of hundreds of rebel cells —mostly small and disorganized. I am pleased to report no Galatian Guard has participated in these endeavors."

"There is at least that," Rafe grunted.

Once in the room, the door shut behind them, leaving them alone. Drago would return to the communications bay to begin the broadcast. Karma immediately checked her appearance in the mirror that had been rezzed into existence by the simulator. She looked as if she had aged over the last two days. Someone else would have tried to conceal her fatigue with make-up, but it was the last thing on her mind. She finger-combed her hair and with a sigh turned to Rafe, who was checking the lighting.

"I have something I want to say to the people, but after, I want you to talk about how we will carry through with our threat to wage war," Karma said.

"Yes," he agreed as they took their seats. "Talk of war should be handled by a warmonger."

The broadcast began. Karma appeared grim as she appeared on monitors and screens.

"Many of you have seen the devastating murders of human citizens for doing nothing more than what all people should be able to do —gather and peacefully protest. But that was one of the rights stripped of us when we became part of The Collective. They have demonstrated they care nothing for our well-being and we truly are under their control.

"Therefore, it is with a heavy heart that our hand has been forced." She turned to Rafe, who paused before speaking.

"The war we intend to wage on the Queens of Galatia will be as merciless as the murders of our human brothers, sisters, mothers...and children." His scales blushed red with emotion. "But I want you to know it is a war that won't happen on Earth. This is a fight we will take to Galatia! It is not to say that you, as humans, will not feel the effects. They will try to hurt us by hurting you. But stand strong because it is not just our freedom we fight for, it is yours-"

"Rafe," Drago interrupted smoothly. "There is another broadcast coming through. It's from The Collective. Your camera is still live, but I will show you the broadcast."

A screen appeared on the adjacent wall and a newscaster was seen, although their face was concealed by a blackout mask. Karma could understand this when being a reporter could be a death sentence.

"Ladies and gentlemen! You have been listening to a broadcast by Rafe and Karma Sigur, but we are also receiving an official live broadcast by The Interplanetary Collective! This is unbelievable, but we will go straight to both broadcasts on a split screen as both parties are live."

Karma could see herself and Rafe on the broadcast, waiting with the same confused expression as the rest of the world. A moment later, Lars Jocavic appeared on the screen.

Everyone in the world knew Lars. He was human and at one time had been a spokesperson for government programs all over the world —generally encouraging humans to register for various programs which generally resulted in people being placed in unfair jobs based on their color and race and not on their abilities. It had been a happy day when he was retired. He had been old back when Karma was a child, and despite his snappy suit and makeup, he looked as old as death.

Karma wondered why they weren't using Mayva. At least she appealed to the men. Lars only appealed to geriatrics with old money.

Lars grinned broadly, showing off big fake teeth. "My apologies for our late response. Many of you know me. For decades, I have worked tirelessly on behalf of the humans of Earth in conjunction with The Interplanetary Collective. I have always been a spokesperson in support of humans and human rights. I have assisted in the implementation of programs that have allowed no humans to go hungry and homeless-"

Karma rolled her eyes and snorted.

Lars chuckled. "Mrs. Sigur, I see that you disagree. But know that the programs are in place despite attempts by other forces who have misused them—namely high-ranking government officials who have illegally—and may I add, immorally utilized those resources to benefit themselves.

"We intend to swiftly deal with those officials that have tarnished our good intent!"

"You are a bit late to speak about these matters when the topic of war is at hand," Rafe stated.

"The Interplanetary Collective has accepted your offer for human and Galatian male representation. There will be two human delegates and, of course, Lt. Sigur, you will be the male Galatian who will serve opposite one of the Queens.

"Karma Sigur, you will be one-half of the human delegate. And I will be the other half. So, you see, there is no need to talk of war. We will talk of restoration, repair, and rehabilitation—on all parts."

"I am surprised Mayva Heath has not been offered the second delegate position," Karma said.

Lars looked surprised. "Well, I'm sure, like everyone else, she is watching these proceedings with high hopes for the best outcome. And with that-"

"You've been retired for many years. I'm just surprised The Collective isn't promoting Mayva Heath. She was popular among those who support your agenda. In fact, the last time I saw her, she was being carted to prison for falsifying information to The Collective.

Lars blinked in shock that this "secret" was revealed in such a way.

"To be honest with you," Karma continued. "The spokespeople that The Collective aligns themselves with aren't always the best choices. With all due respect, you're retired and even during your prime, you supported programs that completely disregarded the human rights of people of color; people that look like me, people that aren't *white* men."

Lars opened and closed his mouth, not accustomed to being spoken to in such a manner—at least not on air in front of others.

"So, the alternative is a woman who turned on friends that she was raised with since being served up into institutionalized prostitution well before the legal prostitution age. A woman who watched her friends murdered—not to mention the murder of an unborn child. *And* then she is found to be a liar by the same Queens that you support."

"That's—well—none of that is true!"

"Tread carefully," Rafe growled. "We were involved in a parley that might have been recorded... "

Lars quickly recovered. "I just mean Mayva Heath has been exonerated of all guilt and has been released—"

"But *you* still supported a system of virtual enslavement-"

Lars's face turned red. "Now that is not true! Our programs were successful until the greed of others-"

"So, none of this was set up so the rich could get richer? Schools in the inner city weren't built using subpar material and the meal plans aren't based on garbage discarded by upper-class schools—"

"But that's not our fault! That is the fault of people that were supposed to be placed in power—"

"Placed in power by you! You and The Interplanetary Collective!"

"I will not be held responsible-!"

"I think the point my wife is making," Rafe interrupted. "...is that we do not accept your offer to serve as the co-human delegate on the grounds that you cannot properly represent human rights. You are not trusted, Mr. Jocavic. No one that has aligned themselves with The Interplanetary Collective will be trusted."

"But that is unfair!" Lars sputtered. "It doesn't help anyone if the human delegates are one-sided. And you don't represent the thoughts of all humanity, Mrs. Sigur! Not even factoring in Government repre-sentatives, until this happened the majority of rebels wanted you and other consorts dead! That is a large segment of the world!"

Karma said nothing. Rafe said nothing. Lars calmed and smiled. "Perhaps another parley is in order. One where the representatives of The Interplanetary Collective can discuss an equitable-"

Karma shook her head. "It's not for the non-humans of The Collective to decide the human delegation! Don't you get that?! This is to benefit *us*! Not *you*! They don't get to decide. Humans of the world, make your wishes known! Be careful, but put the word out. We are listening." Karma raised her hand, indicating the end of the broadcast.

Lars began sputtering again once their feed disappeared. "Well," he finally said. "Efforts for fair representation have been rejected. It seems all Karma Sigur wants is a war. We are trying our best to avoid this. Please stand by." Lars disappeared, having the last words.

"Asshole," Karma said. "My Mama and Daddy always hated him! He's a snake in the grass!"

Rafe pulled her into his arms. "You did good. Very good. You never cease to amaze me."

Karma blew out a long breath and relaxed against her husband. "So, does this mean we aren't going to have a war?"

"I believe the ball is in their court. They've countered, and we have rejected."

"Not so fast," Drago said over the intercom. "Look at this!"

The broadcast screen came to life, and on it was a face Karma recognized. Her father's.

"We have seen the sly way The Interplanetary Collective tries to insinuate themselves. That idiot Lars Jokavic said at least one true thing; prior to the attack on my daughter and her family, the rebels were in agreement that all alien influence needed to be irradi-cated from Earth." James Chambers paused. "And now we agree that humans are the victims of an unjust

regime. The Resistance is no longer targeting consorts, government officials, or any other humans. Our aim is to target those aliens that have enslaved us. That fight begins with The Collective!

"Just as my daughter threw down the gauntlet, I throw down my own. On behalf of the rebels of Earth, you will make me the second human delegate or you will suffer the consequences as we cut you down to your knees!"

James smiled and Karma's heart thumped as she recognized the daddy she had loved and respected before his disappearance.

"I'm sure you underestimate our power because we're just *poor, basic humans*," he said mockingly while using hand quotes. **"But we've been out there in the big wide universe, and we know your weaknesses—namely, your enemies who have only held back from attacking you because of the Galatians Guards."** James chuckled.

"Don't take too long to respond. We are in parley with groups of aliens that hate the Malnamanian, the Tybernees and *you* as much as we do."

James winked, and his screen went blank.

Chapter Thirty-Six

M heard someone moving around. She opened her eyes from her position in the cozy nest where she'd slept the night before and was happy to see Mama and Papa. Mama was holding little Runnar on her hip and the babe was cooing and eating his fist. Papa had climbed into the pool and was checking the chrysalis for Uncle Haru and Uncle Dorf.

Mama! Papa! M leaped up, and in the process woke up Bain and Kelsie. Tam was already awake and drinking coffee while her feet swished around in the pool water. Kemistry was perched on a rock, preening her wings.

Karma knelt and gathered M into a big hug. She kissed the top of her head and then wiped a smudge from her cheek. "Did you take a bath last night?"

M shook her head no. She quickly pulled from her mother's grip, stripped down to her undies, and then climbed into the pool. Rafe went under the water and gripped his daughter from behind, eliciting loud laughter from her as she was lifted into the air.

"Mom," Bain said in excitement. "Can I take a bath in the pool, too?"

"Yes, and say good morning to your Dad. He's lucid right now," Kemistry replied.

Bain quickly stripped down to his undies and excitedly leaped into the pool, despite being sound asleep only seconds before.

Kelsie looked on in disapproval. "How is that a bath when you don't have any soap?"

"The Galatians bathe in it," Bain said before submerging under the water to join M and her father. Kelsie continued to look dubious.

"It's fine, sweetling," Kemistry replied while hopping over the rocks to her daughter. She gave her a good morning hug embracing her with her soft wings. "The minerals in the pool act in the same way as soap. But I don't want you to get in there until after your lungs are developed. I don't want your mechanism getting wet—especially not when we're so far from your surgeons."

Kelsie snuggled against her mother's warm body. She didn't admit how much she wanted to swim with her friends, but cuddling with Mom was the next best thing.

"Good morning, Dad," Bain said when he was next to the oversized chrysalis. It was still strange to him. He'd never gotten the opportunity to even see a Galatian molt, so seeing his father embedded in the thick white cocoon was a little unsettling.

"Can...can you breathe okay in there, Dad?" he whispered before reaching to touch the strange substance with his fingertips. He wondered if his father even knew he was there. What if it was all a big mistake and his father was suffocating? What if he was dying in there?!

Bain felt a panic attack coming and had a desire to rip and shred at the substance trapping his father. M and Rafe looked over at him and the wide expression on his face. But just then, there was a humming sound. It was faint, but unmistakably coming from the cocoon. It swayed gently, and seconds later, Bain smiled.

It was his song! It was the song Dad had made just for him when he was sad and scared. And instantly, Bain knew everything was okay. He flung himself onto the chrysalis and held onto it tightly.

When are you going to come out, Dad? I miss you so much... He was able to hold back the tears, but his eyes stung.

Rafe placed a gentle hand on the boy's head.

"Dorf can hear everything you are saying, Bain. And he misses you, too."

"You can understand him?" Bain asked while still holding onto the gently swaying cocoon.

"I can. Because of his symbiot belt. He's still wearing it and we can speak. Your dad says he can feel you and your sister and your mom and he misses you, too. He is ready to come home to you, but has to wait for the chrysalis to tell him it's time."

Bain closed his eyes and pressed his face against the foreign substance before he finally released it and wiped his stinging eyes. M placed a hand on his shoulder and instead of being ashamed for his show of emotion, he knew his friend understood.

"Come on, children," Rafe said while swimming to the pool's edge. "It's time to get out. There are some things we need to talk about."

M and the others looked at him curiously before turning to the other adults in the room. It was obvious from Tam to Kemistry, not to mention the expressions of Karma and Rafe, that something important was happening.

Tam gathered some towels and offered them to the kids while Rafe quickly slipped on his skirt and then boots. Meanwhile, the children had gathered around Karma, who had taken a seat on one of the rolling doctor chairs. Once he was dressed, Rafe took the baby from her and used the claw of his index finger to carefully stroke his sleek curls.

Kelsie gave her mother a questioning look and Kemistry nodded and smiled, letting her know that no matter what, everything was going to be okay.

Karma looked at them, her expression a strange mixture of dazzling intensity. What M saw was a woman who looked like a warrior who could go up against any foe and whether she won or lost, she would always look like the better individual.

All of this time she'd been trying to emulate Papa, but maybe she should have been trying to encompass Mama's spirit...

Karma looked at Kelsie and Bain. "Your mom thought it would be a good idea to get you all together to have this talk." Kelsie and Bain watched her solemnly. And M knew this was about the Black Mask. Had she found another way to escape? Would she find a way to finish the job that had taken the lives of so many?

I should have finished her...

"First, let me say that none of you have to ever worry about Ragna. She is dead."

How? M asked in shock.

"I killed her. I shot her, and she is gone forever."

M let out a long sigh. She hugged her mother and without her knowing it was going to happen, tears came to M's eyes. She began to sob softly.

"It's over, baby. It's over." Karma gathered her and rubbed her back. After a few moments, she kissed the top of M's head. "There's more. Even though she's gone, there is a lot more."

M pulled back and searched her mother's face.

Dr. Garry?

Karma sighed. "Ragna was pregnant. It happened when Dr. Garry stole her."

"Ewww," Kelsie said before slapping her hand over her mouth.

Karma just smiled. "There's more to it. Ragna tricked him. But the main thing is, Dr. Garry was able to save the baby. That is why Nanny left yesterday. It was to help Dr. Garry. I checked earlier and the baby—who is just a little embryo — is stable and doing well."

"Is it going to be like Runnar?" Kelsie asked.

"A hybrid human-Galatian. Yes," Karma replied.

So, you didn't kill Dr. Garry? M asked happily. **Please, don't kill him, Mama. Let him raise the baby.**

Karma looked at her in dawning understanding. She wasn't

raising a blood-thirsty child. Somewhere in the back of her mind, Karma had feared her child would be consumed with violence and fighting. But this little girl had a healthy understanding of self-preservation; if you were a danger to her, you had to go. And that was all.

Karma smiled and gripped her hand. "Don't worry about Dr. Garry. As long as he does the right thing, he will be okay."

Rafe's expression darkened, but he held his tongue. That would be the first untruth Karma had ever told their daughter. As far as he was concerned, Garry Brookstone was far from 'okay'.

"Even though we've handled Ragna, it doesn't mean everything is settled. Back when we were on Earth, you remember my father figured out how to find us. At the time, we felt it would be better to relocate. In the time since I last saw my father, he became the head of a Resistance. Do you know what the Resistance is?"

Kelsie was the only one to nod yes. "They are humans who don't like aliens."

Karma nodded. "Moreso, they don't like humans and Galatians to be together. Which means they don't like consorts, either."

M looked at Tam. **But Aunt Tam joined the Resistance**.

Tam nodded. "But only to find out their secrets. We needed to know how dangerous they were to our fight. We needed to understand their numbers and alliances."

"Tamsyn was very helpful," Rafe added. "But there are many cells around the world. However, Karma's father is part of a very large and very dangerous cell. And when they were able to locate us, I knew we could easily become a target."

But that is Mama's own father. M looked at Karma. **Your own father wouldn't hurt you, would he?**

Rafe made a "hmphing" sound before Karma answered. She gave him a quick look and answered.

"It's complicated. I know my dad cares about me. But he's made it clear that he hates Galatians and all aliens. Aliens are part of our family. My son is part alien..." A sad expression came over her face. "Besides, I thought he was dead for a big portion of my life and he never tried to contact me to let me know he was alive, even though he knew where I was and what my life was like.

"Anyway, after we left Earth, your dad was contacted by the head of the Galatian Queens. They call her The Most Exalted. They wanted to have a parley—or a talk in order to stop any war from happening. But in truth, she was trying to set up your dad for Ragna's disappearance. She got Mayva Heath to lie and to say she saw your dad kill Ragna.

She's a liar! M snapped.

"Yes," Rafe answered. "Because by that time, the good Dr. Garry had already stolen Ragna," he said with perfect sarcasm. "It meant we had to go out and find them so that I could prove my innocence. Otherwise, I would be hunted by The Interplanetary Collective."

"But you killed her," Bain said. "Is Uncle Rafe going to keep being hunted?"

"No, honey," Karma said. "Because my father spoke up and showed a video of his Resistance group capturing Ragna. And for all the world knows, she is still being held captive by that group."

The children smiled, recognizing that they had won an important battle.

Tam smiled as well. "What Karma failed to say is that even before her father spoke up, humans all over the world rallied for her. She gave an interview, and it turned the tide so even the rebels began to side with us. Karma let the world know what we are fighting for isn't just the right for humans and Galatians to be together, but the right for Galatians to make their own choices and not to be ruled by the queens.

"And that is no different from demanding equal treatment among humans." Tam's face grew stern. "No human should be hungry or mistreated because they weren't born a white male or don't have a government job!

"Because Karma stood up for herself, it made others in the world want to stand up for themselves and for others that have been mistreated." She gave Karma a look of admiration. "She's an important woman on Earth. Because of her, everyone is willing to fight for what's right. All over Earth, people are joining our cause—and that is all Karma Sigur."

Karma looked embarrassed as she shook her head. "It's all of us-"

But Tam refused to give her an out. "No. From day one, you have always done the right thing and have always looked out for the underdog; me, the children from the orphanage, the homeless, even the paparazzi who wanted to stalk you."

Karma shook her head but smiled. "Fine, but regardless of what brought on the fight in people, the world is ready and they are fighting and defending themselves against the bad military who is being controlled by The Collective."

"They aren't the same military who work with us," Bain said. "Our military is good."

The bad ones hurt the poor and the homeless, M said solemnly. Kelsie listened quietly, a haunted look on her face as she remembered things that were best left unsaid. Luckily for Bain, he had been born to a wealthy family and had never been exposed to the corruption of the government-run police and military. Even Tam, who was born to a well-off Hispanic family, was still raised in a province of Mexico that saw a great deal of abuse and corruption against people of color—people just like her.

M was watching her mother with a knowing expression. Mama hadn't said the most important thing. She was building up to something terrible.

"Everything happening is very important—not to just our family, but to all the humans of Earth and all the male Galatians in the Universe," Karma continued. "Rafe and I made a broadcast declaring we would wage war unless The Collective met our demands, which was to allow human delegates onto The Council along with a male Galatian.

"They have agreed to our terms. Your father will be the first male Galatian delegate to serve on the Interplanetary Collective. And I will be the very first human delegate. My father has requested to be the other."

Your father…M said. **I thought you didn't trust him?**

Karma sighed. "You're right. My father is going to have to regain my trust. Also, we might have dodged a war for now, but I don't think The Collective will easily give up their control of either the Galatian Guards or of humans."

And there it was, M thought. That was the dangerous part.

Chapter Thirty-Seven

"I need to get out of here! My family needs me."

"You cannot rush this, Dorf," Haru stated. He sat on a large rock while Dorf paced over the soft purple grass.

Haru wasn't sure why they always conjured images of Galatia. Perhaps because there would never be a planet more beautiful to him, and while they were in stasis, Dorf allowed him to take the lead —well, with the exception of the frequent concerts where Dorf was always a one-man show.

"Did you hear my boy?" Dorf stopped in front of Haru, hands on his hips. "He was in tears."

"I did not. I can hear Tam and sometimes Rafe. But I spend my time here recuperating. To the outside world, I am in a deep sleep. You, on the other hand, stay wide awake listening for news of the outside world."

Dorf scowled. "But how can you not?! The world is in shambles-"

"And we are well taken care of. Dorf, I have done this for decades. If you continue to fight the process, you will only prolong it. And if you prolong your healing, you also prolong mine."

Dorf closed his mouth, biting back his angry retort. Haru was right. He wanted to see his woman just as much as Dorf did. He looked down at himself but couldn't gauge how he truly looked; how much he had healed. In this fever dream existence, he looked however he imagined. Sometimes he was as tall as Haru, while at other times he had two sleek wings which allowed him to soar with unimaginable speed.

Dorf plopped down on a nearby rock. "How long have we been here?" His voice was resolute. "I can't tell. It seems as if it's been forever."

Haru tilted his head in deep thought. "Less than a week—and much too soon to complete the process. Just relax and disconnect. Things will go much smoother...for the both of us."

Haru closed his eyes and began to meditate, chanting softly in Japanese. Dorf allowed his friend to pull him into the meditative state so they both sat and chanted in unison as the sun began to set over the soft lavender sky.

"I almost wish we had gone to war," Marisol said while pushing back sweaty red curls from her face. They were in his bed and Kendrick was on his side watching her, but at those words, he froze.

"Have you ever fought in a war?"

"No. But it's fighting, which is better than sitting around here waiting for something to happen."

He analyzed her words, trying to understand them. On some level, he recognized that she was simply stating her displeasure with the prolonged downtime. On Earth, there were always missions, even if it was simply training recruits. There were frequent skirmishes with local rebels or unruly space pirates. The soldiers who served alongside the Galatian Guards weren't just relegated to Earth. They saw plenty of intergalactic combat.

Yes, joining the Service was perfect for those who loved to fight. Still, only a naïve person would wish for war out of boredom.

Kendrick sat up in bed, swinging his legs over its edge. "We should go. There might not be a war, but there is much work still left to be done."

Marisol padded to the bathroom naked. "Thanks for calling for me. I needed this. I ain't had a man in years and now it seems like I can't stop thinking about it." He heard the water run as he fastened his skirt.

"I hope you ain't trying to keep this a secret," she continued, "because the girls all gave me the side-eye when you called for me." She chuckled. "I ain't saying a thing about it, but you should know that all the girls want a taste of Galatian prick."

"Aye," he said simply. Humans did a lot to get just a glimpse of a nude Galatian. But despite being of the same species, sex between them was discouraged except in the case of the consorts. He felt a bitter flash of anger that someone would dare place rules on who he would share his life with. Even now, he was hiding what any adult should be free to share with another. He hid so much; his love of human culture and now his sex life. Would his brothers even care?

"So," Marisol continued in her deep southern twang. "You sure you can't put just a little bit of your prick in me?" she called.

Kendrick paused again. "I made you cum three times and you still want more?"

She poked her head from the bathroom, a washcloth in her hand. "I like your tongue and tail when you stick it in me. I really like sucking you off. But I *love* fucking."

Kendrick said nothing as he fastened his skirt.

"You know I can take birth control-"

"We don't believe in birth control. We have had this discussion," he said dismissively.

"Okay, Commander." She turned to head back into the bathroom and he was behind her in a blink of an eye. She swung around in surprise and he admired her quick reflexes.

"There is no commander within these rooms."

"That was sarcasm," she smiled. "I know we're...*special* friends."

He eyed her fleshy pink breasts with its spattering of freckles. Maybe they could spend a few more moments before returning to duty...

"Look," she said hesitantly. "I have another question for you."

He paused before taking her into his arms, hoping she wasn't going to ask for his prick. It was honestly becoming tiresome. "Ask."

"Since you don't want to put it in me, is it okay if I do it with another guy? I mean, we can still do it your way-"

Yeah. He was certainly tired of her. "I have no problem with that." He released her and then returned to the bedroom to continue dressing.

While Rafe and his men were busy monitoring and networking with their allies, Karma was in the sick bay with her sisters and the children. It was the only way for her to have a meeting with all of them present since Kemistry and Tam wouldn't leave the pool with Haru and Dorf.

"Thank you for watching Runnar," Karma said to Justina as she jostled him while he sat propped on her hip. Justina eyed the baby in his mother's arms.

"I enjoyed it. I know nanny's busy and you will be too. I'd love to keep him whenever you need."

Karma smiled. "I will take you up on that. The Collective hasn't yet responded to my father's demands. When they do, I think things will happen fast."

M peeked up at her mother from the laptop computer. She was supposed to be doing her lessons. Aunt Daya was in teacher mode, keeping the children preoccupied or trying to. But even with their headphones, the children had a difficult time paying attention. And M, with her enhanced hearing, could understand every word the adults were saying.

Justina had lowered her voice, but M could still hear. "There's no way your father can afford to be around The Collective after he's admitted to taking Ragna. If they wanted to arrest Rafe just under the suspicion of taking her, just imagine what they'll do to him."

"I know," Karma agreed. "But I don't think my father intends to allow himself to be at their mercy. None of us can."

"I had my doubts about your father," Maddie said. "But I hope you give him a chance. He obviously cares about you."

Justina reached for Rex, who went to her readily. Justina beamed as she lifted the bigger baby and hugged him. Adrian was standing guard by the door and hid a smile at Justina's delight.

"I don't have any doubts he cares about me. It's the Galatians in my family I'm worried about. But I will give him a chance."

"So, you're going to tell him about Runnar?" Justina asked.

"Not anytime soon. He has to prove I can trust him." The women nodded in agreement.

Karma looked over at M, who continued to pretend to be absorbed in her lesson. "Rafe said we can go back to the villa, but I think I need to stay here in case..." She shrugged.

"I can't leave until I know Dorf is okay," Kemistry said.

"Same here." Tam replied.

"I don't mind taking the children back to the villa," Justina stated. "They have to be bored silly on this ship. And I can keep Runnar. We did fine, together."

"I'll help with Runnar," Maddie said.

Daya walked over. "I'll help, too."

Karma looked doubtful. "It might be a few days..."

Maddie smiled. "We're a village and a family. We got you, sis."

Karma smiled. "Okay. Thank you."

Adrian was in charge of getting them to the villa. The Edenites might not know much about the happenings on Earth, but they knew something important was happening on the huge spacecraft that had settled in their territory.

Galatian sightings in Eden were commonplace, although they were aloof and far from friendly. The Galatian Guards were peace-keepers, preventing space pirates from trying to destroy their world as Earth had been destroyed, and not considered residents.

There were reports of other alien life forms sightings around the craft, many of which wore the uniforms of the Galatian Guards. It meant they were intelligent, even if they looked like walking boulders or prehistoric birds.

The rumor mill also whispered that the beautiful women who had rented the seaside villa were really consorts and their Galatian Guards were actually their mates.

However, people with common sense knew that even as backward as Earth was, no one would still willingly mate with aliens. That practice had been barbaric generations ago and surely Earthlings had advanced, at least in some ways.

When the Earthlings returned to the Villa, the gossip multiplied. But there was no use in trying to get any information from the old couple who worked there. They acted like they owned the place and weren't just working-class servants.

The only information they had about the Earthlings came from a few of the seaside vacationers whose children had claimed they'd met a robot-talking child that fought with robotic precision.

It made the teens the focus of attention and the instant popularity gave them the idea to seek out that pesky Ciprio. He certainly would know all the secrets of the household—and if not, they could force him to find out.

Chapter Thirty-Eight

"You look as if you are in deep thought," Rafe said. They were in the communications room watching several screens as news around Earth was broadcast.

Karma turned to him and offered a soft smile. Rafe looked at the screen she had been viewing and grimaced. Human protestors were being 'punished' for demonstrating. Dead bodies littered the ground as people ran screaming for cover as soldiers wearing Interplanetary Collective insignias fired on them mercilessly.

Rafe could not imagine his woman there among the people who were being cut down in troves. He knew The Collective wanted to make a point, but Earth was still recovering from a huge loss of life from war, famine, and alien trafficking.

"I want this to be one of the first things we address," she said. She glanced at the screen again and sighed. "They've killed thousands, Rafe. *Thousands* in just hours..."

He nodded, knowing he could explain the strategy behind the carnage. But that is not what Karma needed right now. Instead, he grasped her hand and gave it a gentle squeeze.

"We will, my love. We will put an end to it."

"Why is it taking them so long to respond to my father's demands?" She asked in exasperation.

"Because they want to show they are in control. Besides, they don't know if your father was being truthful regarding enemies of The Collective. But the chatter indicates he is not exaggerating. Whether he had engaged in those discussions beforehand is no matter because now there are several enemies of The Collective in touch with Galatian Guards stationed across the Galaxy. They want to attack."

"How is my father's group going to know this? Hell, how is he even supposed to contact us? We need to talk! I need to talk to my dad." She ran her hand through her messy curls.

"We are actually working on that. Drago has left discreet messages in areas where your father or his team would likely pick them up. Obviously, we cannot allow anyone to learn our location—which includes him." He gave her a pointed look.

"I know. We can't trust him—at least not yet."

Rafe sat in the chair next to her, satisfied. James Chambers had allowed his hatred of Galatians known during their last meeting and he wouldn't take any chances he wouldn't kidnap his daughter in some misguided attempt to 'rescue' her. After all, that was something he was quite familiar with.

"I'm also thinking about our kids."

"Eh. They will be okay. They are in good hands."

"Oh," Karma said. "I do not doubt that. It's the fact that they are learning to do well without their mama and papa. Sometimes I wonder if I shouldn't just give all of this up and raise my kids and be a family." She turned back to look at the many screens. "And then I see this and I know I can't let that be the world I leave for my kids."

"We agree. M is intelligent and brave. And Runnar is the best part of both of us. I hear he did not injure his Aunt Justina."

She smiled, and this time it touched her eyes. "He's learned that his teeth and claws can do damage, and I think he learned it by accidentally injuring himself."

"We all do; Galatians, that is."

"I would love to talk to your mother about what it was like raising two little Galatian children."

"My mother has rejected the ways of the Queens in support of me and our cause. I can only imagine that the murder of her first grandchild was pivotal in changing her mind. I think she will be pleased to learn she has more grandchildren."

"It's still strange the Queen mothers would want so much to have their own children, but then limit them."

"It is not much different from human parents that maim their children in support of their religion or culture."

Before Karma could agree, Drago turned from where he was in communication with others over a headset.

"There has been an attack on *Monobosteek!*"

Rafe jumped out of his seat and hurried to where Drago and his team were busily pulling up images. Karma had followed.

"Isn't that where The Collective is located?"

"It is," Rafe confirmed.

"My dad..."

Although Rafe had vowed not to reach out to his old Commander after Einar had sided with the Queens against his own men. But Einar had indicated that although he wouldn't join Rafe's cause, he also wouldn't fight against them.

Did that mean Einar was sitting there in the middle of a war zone, doing nothing? Or was his intent not to defend The Collective against a direct attack by Galatians? Rafe knew for a fact that no Galatians were involved in the attack on The Collective.

Einar looked tired when he appeared on the virtual monitor. He looked around at the room, probably trying to assess Rafe's location. Rafe knew he wouldn't be able to. They were inside of a starship and had blockers preventing location tracking.

"Commander Einar, thank you for responding to my communications."

Einar nodded as his eyes moved over the image of Karma. "So, we are speaking English and not Galatian."

"Yes. My wife should be involved in these talks."

Einar nodded. "I suppose you heard about the attack on the IPC?"

"Yes. It is why I am contacting you."

"And you wonder if I kept my word and did not engage the attackers? We did not, however, they were small and explorative." Rafe gave him a questioning look. "There were no casualties. In fact, it does not appear as if they wanted to actually cause damage. That wasn't their purpose."

Paris and Kendrick had joined the meeting and Commander acknowledged them with a brief nod.

"They attacked The Collective, but you don't think their purpose was to do harm?" Drago asked.

"I know it wasn't their purpose," the Commander replied. His eyes fell on Karma again. "James Chambers deposited a message for his daughter."

Karma's eyes widened. "Through the Collective?"

"Yes. It was simple. He said he left a message for you in the summer place. You understand the message?"

Karma gave a short nod.

"I suppose the Collective is not happy with you right now," Rafe continued, preventing any attempt by Einar to interrogate his wife.

"You would be correct."

"And when there is a genuine attack?" Drago added. "What then?"

Einar took some time before replying. "I don't believe that will be an issue. I will be replaced by someone who is more... accommodating."

None of the Galatians asked for a definition of that statement. Either he was being forced into retirement, or he was going to be put to death. Regardless, that was his business and not theirs.

"There is always room for a good soldier on our team," Rafe said.

The two may have fallen out as of late, but the Commander had always been a highly proficient soldier.

For the first time, Einar seemed surprised. "I thank you Rafe. But there would always be suspicion between us. I respectfully decline your offer."

It wasn't lost on Rafe that he'd declined the offer, not because he didn't believe in the cause, but because he would never be considered an insider for fear of him compromising their mission. Rafe nodded in acceptance, ending their meeting.

"The summer place?" Rafe asked.

"Yes. When I was a kid, we were too poor to go on vacation. So, we'd just have a picnic in the basement of the building. My dad must have left something for me in the basement of my old building."

"That is very obvious. If others were looking for your father—and I'm certain many are— the first place they'd set up surveillance is his old home."

Karma stroked her chin. "Yeah. You're right."

"We will send one of our human allies to retrieve the message. They will be equipped with a video feed to show everything that happens."

"Rafe, I need to be able to leave my dad a message."

"Yes. I will make sure you can."

It was not even a second later that nearly every monitor in the room was interrupted by the serious face of Lars Jokavic, who was evidently the new spokesperson for The Collective.

"Hello, ladies and gentlemen. Recently, there has been much discontent between the citizens of Earth and The Interplanetary Collective.

"James Chambers and Karma Sigur have made it obvious they welcome war. Which is not what any of us at the IPC want. There has been a history of death and

mistrust among us humans. Yes, I do say *us*, as I am one of you! But I too want nothing but the well-being of Earth and its people which is why I have placed my faith in The Interplanetary Collective. I know Earth's history and our planet was dying before our guardians at The Interplanetary Collective stepped in.

"As much as we have demonstrated our desire to protect, we are met with continuous suspicion and now even threats." Lars smiled sadly. "But this is how much our Guardians within The Interplanetary Collective cares for us; they will honor the ultimatum set forth by James Chambers, Karma Sigur, and Lt. Rafe Sigur. To prevent war and more death, James Chambers and Karma will be the new human delegates of The Interplanetary Collective. And Lt. Sigur will serve as the first male Galatian in the IPC."

Karma and Rafe exchanged looks. "He's such an asshole!" Karma hissed. "They don't care about the thousands of people killed by their soldiers! They only care that my father was able to infiltrate their security."

Lars continued. **"We invite the parties to join us on *Monobosteek*, where we will have an impromptu meeting to discuss what we can do to rectify our differences."**

"I bet you do," Karma growled.

Drago made contact with one of their soldiers who made the trip to Karma's old neighborhood. The communications office was crowded with technicians as well as Rafe's crew who were monitoring the feed.

Karma didn't recognize any of the residences, not even the old people, and certainly not the children who played with handmade toys in the front yard of the building. It made her heartache at the sight of their poverty. Once upon a time, she had sent them gifts of food. But that was all she'd done, which was basically nothing. The place was falling apart. The children were dressed in rags, and she could see they were still starving.

Nothing she'd done was good enough! She had to do more—and not just for these people, but for all the poor!

"Go down into the basement," Karma instructed once the soldier had entered the building. He had wisely dressed in rags, but he looked healthy and for that reason, he stood out to her, but probably not to anyone watching.

Once the man was in the basement, Karma directed him to the window. The sun would shine through it, brightening a few feet of space on the concrete floor. But her mom would spread out a large quilt while her father plugged in an old radio. Her job was to place the sandwiches out. She always wrapped them in newspapers the way she thought the rich people had them. Her mother would always bake something special, like cookies or cereal and marshmallow treats.

Their picnics had always been a high point of their summer, and Daddy called it the summer place. As Karma looked at the small dingy basement, she was even more sad they'd so easily made this dirty place home.

Tears stung her eyes when she realized it had never been about the location. What made it special was they'd had fun just being together.

There were crates beneath the window and after the soldier moved one of them, he located an old-fashioned tape recorder. It was so old-fashioned there was no chance anyone could trace it. The soldier didn't even know how to work it. Karma had to tell him to press play.

Hi, baby girl. Smart. Daddy didn't use real names. **I trust you are well. I am sorry about how we left things. I am**

recording this as I sit on the floor right beneath the window. I remember how the light shined through that dirty glass, but it lit up you and your mother with such a beautiful glow. I have never seen anything more beautiful. There was a sigh.

I am sorrier than you can ever know. It is my hope we can rectify so many wrongs in this world, even if we can't rectify our own issues. I know I took a huge license when I offered to serve opposite you. But I don't trust our enemies. And between me and your husband, I know nothing can protect you more. Karma found herself smiling despite the tears that threatened to spill from her eyes.

I want nothing more than to make this world safe so no other person has to go through what you, your mother, or I had to endure. We need to talk; really talk. I want you to record over this tape. Leave me a message. We don't have to meet if you aren't ready for that. But we need to strategize. I love you. If you doubt anything, never doubt that.

Rafe was quiet. "Fine," he finally said. "Short of him coming here, we will meet with your father. I will leave him coordinates for one of our satellite sites.

Karma gave him a big hug. "Thank you!"

Chapter Thirty-Nine

"I know it seems weird," Maddie said. "But taking care of your mate when they are molting is mostly about letting them know you are present." Daya nodded worriedly.

They were in the garden having tea, although Daya was too nervous to eat much. The ladies were there to assure her there was nothing to helping a Galatian through his stasis.

Justina watched Runnar as he sat on a blanket spread out on the soft grass. He had his toys around him but was more interested in reaching for blades of grass or dirt so he could place them in his mouth. For what seemed like the hundredth time, she gently plucked the dirt from his tiny fist and tried to entice him with a teething toy.

"I only went through one change with Paris, but Laylay did all the work." Justina smiled sadly. "She didn't think I was capable when, in truth, I was just going through the motions."

Daya listened intently, hungry for as much information as she could get about Paris—at least the person he had been in the past. She never asked, though. His past with Justina seemed personal, but whenever she offered a tidbit, Daya made sure to pay attention.

"The main thing is, Laylay always made sure he was nourished.

She did her bathroom business there, kept him up to date with news, and sometimes she even seemed to argue with him." Justina chuckled. "It was probably the only time she could get a word in edgewise."

"She sounded like a good friend."

Justina nodded. "To him, she was. We weren't friends until the very end." Justina frowned. "If not for her loss, Paris and I wouldn't be where we are now..." Justina glanced over at her bodyguard.

Sgt. Kelly was too far away to hear them. They were doing double duty guarding the women, babies and the three children who were thankfully playing a quiet virtual game instead of running around.

Maddie got up from the blanket to grab her baby. Since Rex realized he could crawl, he tried his best to explore his surroundings. Maddie had kept him occupied with some vegetables she'd plucked from the ground. Now he wanted to pluck items. He wasn't even interested in Runnar any longer.

After Justina survived her time with the baby unscathed, Maddie carefully allowed the two babies together. The first time Runnar lunged at her son with his mouth wide open and sharp teeth gleaming, Maddie had to force herself not to snatch her baby right back up. But all Runnar wanted was to taste her son. He slobbered on Rex's cheek while the older baby tried to grab Runnar's tail.

They played for a while before both lost interest and went after other pursuits.

"Have you swum in the pool yet?" Maddie asked.

"Paris has taken me to his private pool a few times." She pulled her scarf around her neck. It shielded her head and some of her face from the sun—as well as from the eyes of the guards situated around the perimeter of the large grounds. They were polite and didn't stare —at least they tried not to, but she would always be a bit self-conscious around them. It had taken her time to feel comfortable around the beautiful ex-consorts. And that was mainly because they had been able to overlook the strange and sometimes unsettling appearance of their mates without judgment.

She knew the Galatians didn't judge her, either. She believed Paris when he explained her severe scars weren't ugly to them. But she didn't know if she could reveal herself to a group of Galatian males and do her bathroom business around them as she tended to her man. She wasn't even grossed out by the concept of a Galatian pool where people went to bathe and expel their waste. It was the fountain of youth, for most. For her, the benefits could only be indulged in small increments. Her skin was just too delicate and the enzymes could easily overwhelm her.

"You can move back to the ship where Paris can have a private pool," Maddie explained in understanding. "And there would be a shower nearby for your after-care."

"I think that's the only way I could assist him." Daya forced herself not to feel inadequate. But once again, her injuries made her vulnerable, and now she couldn't properly take care of her mate. What if she had to have one of the other consorts step in? No! Even if she had to wear a protective suit, she'd tend to her mate herself while he was vulnerable.

"Don't worry yourself, Daya. The men will be on the ship and you know they will always help—whether you want them to or not," Maddie said. She quickly scurried after her son, who had taken off after a flying insect.

"What is it like? When the chrysalis forms?"

"Weird," Maddie admitted. "They get into the pool and it begins to form over them like a thick web, but only while they doze. When they wake up, it stops and you can even pull it off. They are so tired though. Sometimes Drago would fall asleep in mid-sentence. Encourage Paris to sleep and remind him it will be over sooner if he doesn't fight it. Galatian men think the world is going to end if they aren't awake to protect it!"

Justina chuckled. "That's the truth. Kendrick isn't even my mate, and he assigned me my own personal bodyguard because he wouldn't be there to protect me."

"There are worse things than having a Galatian protect you," Daya grinned.

"But loving a Galatian isn't easy." Maddie sighed as she brought her runaway son back to the blanket. "Rex and I don't see him enough." She forced a smile. "But it's fine. This fight is to protect us all. It's just there's no telling how long it will last..."

Daya slipped from her seat on the bench to weave blades of grass while Rex watched with interest. "You should go and get some rest, Maddie. We'll watch Runnar."

Maddie sighed sleepily. "I am exhausted. Rex is tireless."

"We'll watch him," Justina assured her. "Runnar's getting tired and will be napping soon."

Maddie didn't take much more convincing. She hadn't slept through the night in ages so she slipped away for some time alone.

"Bochs!" Rex said once he got bored of the grass bracelet his aunt had woven for him. "Bochs!"

"Are you saying, mama?" Justina asked. "She'll be back soon."

Rex just gave her an inquisitive look before turning to the vegetable garden. "Bochs." Justina looked at Daya for a translation. Daya shrugged.

"Do you want a box, Rexie?" Daya asked.

"Bochs!" Rex's face was turning red and he looked ready to cry.

"Okay!" Justina passed him his bottle. "Do you want ba-ba?"

Rex shook his head and pushed the offered bottle away in consternation before grabbing for it and taking a few swigs from it. He then launched it away.

"Not ba-ba." Daya confirmed. "Do you want binkie?" She handed him his pacifier.

Rex shook his head in frustration and pushed her hand away. "Bochs!"

"I don't know what that means," Daya said. "Are you hungry?"

"Maybe we should get Maddie..." Justina suggested.

"No. She needs some rest. We're not throwing in the towel over this." She lifted the fat baby in her arms. "Take me to the bock, Rexie."

"Bochs!" Rex demanded this time opening and closing his little fists, indicating he wanted something. "M!" He finally said. "M!"

"You want M?" Daya asked.

"M!" Rex stared at her with big blue eyes, as if giving his confirmation.

"Okay, we can do that."

M, Bain, and Kelsie were playing a strategy game where tiny spaceships floated in the air, shooting their opponents.

"M," Daya said while carrying the baby propped on her hip. "I could use your help."

Yes, Aunt Daya?

"I think Rex is asking for you."

M smiled and came to her feet from where she had been sitting cross-legged on the grass.

Hi Rex. The baby launched himself at her, and M gave him a big bear hug and held him in her arms.

"Bochs!"

What? M asked. Bain and Kelsie gathered around the baby. Even Adrian had come forward.

"You want a box?" Kelsie asked.

Rex stared at M. His lips trembled and fat tears appeared in his eyes. M stooped and placed him on the ground.

Show me.

Rex quickly took off on fat knees. Everyone followed. When he got to the step leading to the patio, he climbed it with only a little trouble, and everyone seemed to understand by his determined expression not to interrupt him. They followed the baby through the opened doors of the villa while he moved speedily down the corridor toward his quarters.

"Maybe he wants his mama," Kelsie whispered.

No. Mama is easy to say. He wants something else.

"Why did he ask for you?" Bain asked.

M scratched her head. She looked at her communicator. **Because I'm the only other person who can't talk.**

Daya frowned as that was a very advanced concept for a baby who wasn't even a year old yet. Still, they continued to follow him until he finally reached the closed door of his and his parent's quarters.

"Bochs!" He sat on his butt, waiting for someone to open the door. Adrian stepped forward and opened it for the baby.

"Bochs..." Rex said quietly as he hurried to his bedroom.

"Ahh, he's sleepy," Justina guessed, thinking he wanted his own crib. But he ignored his crib and headed straight for his toy chest.

M helped him pull himself up into a standing position so the baby could reach into the little box.

"Toy box," Bain said. "He wanted his toy box!"

But M shook her head. **No.**

She rummaged past a few toys and stopped to grin. She picked up an object and handed it to the baby. He grabbed it happily.

"Bochs! Bochs! Wexie bochs!"

M dropped to her knees as everyone watched in awe.

Yes, Rexie's blocks. She pulled all the colorful puzzle blocks from the toy chest and set them before the baby. He began examining the pieces in deep thought while slowly putting them together. He looked up at M and grinned.

"M."

You're welcome, little buddy

"Uh?" Maddie was standing in the doorway, rubbing her eyes. She had slept for approximately five minutes.

Daya jumped into action and led the sleepy woman back to her bedroom. "Go back to sleep, sis. We got this."

Haru nudged his friend's shoulder. Dorf opened his eyes, nearly forgetting he had been meditating.

"How long have we been-"

"It's time," Haru said happily. "Don't you feel it? It's like energy."

"Uh...no." Dorf looked around. "Everything is the same."

"I guess because I control the stasis. I am awakening."

Dorf peered at his friend. "You're... vibrant."

"Yes! I feel vibrant." Haru looked up. "I am going to release us." And then Haru disappeared.

"What—? Haru?" It was the first time Dorf was left alone in this strange place. Without him, the world was too big and desolate. "Haru!"

Something grabbed him and lifted him into the air as if he had been grabbed by the hand of the Guardian!

Chapter Forty

Dorf felt as if his soul was being yanked from his body. It was much different reading another individual. When reading the thoughts of others, sure he was transported into a lucid place, but he was always aware of his surroundings. But not in this place. Here he felt lost without Haru.

But that didn't last long! Once Haru disappeared Dorf was immediately being pulled out of the strange world where he had resided for what felt like forever.

A cacophony of sound crashed around him as he was somehow pulled from the pool and back to the real world. When his vision cleared, the first thing he saw was Kemistry's beautiful turquoise feathers! He watched, mesmerized, as her wings spread and flapped above him. He realized he was in her arms when he was lifted in the air.

A moment later, he was being placed on a nearby bed. Hospital bed? He blinked the water from his eye and saw others crowding around him just as he realized that he was in an infirmary.

Where...? He tried to speak, but the words wouldn't come.

"Don't try to speak," Kemistry said. Her feathered wings

stroked his face. "We are on the mothership on Eden. It's been nearly five days since you first went into stasis." She smiled. "You changed."

He reached up and pulled the patch from his eye. He could see with both eyes! He rubbed them and then focused on the face of his smiling wife.

Haru was grinning brightly pink. "It is unbelievable. *You* are unbelievable."

Dorf pulled himself into a sitting position, his wings propping him up—*wings?!* He looked down and was first captivated by the vibrant white of his feathers. Despite being soaked from the pool, his feathers naturally repelled water and he easily saw the gleaming white of his sleek body. He flexed his wings and both spread behind him.

Turning in amazement, he expanded them, stretching them to their limits. Haru and Tam had to step aside. Where his missing wing had been felt slightly sore, like an overworked muscle. Beyond that, Dorf felt and looked invigorated.

He launched himself into the air and began to fly around the sick bay. Kemistry laughed and clapped while Haru just watched in awe, his arm around Tam.

I'm flying! I'm whole again! He reached down to touch the symbiot belt around his much trimmer waist. No one but them knew this technology existed. This could potentially change everything...

"We can't tell anyone."

"Why not?" Karma asked. Her smile hadn't left her face since the moment she'd hurried into the sick bay to see Kemistry and Dorf flying around the room.

"Just imagine if others realize the power of this symbiot belt, along with the regenerative abilities of a Galatian, can do the same for other life forms." Dorf was talking while busily eating a smoked salmon salad. "Japoxillian are already endangered."

"Can't the belts be used without a Japoxillian?"

Rafe was already shaking his head. "The belt is an antenna to amplify the reach of the Japoxillian. And just as importantly, the belt is formed based on a specific Galatian. Only Dorf and I can speak mentally because my belt links us."

"But Haru's stasis fixed Dorf," Tam interjected, "and they aren't linked by the belts."

"True," Kemistry added. She snatched a piece of Dorf's fish and popped it into her mouth, chewing while she explained. "The belts can never be mass produced. They are created based on a mental link between two; a fond Galatian and a Japoxillian. If this technology is to be used by others, they'd have to get their hands on a belt made for two symbiotically linked beings.

"And there is no telling whether it will work on other species," Drago said thoughtfully. "The link can exist between us, but if others find out about this ability, they will try to force it to work for them—even if it means enslaving the Japoxillian for their own purposes."

"You're right," Tam said. When parents sold their own children to be married to aliens just to further their own social standing, then anything was possible.

"Others have long stolen our kind to use us as their personal translators." Dorf's voice was quiet and Karma remembered his first wife was kidnapped just for that very purpose. And when Rafe's team finally located her, she was killed in the line of battle.

"We can speculate about this later," Dorf continued. "But I have been out of commission. I want to be caught up on what is happening and then I want to go to the villa and see my kids."

Paris and Kendrick joined the impromptu meeting. Paris's mouth hung open when he saw Dorf's transformation. He'd known the

Japoxillian for decades and Dorf looked like he did when they'd first met! His fur virtually gleamed and his feathers were sleek. Best of all, his wing had returned, his eye was no longer missing, and all scars had disappeared.

He was renewed in the same way Galatians renewed. How long would this last? Galatians had to rejuvenate once or twice a year—more often if they were injured. He wanted to poke his friend just to make sure his changes were solid.

"How is this possible?" He asked in total awe.

"I can venture several guesses," Dorf replied. "But that question is best addressed by the scientist who made the symbiot belts possible. And for now, we are keeping this to ourselves."

Paris rubbed his chin. "It was the belt. Dorf, do you still have me and Laylay's belt?"

"I do. I kept everyone's belt. It's in storage. Why?"

He headed out the door. "I need my belt! I'm going into stasis soon, and I'm going to bring Daya with me."

"Wait!" Karma called. "You can't put Daya in the pool for close to a week with no air or food."

Paris halted and turned to face his friends. "I do not know, but Dorf is healed. It must be capable of working on Daya. And before you object, just know she suffers in silence. She suffers in ways she never reveals—not even to me." He gestured to the door, his color darkening. "And now that the prick doctor can no longer be trusted, I would never allow him to touch her, even if surgery was a viable option right now.

"Don't you see, if this works for Daya, she could be completely healed within a week!"

Karma frowned, seeing how amazing it would be if this worked for her. But on the other hand, she could be trapped in an impenetrable cocoon in horrible pain, suffocating, drowning, dying...

"I'm going to the villa with the belt!" He stormed out of the room.

Dorf hopped up after exchanging looks with Kemistry. "We're going back, too!" The two Japoxillian followed Paris.

Haru took Tam's hand. "Show me our home." Tam blushed and then quickly nodded. They left the room too, so there was only Kendrick, Drago, Karma and Rafe remaining. Everyone looked at each other.

Kendrick spoke in a solemn tone. "I'm staying here on the ship. There is no need for me to return to the villa."

Karma was alarmed he felt that way. "Kendrick! Your home is with us. Not having a mate doesn't change that."

"Brother, we need you now, more than ever before," Rafe said.

Kendrick looked amused. "I know you do. But I'm more useful here with you and Karma. Drago needs to go home and soon you will, too. You have children to see after. I will manage the ship."

"But-" Karma began.

"He is right," Drago said. "He can best protect us all from here."

Kendrick nodded. Karma looked from Drago to Rafe to Kendrick. She hurried forward and gave Kendrick a hug. He looked down at her in surprise and slowly returned it. After a moment, he glowed a soft pink. It was nice to be touched with no ulterior motives.

Kendrick was tired and hungry. He decided to grab something to eat from the canteen and then maybe retire to his quarters to listen to music. He should take advantage of the downtime while Drago and Rafe were still aboard the ship. Soon, he would be running things once they returned to the villa.

He knew he had made the right decision, although it pained him that he had chosen to lead a solitary life.

He dismissed thoughts of Marisol. She treated him like a fuck boy and he had no interest in that.

Once inside the lunch hall, Kendrick realized just how late it was. Chow was over and the room was nearly vacant. There was one person sitting at a table concentrating on cards spread out in front of her. She looked up and smiled.

"Kitchens closed, but I can whip you up something pretty quick."

He paused at the informal way she spoke. There was none of that "Sir" and "Lieutenant" business which sometimes made things awkward when relaxing with others. That was when he noticed she wasn't even dressed in the normal military attire. It suddenly snapped in place. Some of the staff workers weren't enlisted, but were subcontractors.

"I don't mind getting something from the vendor."

The woman made a clucking sound. "Not much of a selection there. We're having trouble getting stocked. Folks here in Eden don't use vendors and don't understand the concept. I'm waiting on a shipment from the *Ulternaron* traders." She stood and stretched her back as if she had been sitting there for a time.

"Besides, you won't find fresh ____ anywhere but in my kitchen."

Kendrick's eyes widened. Did this human just speak in Galatian? "How did you learn that word?"

She smiled easily. "It's best to learn the words for the food you are preparing. There are enough Galatians stationed on this planet that getting my hands on authentic Galatian ingredients isn't completely impossible—especially if you know the language and who to speak to.

Kendrick warmed up to the human. He liked the way she talked freely and not stiff and formal. She was brown and little, with rounded curves that certainly indicated she was not a youngster. Thick black hair hung in inky black coils that reached her shoulders. A shock of white was nestled at the peak and he didn't think she did that for style purposes because he had never seen another human with a streak of white running through their completely black hair.

She headed to the kitchen and turned before reaching the door. "You want some beast or *ctullian* broth with that?"

Again, he was awestruck. "Beast if you got it."

"I always got beast on hand. I just roasted one yesterday." She went into the kitchen and called out to him. "Make yourself comfortable. It won't take long to heat up."

Kendrick sat at the table where she had been playing cards. He peeked at them, not knowing the game. He'd watched several human card games, but not when the human played alone.

Kendrick realized he was in luck. He'd just met a human who wasn't intimidated by his status or his alien qualities. That meant he could probably ask her questions about the human experience.

"I am Kendrick, by the way," he called out, realizing he hadn't introduced himself.

"Yep," she called back. "Lt. Kendrick Washington. I've been preparing your meals since you've been on this ship." She appeared in the doorway holding a huge tray.

"Told you it wouldn't be long—no, no, I got it. Go on ahead and sit back down," she said when he rose to help her. "I do this all day, every day."

She sat the tray in front of him on top of the cards. Once her hands were free, she offered him a shake. He accepted the hand and shook it carefully, although the woman had a firm grip.

"I'm Deedra; unofficial culinary Mess Sargent." She took the lid from the bowl of large squirming grubs. "Eat up. I told you I got some fresh ones."

And eat up, Kendrick did!

Chapter Forty-One

Haru wanted to know everything Tam did while she was with the Resistance and Tam wanted to know everything that happened while he was in Galatia. Haru was reluctant to reveal all he'd had to do in order to succeed with his mission.

But Tamsyn was no wilting flower. She understood that in playing the role of a traitor, he would have to reunite with his bound mate. And while Tam understood the necessity, she had a much more difficult time believing someone like Haru would prefer her over a Galatian Queen—someone who he'd been sworn to since childhood.

"You are quiet," Haru said as they sat in the back row of the transport. She forced herself to meet his eyes, feeling shy around him again. Haru was her first love. While in consort school, she had never imagined falling in love with the Galatian she was enslaved to. She'd done it for her family, for the status and obviously for the lifetime of riches. The teachers made it seem as if everything involved appeasing them. But nothing could be further from the truth.

This oversized, powerful alien was the first to ever give her individuality. He encouraged her to find her truest self and assuring her he much preferred her to the carbon copy consorts that had been part of the Galatian Exchange since the very beginning.

When she said she wanted to learn to be strong and to fight, he trained her. And when she offered to join the Resistance, he did not take away her right to decide this for herself despite his fears.

Haru was everything she could ever desire in a mate, and she loved him almost obsessively. But what did she bring to the table? She would never be as strong as a Queen, or the best fighter, or even the best looking. She wasn't-

Haru touched her chin. "Speak to me Tam. I have missed everything about you in my time away. Thoughts of you are what kept me going when I wanted to fight, argue, defend who you taught me to become-"

Her eyes widened. "Me?"

He tilted his head in confusion at her surprise.

"I never knew what life was until I met you and you showed me what it was to want more than the limitations others place on me. I have fought wars, killed enemies, respected my station in life, but I never lived until you showed me what that truly meant."

Her smile covered her entire face, and she came up on her knees and wrapped her arms around him.

"I missed you so much. I...I wondered if you would find regret in mating with me."

He pulled back and stared into her face. "Regret? My Tam, you are the very best thing that has ever happened to me. Before you, I was little more than a robot! Why would you want me when I am only now learning how to be a true person? You could have chosen your own kind-"

"Haru," she placed her lips on his, stopping those terrible words. "You *are* my kind. You and I, my love. That is what I want." They were two new beings trying to find a way to grow into something that should have never been stifled out of them.

He held her close to his hard body, his scales more vibrant than she'd ever seen. And to her, Haru was the most beautiful being she'd ever laid eyes on.

"I love you Tamsyn Felicidad Hernandez-Bano," he said between kisses.

Tam shook her head quickly. "No. Tamsyn Felicidad Bano. Bano is my name."

A warm pink glow tinted his scales as a slow growl rose from his throat. "How close are we to the villa?"

Kemistry and Dorf were in the front seats. He was staring longingly out of the window, his wings twitching to be used, while she insistently whispered that flying to the villa was out of the question. The humans of this planet had never seen a Japoxillian and would likely shoot him!

"I need practice. I was a bit wobblily back on the ship."

"In time, dear," she said proudly. He placed his new wing around her, encasing them in soft white feathers. They placed their heads together and rode in contented silence.

Paris had no patience. The moment he saw the large oceanfront villa at the next crest, he leaped from the open-air transport and went sprinting home. Dorf's breath caught in his chest as he watched his friend leaping and charging through the tall purple grass.

Kemistry made a clucking sound of resignation. "Fine. Go join him." Dorf gave her a quick peck and then he dived out the door and went soaring through the sky along with his friend.

Daya was expecting his arrival, but in the manner of the Galatian, he'd simply said. "I'm on my way home."

And she'd said, "I will see you when you get here."

And then he had nodded, and the communication ended.

She would soon realize the conversation they were about to have was the furthest from her imagination.

Daya was laughing when she saw him appear over the side of the cliffside overlooking the ocean.

"Babe, you just scared the *bejeezus* out of the guards!" They were scurrying and trying to regroup as if his sudden appearance was an enemy invasion.

He ignored the others, who were all waiting in the courtyard for the arrival of the truck. He grabbed hold of her wrist.

"We need to talk," And then he pulled her into the villa.

The children looked on in awe. "Is Aunt Daya in trouble?" Kelsie asked.

M shrugged, not believing her wonderful teacher could ever do anything wrong.

"Paris, what's gotten into you?" Daya asked as she hurried to keep up with him. "We just had sex before I left the ship," she whispered.

He turned his head to look at her instead of using his tail to do so. "Daya, soon we can make love without fear of me tearing you."

She looked at him in confusion. "What are you talking about? Paris?"

He hurried them to their quarters and once they were inside; she plopped down onto the sofa before even removing her veil.

"What in the world?"

He got down on his knees in front of her. "Dorf is completely healed."

She turned to look at the door as if she wanted to go right back out there to see him. Paris took her hand in his, examining the scars on the back before he met her eyes again and continued.

"It may be possible that with a symbiot belt, another individual can molt with a Galatian! And the healing properties aren't just exclusive to the Galatian, but to whoever is in the chrysalis! What if you were to molt with me, Daya! The chrysalis might be able to heal your scars."

"What? A human go into metamorphosis? But that's not possible..."

"Why?" he asked insistently.

"Well, for one; I can't breathe underwater."

"Neither could Dorf."

She placed her fingers on her lips. "The water eats away my skin after a fairly short amount of time."

"Yes, but that is only specific to your condition. Humans can benefit from the Galatian waters and the chrysalis will heal you."

She continued to look as if she was in a state of disbelief. "But I'm not a Japoxillian. I don't possess the power they have to harness their abilities."

He pointed to his temple. "Their abilities are to read into your emotions. Their abilities have never been to molt. Japoxillian don't go into stasis."

She thought about that. "Has anyone ever tried to molt with another?"

Paris slowly sat back on his haunches. "There have been others caught in the chrysalis—generally water creatures."

"And what happened to them?"

"Well, they were absorbed by the chrysalis and turned into food for the Galatian-"

"But have two Galatians ever tried it?"

He looked down reluctantly. "Generally, we would break free if two were beginning to be joined by one chrysalis. But...it has happened with the elderly. They were absorbed." He looked at her again. "But they weren't wearing a symbiot belt, and that's the difference! Dorf wasn't absorbed."

She studied the hope on his face. "I don't know, Paris," she finally said reluctantly.

He paused and then kissed her fingertips. "You do not have to do this. We can...experiment more. I'll molt again within a year and we could try it then. But it worked for Dorf. And my love, you would never have to stop yourself from smiling out of fear of bleeding through cracked skin." He picked up the veil. "And no more of these!" He calmed and spoke quieter. "But more importantly, no more pain." His eyes narrowed.

"What Garry was going to do to heal you would have been nothing short of torture. And it would have lasted months. Daya, love, in mere days, you could be the way you were before that monster put his hands on you!"

Daya closed her eyes and then formed a teepee with her fingers right before her face. *Dear Guardian, what if this could really work?*

She finally opened her eyes. "And if it doesn't work for me?"

"We will shred that chrysalis to ribbons in order to get you out!"

Could she really be whole again in a matter of days? She nodded. "Let's do it."

The End...

RAFE
HARU
PARIS
KENDRICK
DRAGO
TITUS

TGE Master Key and Emotional Colors

TGE MASTER KEY
THE GALATIAN GUARDS

NAME	FAMILY	EARTH'S ORIGIN	BOUND MATE	JAPOXILLIAN
RAFE SIGUR	-WIFE: KARMA CHAMBERS -CHILDREN: RUNNAR. ELIJAH JAMES, M (EMMY) -MOTHER: JADORITY -BROTHER: GILA	ICELAND	RAGNA	SIR DORF (KNIGHTED)
DRAGO ENGSTRÖM	-WIFE: MADELINE (MADDIE -CHILD: REX -MOTHER: BIRTA	ICELAND	ISYSS	KEMISTRY
TITUS GRAYSON	-MATE: POLAT -MOTHER: NO HUMAN NAME	SCOTLAND	FILENE	BROMHILD
KENDRICK WASHINGTON	-MATE: AURAS -GIRLFRIEND: ? -PARENTS: NO HUMAN NAMD	NORTH AMERICA	EVORA	POGO
LEOLO SANCHEZ	MATE: JAYNE (REJECTED) -MOTHER: NO HUMAN NAME	SOUTH AMERICA	NOT NAMED	SOLOMAR
PARIS FRENCHMAN	-MATE: JUSTINA -WIFE: -MOTHER: URSA	FRANCE (EU)	THALIA	LAYLAY
HARU BANO	-WIFE: TAMSYN (TAM) FELICIDAD HERNANDEZ-BANO -MOTHER: LEPHORA	JAPAN	CAEDA	NAO

GALATIAN EMOTIONAL COLORS

COLOR	EMOTION
GREEN	NEUTRAL STATE
WHITE	FEAR FOR SOMEON THEY CARE ABOUT (NO COLOR FOR SELF-FEAR)
YELLOW	AMUSED
PINK	SMILE. AMUSEMENT
ORANGE	LAUGHTER, EXTREME PLAYFULNESS
PURPLE	ANNOYANCE
BLACK	DISAPPOINTED ANGER
RED	RAGE
BLUE	SEXUAL AROUSAL
KALEIDESCOPE	ALARM. ANXIETY

Pepper Pace Books

STRANDED!
Juicy
Love Intertwined Vol. 1
Love Intertwined Vol. 2
Urban Vampire; The Turning
Urban Vampire; Creature of the Night
Urban Vampire; The Return of Alexis
Urban Vampire; The Final Battle
Wheels of Steel Book 1
Wheels of Steel Book 2
Wheels of Steel Book 3
Wheels of Steel Book 4
Angel Over My Shoulder
CRASH
Miscegenist Sabishii
They Say Love Is Blind
The Throwaway Year
Beast
A Seal Upon Your Heart

Everything is Everything Book 1
Everything is Everything Book 2
Adaptation book 1
Adaptation book 2
About Coco's Room
The Witch's Demon book 1
A Bubble of Time
Awakening
1954
The Galatian Exchange Book 1: Karma and Rafe
The Galatian Exchange Book 2: The Family
The Galatian Exchange Book 3: The Enemies
The Galatian Exchange Book 4: Strike of the Black Masks!

SHORT STORIES/NOVELLAS
~~***~~
The Way Home
MILF
Blair and the Emoboy
Emoboy the Submissive Dom
1-900-BrownSugar
Someone To Love
My Special Friend
Baby Girl and the Mean Boss
A Wrong Turn Towards Love (An Estill County Mountain Man
Romance)
True's Love (An Estill County Mountain Man Romance)
The Miseducation of Riley Pranger (An Estill County Mountain
Man Romance)
Christmas Redemption (An Estill County Mountain Man Romance)
The Delicate Sadness
The Shadow People
The Love Unexpected
The Vinyl Man

Punishment Island
Super G

COLLABORATIONS
~~***~~

Sexy Southern Hometown Heroes
Seduction: An Interracial Romance Anthology Vol. 1
Scandalous Heroes Box set
Secrets of the Elite

WRITTEN UNDER BETH JO ANDERSEN
~~***~~

Snatched by Bigfoot!
Bigfoot's Sidepiece
Mated to the Bigfoot!

WRITTEN UNDER KIM CHAMBERS
~~***~~
The Purple World book 1

About the Author

Pepper Pace creates a unique brand of Interracial/multicultural erotic romance. While her stories span the gamut from humorous to heartfelt, the common theme is crossing racial boundaries. She writes in the genres of science fiction, youth, horror, urban lit and poetry.

For More Information About The Author

Sign-up to the Pepper Pace Newsletter!

http://eepurl.com/bGV4tb

www.ingramcontent.com/pod-product-compliance
Lightning Source LLC
Chambersburg PA
CBHW060233100726
47907CB00003B/616